# SHADOW OF THE OWL

Amanda Orneck

Gold Leaf Books

TONEY, ALABAMA

Copyright © 2015 by **Amanda Orneck**

All rights reserved. No part of this publication may be reproduced, distributed or transmitted in any form or by any means, without prior written permission.

**Gold Leaf Books**
**115 Spirit Drive**
**Toney, Alabama 35773**
www.goldleafbooks.com

Publisher's Note: This is a work of fiction. Names, characters, places, and incidents are a product of the author's imagination. Locales and public names are sometimes used for atmospheric purposes. Any resemblance to actual people, living or dead, or to businesses, companies, events, institutions, or locales is completely coincidental.

Book Layout © 2015 BookDesignTemplates.com

**Book Title/ Author Name**. -- 1st ed.
ISBN 978-0-9968435-1-5

For Xander

# CONTENTS

- BOOK ONE .................................................................. 1
  - CHAPTER ONE .......................................................... 3
  - CHAPTER TWO ......................................................... 33
  - CHAPTER THREE ...................................................... 63
  - CHAPTER FOUR ....................................................... 99
- BOOK TWO ................................................................ 113
  - CHAPTER FIVE ........................................................ 115
  - CHAPTER SIX .......................................................... 135
  - CHAPTER SEVEN ..................................................... 159
  - CHAPTER EIGHT ..................................................... 175
  - CHAPTER NINE ....................................................... 203
  - CHAPTER TEN ........................................................ 225
  - CHAPTER ELEVEN .................................................. 243
- BOOK THREE ............................................................ 273
  - CHAPTER TWELVE ................................................. 277
  - CHAPTER THIRTEEN .............................................. 315
  - CHAPTER FOURTEEN ............................................. 331

# BOOK ONE

The lady sleeps in darkness, though the world, it burns around her.
It's best she does not wake because the flames still lick her bower.
The castle on the mountainside remembers how she glowed,
How tears she cried for her doomed realm upon the flagstones flowed.
The very stones do weep and mourn, each grain of sand wails on shore, for evermore
the lady sleeps.
Oh, how the halls did echo long with her warm peals of laughter,
And every plant did bloom within her never-ending summer.
Now, silence reigns and winter chills for, in the ground on which it snowed,
the lady sleeps,

The ashes of her home are gone; in winds of time, they scatter.
And only mutes remain to sing of her unfettered power.
Will no one rise to walk the path our Warrior Queen has strode?
Will no one come to save the realm whose lives will soon erode?

While still we search for miracles down every lane and road, the lady sleeps.
   *-Anonymous*
   *Year two of the Occupation*

## CHAPTER ONE

The people of Shadowhaven were said to take in anyone, but he knew that only made the kingdom weak. All his life, he had watched as the strength of the elves was diluted by the human taint pouring in from the North. Vortrev Venturil longed for the days when his ancestors roamed the land, mastering it with their elemental magics. But that was before the humans arrived, bring with them the stench of the magicless, infiltrating the elven population the only way the weak know how to conquer—through the machinations of seduction. If that weren't a form of guerilla warfare, he didn't know what was.

The new generations of Shadowhaven were already showing themselves to be little more than mutts. Sure, some had magic, but it was a bastardized form that hardly held to the elements at all. Vortrev's people, the Kir'Tazul Well Keepers, could trace their lineage all the way back to the Great Ione himself. Vortrev's magic was the strongest of all elves, being an Air Weaver, as it was common knowledge that air was the most difficult element to harness.

He would never have known his truly special connection with the Father of the Elves had he not snuck into his father's study and stolen the Wind Flute. His father had kept it as a relic of past generations, handed down he said, from his great ancestor Abbator Venturil, Lord of the Winds, who had been given the ability to Weave Air from King Ione himself. But his father lacked vision, seeing the precious relic only as a trophy of a bygone era. Vortrev knew it was more.

In the light of a full moon, Vortrev stood on a white sand beach. Here the coastline of Shadowhaven was clean, unsullied by any of those hideous human houses that cluttered the streets of the capital city. Here he was far enough away from the castle that he could breathe free of the stench of humans. One needed clean air to properly work great magic. Like a fine feast, only the best ingredients would do. Filling his lungs with clean, salty air, he pulled out his stolen flute and began to play.

Air Weaving didn't require an instrument, but finely crafted flutes embellished and focused the power into something lyrical and pleasing to the ear. Air Weavers were the only elves to use instruments in their magic, the others only using their voice in spell song. Yet another reason they were superior. Only a truly great elementalist could control both a musical instrument and a force of nature at the same time.

Now, the Wind Flute was another animal altogether. Power throbbed through every carving along the shaft of the thing, and even whispering through it brought the strength of zephyrs under his command. Vortrev closed his eyes as he felt the magic flow through him and out through the intricate carvings of the flute. Before him danced a mighty whirlwind, carving shapes into the sand. He switched octaves, and the wind funnel split in two, the twin cones turning circles around one another as they skittered down the sand. The pas-de-deux continued its circuit out over the water, picking up delicate strands of water to mix with the sand and air.

*I am Abbator Venturil come again!* Vortrev thought, watching the air swirl with his crafted magic. The sea itself seemed to agree, for a dark shadow was spreading under the waves as if the ocean were bowing in acknowledgement of his prowess. But the more he watched, the darker the water became, the shadow began to rise like the body of a behemoth, staining the water from below. Vortrev swallowed a sudden dryness in his throat, and the music faltered. The whirlwinds skipped jerkily across the water once or twice, weaving at odd angles.

Below them, the darkness rose in peaks, like taste buds on a gargantuan creature's tongue, tasting the salt of the sea. First one orbicular blemish broke the surface of the water, then another, then hundreds, and then thousands, miniscule pin pricks in proliferating numbers, spreading down the coastline out of sight. Vortrev thought they looked like the noses of fish, but as they continued to rise, he realized these were not fish; these were the heads of men rising from the water as easily as they were pushing through fog. First the helmets appeared, then shoulders, soon, entire men were striding up the beach, water cascading off them in sheets. They marched from the sea as if made of it, as if formed from the waves themselves, to blight the virgin sand with their dark intentions.

Vortrev stopped playing altogether, and backed away, hoping he wouldn't be noticed. The twin funnels ran down the beach like two errant children disobeying their father. They played along the bodies churning up out of the water, spinning circles through the crowd of armored forms. These weren't elves, he noticed with alarm. Even in the darkness he could tell their faces were too angular, their ears under their helmets too long and pointed. Their skin looked black in the moonlight, and was shot all over with iridescent veins like one might see on the interior of a cavern wall. Pale lavender eyes glinted in the moonlight from under hooded lids. They did not belong here, surrounded by the peace of a moonlit night.

Then, all at once, the mass of warriors began to march northward as one. They came toward him, strange curved swords drawn, creatures that looked as if they were made of shadow itself. Vortrev was caught between the water and the dunes, and, in one last vain effort to defend himself, he put the Wind Flute to his lips, but his fear silenced his magic. A sword carved a path through the moonlight, coming down to cleave the Wind Flute and its player in twain. Had he lived long enough to think it, Vortrev might have been honored to be the first casualty of the siege of Shadowhaven. Instead, he fell soundlessly, his broken body shattered by the boots of the invaders. They drove the shards of his precious relic carelessly into the sand, as they flowed incessantly up the valley toward the unsuspecting capital.

Two hours later, behind the main gate of Haven City, two gatekeepers stood stolid and immovable. Sisters in arms, if not sisters in blood, the pair nevertheless could have been twins, so alike did they look. Their keen blue eyes scanned the shadow-cloaked city, crowned with the castle like a diadem. Their golden-white hair lay wrapped in leather at the base of their necks, their armor glinted dully in the moonlight. Though they had seen little warfare themselves, they could smell it on the air, they knew something malevolent was outside, and they waited in silence for the onslaught to begin, just as the archers and Fire Callers awaited their orders.

Out of the darkness of the city, a figure emerged, tall and imposing in flowing purple robes. He was no soldier; this was a male who had never received the training of war. But why should he? He was, after all, the Chancellor. Truth be told, he was their polar opposite in every way, a male of power whom others served. His blond hair lay unbound and untamed around his shoulders, held only by the golden circlet on his brow indicative of his position. As he approached, he smiled coolly.

"Unlock the gates, children." Chancellor Arndorn did not mince his words. He was busy and had much to do. "Return home for the evening. You have worked a long day," he said with a hint of kindness in his eyes and tone of voice as he folded his fingers in front of him, "and you deserve some rest."

"Chancellor, the armies of our enemies stand outside this very gate," the younger soldier said, lifting her chin in pride, her stance stiffening. It was clear by her demeanor that she felt their original orders superseded whatever the official might have to say. What did he know of the city's defense?

"Do you not trust the wisdom of the advisor to our king? By the order of our Warrior Queen, I command you to open the gates and stand down," he shouted so that the soldiers atop the battlements could hear him. His commanding voice reverberated dully on the stone of the walls, off the metal in their armor. Then, more softly, he added, "We must be open to negotiations; give peace a chance."

The pair sheathed their swords and turned to face the gate, a pair of doors several stories tall, elegantly carved with the scrollwork of a master Stone Weaver. They had been bound to this gate, lived with it day and night, and felt its urging them to resist their orders. There was an insistence in the stone, a pleading that they do not open up the gates and let danger prey upon the city they had sworn to protect. But the Chancellor had ordered, and the punishment for disobeying his orders was too heinous to imagine.

As they placed their hands on the cold stone, the elder soldier lifted her face and her voice to the gate, a low alto harmony rumbling out of her. The younger soldier joined her after only a second's hesitation, her lilting soprano melody weaving in with the first voice. The magical lock resisted the musical coaxing, and then finally, as if in resignation, released itself to the song and opened. The massive gates swung outward, opening the city to whatever lay outside, letting the song's last echo slip away on the evening air.

With a slow nod to the Chancellor, the soldiers slip into the night. The elder began to head toward her home, but was stopped by a hand on her elbow. "He's up to something," the younger mouthed, and led her partner into the bushes to watch.

"The armies of our enemies," Arndorn murmured under his breath as he turned toward the opening in the gate, his blue eyes glinting darkly, "are already here."

From their vantage point, the soldiers could see a short, rotund human step through the gates, his dark hair and eyes a stark contrast to the brilliant colors of his robes. The newcomer stepped forward, paused a moment, and then embraced the Chancellor. "Ah, Arndorn, at last we meet. Your generosity will never be forgotten." He patted the pocket of his robe, nodding conspiratorially.

"My lord, Sargon," Arndorn bowed, his haughty air instantly covered by a mask of subservience. With a second sweeping bow, he waved a hand to the city beyond. "Haven City is yours."

Sargon smiled, his dark eyes sparkling. "I've always wanted a city; you're too kind. Whatever shall I do with it? Oh, right." He turned to a lithe figure with dark gray skin and deep blue hair standing at his shoulder, grinned, and said, "Burn what you will, but the castle is mine. Welcome to Shadowhaven men; the time for restraint has passed." The lithe figure smiled, revealing a mouth full of pointed teeth, and then broke into a full run. Behind him, his cohorts moved as one, a great beast unleashed upon the unsuspecting city.

The pair of soldiers knelt frozen in the underbrush, not daring to move. The elder turned her eyes to the younger, a decision written on her features. The younger nodded. As the last invaders flooded into the city and the fires and screams began to pollute the night, the pair of soldiers slipped out of the gates unnoticed, and headed north, leaving their home behind, melting into the night.

The pain was deep, dark, and tasting of the sea. It woke her, gnawing at her belly with the frenzy of a wolf gnawing at a fresh kill. For a moment, Mylena didn't know where she was, who she was. There was only the pain, starting from forever and continuing on into eternity. The darkness around her bed gave her no indication of place, so she clung to the sweat-soaked sheets as her only anchor in the sea of torment. *What is this?* It was the only coherent thought in her head. *Am I dying?*

For a time, she lay there, drenched in her own pain, scarcely breathing. If she played dead, maybe the pain would stop, would think her not worth the trouble. The pain was clever, though, and found her even as she lay stock still with her nightgown bunched around her. New tears ran the tracks of dried ones that had traveled her cheeks in her sleep, leaving their sticky residue in her eyelashes. Her next instinct was to get away from the pain. If it could find her when she lay quiet, maybe it couldn't find her if she left the bed.

Mylena crawled out from under the pain and stood, mangled by sleep, on the wolf-skin rug. Her knees wobbled as if she had spent the night riding horseback. *Must have been one devil of a beast,* she thought darkly, running a hand over her eyes to clear her vision. The room around her was still cloaked in blackness, shapes barely distinguishable in the dark. Behind her was the four-poster bed, swathed in filmy gauze. To her right, the ever-blooming narcissus bobbed their heads in drowsy acknowledgment of their mistress, and behind them, stood the mirror dressing table that reflected only darkness. Night then, or near to it. The soaring windows confirmed this, showing only a dark, rolling sea below. Mylena felt as if she had a dark, rolling sea within her, and she wished vehemently that it would leave.

She walked to the window and put her palm against the glass, and then, as another wave of pain hit her, rested her cheek against it as well. There was comfort in the cold response of the window, the unyielding pane of glass barely warmed at all to her touch. The sensation of outside stimulus soothed her, brought her out of the pain for a moment, and held her in a sort of stasis between moments.

"Your Highness?" Came a throaty voice slurred with sleep, shattering Mylena's stasis with its harsh reality.

Mylena turned from the window to see who it was, but another wave of pain slammed her back against the window, and she shut her eyes in trying to block it out. When she opened them, she saw Muirinn, her lady-in-waiting, holding up a candle, her beady eyes pinched with worry. *Ugly as she is stupid*, Mylena thought bitterly, wishing very much that she could tear the pain from her own body and fling it away, preferably toward the maid.

"Oh, Highness, look at you!" Muirinn exclaimed as she approached. The concern in her eyes had shifted into full panic, and Mylena felt her own alarm rise in reaction.

Holding up a warning hand to the servant lest she rush forward and only bring on fresh waves of pain—who knew how this monster worked? Maybe it fed on groups and got larger and more menacing—Mylena looked down at the nightgown she wore and the dark red stain that was spreading across the silk fabric. *So it's happened then,* she thought with an odd sense of detachment. When she realized Muirinn was still staring at her, the detachment quickly faded, replaced instead by a strong mix of humiliation, irritation, and longing: humiliation that she should be in this state, irritation that she had to share this important moment with the cow-eyed servant girl, and an overwhelming longing to run for her mother.

The last emotion won out. "Where is my mother?" she asked weakly, her bravado quickly fading.

"Her Royal Highness is in the queen's chambers, Highness. Here, let me draw you a bath."

Muirinn went to light the braziers against the walls of the bedroom, methodically tipping her candle against each in turn. As she retreated into the adjacent bathroom, Mylena went to the dressing table and picked up the ivory-handled brush. She was unaccustomed to brushing out her own hair, and as she ran the brush through the mass of red curls, she seemed to be doing more harm than good.

"Here Highness, let me," she heard behind her, and Muirinn took the brush from her and ran it swiftly through Mylena's hair with practiced skill.

Feeling awkward standing there as the short maid cowed her hair into submission and then plated it into a long, fiery coil, Mylena bit her lip and asked, "Muirinn, does it always hurt like this?"

"For some," Muirinn responded frankly, as was her way. "But the first moonblood is always the worst."

Heading into the bathroom, Mylena tugged closed the velvet curtain that separated sleeping area from bathing area. Shrugging out of the soiled nightgown, she dropped it on the floor and gingerly stepped into the steaming water. The copper tub was warm to the touch, and she slid her aching body below the surface with a contented sigh. As the heat wrapped itself around her clenching muscles, the pain started to dissipate, leaving her nerves tingling from overwork. Closing her eyes, she let the heat work on her body, and her mind drift along a tide of relief.

When she opened her eyes though, the room around the tub was dark as if the candles had been snuffed out. The only source of light came from around her, a pulsing blue glow emanating from the water in which she floated. The pulse of the water beat all around her, as if the liquid itself were alive.

Afloat in this womb of magic, she felt the water undulate with inner power. Warm and slightly viscous, it flowed around her, turning her skin blue in its reflective glow. *The Well of Zyn,* she thought reverently, *my people's greatest treasure.* Somewhere in the back of her mind, she felt the strangeness of her bathing in the sacred waters, feeling their warmth course through her. But a feeling of peaceful power was charging up and down her bones, and she was loathe to remove herself from the sensation.

Across the room, she saw movement. Figures were approaching, and as they neared she saw they were her parents. Hand-in-hand, they walked, their faces pale in the blue light reflecting from the Well of Zyn. Together, they stopped at the edge of the pool, dropped to their knees, and reached out to her. Mylena reached out toward them, but when her hands touched theirs, they melted, becoming nothing more than black ooze on the stone floor.

"No, Mother! Father!" Mylena cried, and the ooze responded, flowing toward her. When it hit the Well of Zyn, it began to smoke, black steam stinging her eyes; she felt the pool around her shudder in pain. It was dying; she was killing it, just as she had killed her parents.

Mylena awoke with a scream, sitting bolt upright in the now tepid water of the bath. Shivering with the memory of the vision, she stepped out of the water to find a towel and gown laid out for her, as well as a small pile of rags for her personal hygiene. Drying off and dressing, Mylena tried her best to push the images from her mind, but they kept floating to the surface. *What does it mean?* She had only been to the Well of Zyn three times in her entire life, and no one bathed in it—the magical shield her parents had erected around it made sure of that. Perhaps she was just tired and sore, and random images had come to mind. Yet, the memory of her parents melting at her touch did not feel like a random image. As she left the bathroom and stepped into a pair of calfskin slippers, she saw no sign of Muirinn. The maid must have slinked back to bed. At least someone would get some sleep.

Mylena's apartment was a small set of rooms situated on the West end of Castle Illuminata. Hurrying down a small spiral stair, she turned left at the landing and sped down the hall toward the royal apartments. Here a large pair of finely carved doors stood closed, their handles forming two halves of an owl's head, majestic in gold. Before the door, stood two guards, who snapped to attention as she approached. These were from her mother's guard, young women chosen out of the Haven City populace, and charged with her protection. They had rarely seen action, and had the sort of kind, soft faces you would expect from perennial bodyguards with nothing to do.

"Ryban, I would see my mother," she said without ceremony. She was in too much pain for formalities, and it was too early for courtesy.

Nodding, the right-hand guard stepped aside and pulled on the right-hand section of the owl's head, opening the door so Mylena could make her way inside. From here, the hallway continued unbroken save for a few steps, but the furnishings were richer here, and the plant life more exotic. She had once asked why Castle Illuminata was filled with plants and flowers, but her mother had only smiled saying they were a gift from her father. If so, then her father was a very prolific gift giver.

At the top of the steps, a second hallway branched, with one section leading to her father's study and laboratory. She turned her back on this and instead took the passage that led to the royal sleeping chamber. Normally, the sound of snoring rumbled down the passage from her parents' bedroom, but now only light greeted her as she pushed open the door. The large expansive royal bedroom was crowned by a massive bed that stood on a plinth in the center of the room. At the foot of the bed stood a low bench, and it was here that Mylena found her mother, dressed in her ceremonial armor and reading a rather large scroll. Gilded by the candlelight radiating from a half dozen candelabras stationed throughout the room, Queen Saebariel Yslela was a sight to behold. Everything around her was golden, from the free flowing tresses of her hair to her eyes, glinting like pools of molten gold in the candlelight. The strong lines of her chin and nose matched those of her delicately pointed ears, ears Mylena had envied all her life. Mylena self-consciously tucked a loose curl behind her commonly round ear. What was the use of being half-pixie if you didn't have the ears to show for it?

As Mylena approached, Saebariel looked up from her reading. In an instant, she was on her feet, the scroll abandoned on the bench behind her, her face alight in a huge golden smile.

"Dear one," Saebariel said, wrapping Mylena in a hug that pressed the girl to her golden breastplate and reminded her exactly how much shorter she was than her mother's six foot height. The queen pulled the girl from her and held her at arm's length, her eyes looking deeply into her daughter's. "What's wrong? Why are you up so early?"

Mylena yawned slightly at the reminder of the early hour, and then shifted on her feet a little. She was unsure how exactly how to start this conversation. *Hello Mother, I'm a woman now?* Or perhaps *I've been bleeding like a stuck pig all night, how you are you?* Dropping a hand to her belly and feeling the clenching muscles respond with a wave of pain, she settled for a simple "It's begun."

Cupping her daughter's chin in her hand, Saebariel kissed her on the forehead and then led her to the bench. Resuming her place she pushed the scroll onto the floor and patted the vacant spot beside her. "Sit down my love. This is an important day for you."

Mylena sat down gingerly and looked up at her mother, still towering over her even when seated. "Important hurts."

Her mother smiled knowingly. "Well you're a bit of a special case, what with your father being human and me being, well, me," she twinkled a bit as if her heritage were a great secret. As if anyone walking into a room full of blooming flowers and trees wouldn't recognize something out of the ordinary about how the plants fairly glowed when her mother was nearby. Her mother might be able to pretend that she was just a regular old elf, but the rest of them could read her true pixie origins in every expression and gesture.

So what did that mean for Mylena? That mixing pure pixie blood with human meant the moonblood rode in on a wave of pure pain every month? Is this what she had to look forward to the rest of her adult life? Sometimes, being special and unique was a blessing, but today, it seemed only a curse.

Her mother was watching her, Mylena realized, and blushed, knowing all her thoughts tended to end up written on her face. "The pain didn't come with anything extra did it? The day I first received my moonblood, I woke up in a hole in the ground. Abilities often manifest when great change happens in our bodies."

Mylena swallowed hard and thought back to the image of a puddle of steaming black ooze floating toward her across the surface of the Well of Zyn. "No," she lied, "I guess I'm more human than you thought. Maybe I won't have abilities at all."

"Oh I doubt that, love. They will come, and soon, I should expect, now that you're a woman. I can't wait to see what you will become." Her mother smiled meaningfully.

"I'm only seventeen," Mylena objected. She didn't like where this conversation was headed.

"True, and today the Festival of the Elements begins, so we best get you ready for that. I have a surprise for you. I was going to wait until later on this morning, but since you're here…" Her mother stood and crossed to a small alcove hidden behind a velvet curtain. The dawn bloomed behind

Saebariel as she passed in front of the windows, almost as if she was drawing the sun up with her very presence. Mylena cocked her head to one side, wondering if pixies had the power to control the sun. Maybe they could. They were magical creatures after all, one of the founding races of the world, as far as the legends went. Maybe they had the moon, the sun, and the stars in their sway.

Her mother returned to the bedroom proper carrying something over her arms. As she approached, dread began to gnaw at Mylena, even as her mother's smile grew. She was holding a gown, a wonder of pale peach cotton. Standing, Mylena turned with arms outstretched and allowed her mother to undress and redress her, doing her best to ignore the nagging feeling at the back of her mind.

This was one line of thought that didn't seem to escape onto her features, because her mother merely grinned and drew her toward the full length mirror that stood in the corner of the room. "There, now you look every inch the princess, ready to hold court. Now, all you need is a tiara."

"I'll braid my hair instead," Mylena said, feeling suddenly very surreal. "I have a feeling it will go perfectly with the gown. Thank you, Mother." Turning, she stood on tiptoe so that she could kiss Saebariel on the cheek. "I love you."

"And I you, dearest. Don't look so sad though. Today is a happy day, a day of celebration. The Festival of the Elements has been held this week for thousands of years, and we are fortunate to be a part of it. I—" she broke off as her husband came barreling through the door.

"Oh good, you're both here," he said absently, slamming the door behind him and locking it with a flick of his wrist. "We have a problem."

"Banquet running behind schedule, Thaniel?" Saebariel came up to kiss her husband in greeting, but he merely took her hand and stood facing Mylena, his face blank. The knot in Mylena's stomach doubled in size.

"Ships landed off the coast this morning, offloading soldiers onto the shore," he said curtly, gesturing toward the open window. This particular room overlooked the lee side of the mountain Haven City perched on, so Mylena couldn't see what he was describing, but his gesture said it all.

"By the El," Saebariel whispered, her body tensing for a fight, "we're under siege?"

"No, the invading army has entered the city. The gates were...left *open*. They are already here."

Mylena found herself standing still in the middle of a vortex of movement. Her head buzzed, her fingers tingled, but she could not get her mouth to open. It was happening, just as she had dreamt it: First the dress, and now danger was rising up to swallow her family whole. She had to say something, but how? Her parents were in the middle of a heated discussion across the room. Her father was trying patiently to explain the dire situation they were in, while her mother was strapping on the rest on her armor.

"Thaniel, those people out there need me," Sabariel was saying, reaching for her short sword.

Snatching the sword from off the chair where she had left it, Thaniel held the weapon behind his back. His actions might be playful in a different context, but his expression was completely serious.

"Ella my love, they do need you. Alive. If you head out there and face an invading force by yourself, what do you think will happen? How long will your people have you once you take on a thousand men?"

As they spoke, Mylena approached the window. Pulling the curtains aside, she looked down at Haven City, wrapped around the mountain like a ribbon. Below her directly was the trade quarter, whose businesses would just be opening for the day. Even through the glass she could hear the screams of the citizens, smell the smoke from the fires. As dawn started to brighten the sky, she saw rows of buildings ablaze, and small dark figures running through the streets.

"They aren't men," she whispered as if speaking to the window itself. The sound nevertheless carried to her parents, who joined her at her vigil.

"What, my heart?" Mylena felt her mother's hand on her shoulder, and turned to see her father also stood beside her.

"They aren't men. Look, their skin looks like stone, and their eyes...they're purple."

Over her head, Mylena felt her parents exchange a meaningful look. Together, they pulled her from the window. Her father brushed something from her cheek, and only then did Mylena realize she had been crying.

"This is bad," he said, never one to sugarcoat things. "We are in a dark hour, but we have each other. There's no use worrying. We'll get through this, and be stronger for it."

Nodding absently, Mylena's mind filled with images from her dream. *Hand in hand they stood before me, and when I touched them, they melted into black pools at my feet.* It wasn't worry she felt, but foreboding. *I need to tell them, tell them what's going to happen.* The ache in her deepest muscles returned, and she groaned slightly and bent over at the return of the pain. When she straightened up again, her mother was holding out a steaming cup, her eyes worried. Taking the offered cup, Mylena retreated to the bench beside the bed, keeping her eyes averted. It was the universal signal that a teenager doesn't want to discuss something, and her mother heard it loud and clear. So she turned back to her previous battle and let this one be.

Mylena sipped her hot cider and chewed on her thoughts, watching the interplay between mother and father. She would wait for the right time to tell them about the dream. After all, they were safe enough in the queen's apartments, as long as the doors held.

"Thaniel, give me my sword. I'm not just going to sit here while they sack my city."

"Our city, love, and no. I am your husband, and you will obey me in this."

"I am your queen, and I order you..." she stopped. She had been pacing the room like a jungle cat, eyes on fire and body coiled and ready to strike. Now the fire calmed, and she looked down at Mylena. Something she read in her daughter's eyes changed her mind. "No, I don't order you. Oh, Thaniel, where is my Guard at a time like this? By the Grove, they're burning the city!"

"You know where they are. Sent on a mission of peace. Sent north so that we could prove ourselves autonomous and civilized to our mother nation, to Eidalore. Sent—" Thaniel broke off as the doors opened.

"...by me." The queen's Chancellor swept into the room looking regal and triumphant. His golden hair flowed well past his shoulders, held only by a thin purple ribbon on his temple. The ribbon matched the luxury of his robes, which pooled at his feet like dark, ominous clouds. Arndorn tucked his hands within the belled sleeves of his robes and smiled just like a cat that had cornered a lizard in the garden.

Arndorn, who had been the most loyal of her mother's councilors. Arndorn who had lived with the family since before Mylena was even born. Arndorn, who was full of smiles and warmth and loyal advice. Well, he was smiling now, but there was nothing warm and loyal about it. The look of menace in his eyes sent shivers up Mylena's spine, and she crossed the room to stand behind her father. He spread an arm in front of her protectively, and she realized, as he did so, that he was still holding her mother's sword. Hope blossomed within her as she turned to face their betrayer.

Saebariel too was facing Arndorn. In that instant, the entire family had aligned themselves, both physically and mentally, so that they were united in the far corner of the room.

"What is going on, Arndorn? Surely not you?"

"All these years, you never saw me. Son of the Clan leader of Kir'Tazul, and I wasn't good enough for you. You see me now, don't you?" Mylena realized he wasn't talking to her father, he was totally focused on Saebariel. What did he mean by "not good enough?"

She felt her father's arm in front of her push her back a step, then two, so slowly that Arndorn wouldn't notice. At the same time, Saebariel stepped forward toward Arndorn.

He continued to speak, his words gaining a frantic speed as if he had been holding them in for a very long time. "I know you, Saebariel. I know your secrets, and it is those secrets that will be your undoing." He reached back and opened the bedroom door, revealing the antechamber filled with gray-skinned figures in black armor. Too tall to be men, their eyes glowed purple even in the dim light of the room.

Her mother turned to face her father and embraced him frantically. She kissed him deeply, hungrily, and Mylena was too alarmed at the situation to even remember to be embarrassed at her parents' tendency for public displays of affection. Instead, she focused on the sword, and her mother's hand as it wrapped around the hilt still hidden behind Thaniel. With her eyes locked on his, she nodded, unsheathing the sword in an arc above his shoulder as she spun on her heel. Then the chaos began.

Everything sped up then, and Mylena couldn't focus on any one thing, so that she saw the events in flashes and parts. Her father pulled her toward the far wall; her mother screamed in rage, a scream that turned into spellsong. She was raising a wall between them, even as Arndorn and his minions rushed forward to grab her, the stone continued to seal them in. Mylena heard cries of pain as her mother fought back, years of battle training all culminating in that one moment of what must be brilliant swordfighting.

Through the barrier, Mylena heard her mother call, "Thaniel, I love you!" And then her father was opening a door she never knew existed, and, as the door slid closed behind them and they disappeared into the secret heart of Illuminata Castle, Mylena couldn't help but wonder *why didn't she say goodbye to me?*

With most of the city guard sent home per Arndorn's instructions, Haven City was laid open to the savage forces. Bloodthirsty villains who had spent too much time at sea, burned, pillaged, and murdered with abandon. The city soon began to burn, the screams of the inhabitants rising with the smoke into the night air. Their leader, the Lord Sargon, and his procession, swept up the hill into Illuminata Castle and entered without issue, thanks to his new second-in-command.

As he stepped across the threshold, Sargon announced coolly, "I want the royal family kneeling before me, bound and gagged within the hour." He dropped his ever-present smile for an instant so that the brigands under his command would fully understand exactly how serious he was.

"My lord," Arndorn began quietly, "there has been a challenge. I will require a few moments to collect all the members of Saebariel's family." He snapped his fingers, and the small group of invaders who stood beside him melted into the shadows, to begin their search of the castle.

"Meanwhile, Arndorn, my friend," Lord Sargon said, not dropping his ubiquitous smile, although his dark eyes flashed for a brief moment with irritation, "there is the matter of a certain cavern we must explore. I would hate to come all this way and be disappointed. You do know of the Well's location, I presume?" This time, the stare angled up at the elven chancellor, and Arndorn couldn't help but squirm internally, seeing Sargon suddenly no longer smiling. Sargon's eyes were dark pools filled with darker intentions.

"Of course, my lord. The research I sent you was done by the king himself. Everything it documents about the Well of Zyn is entirely accurate. The Well resides within a cavern underneath this very castle. If you wish, I can take you there now."

"Oh I wish, I wish," Sargon replied silkily. He fingered his narrow beard and gestured for Arndorn to lead the way. The chancellor oozed through the main foyer of the castle, his purple robes silently caressing the polished marble floors as he went.

Much like the kingdom of Shadowhaven itself, the castle was a new construction, built once the kingdom had been formally established some twenty years before. Songs had been sung and tales written of the deep and undeniable love between King Thaniel and the Warrior Queen Saebariel. Once they had sworn to bind their lives, a kingdom arose out of the beauty of their union. Thaniel thought it fitting to erect their castle on the site of the Well of Zyn, and created around it the first elven city.

Some thought it mad, the intention to stay in one place forever. Had they not moved their people in the traditions and pathways of their ancestors for thousands of years? Combining the two races was madness enough, but a madness they knew would not be soon erased the day the king set work on building Illuminata Castle.

*And now,* thought the Chancellor, *shall we change again, or be lost to the histories of men?* He plunged through the passageways of the castle, arriving at last at the throne room, his mind on the history of this magnificent building. It was this structure that first gave him the idea that perhaps the elves had little concept of how to truly use the powers at their disposal.

It seemed to him as he walked through the castle he deconstructed it with his mind, tore it down stone by stone. When he finally reached the throne room with its secret cavern below, Arndorn had removed all traces of Thaniel's reign from his mind. In its place, stood a new temple, dedicated to the worship of Arndorn, the new god-king of the elves. With the humans eliminated, he could return his people to their proper traditions, he could rebuild what Thaniel had perverted the day he stepped onto the shore and started this travesty they call Shadowhaven.

As they entered the throne room, a group of Sargon's warriors came in dragging an elven woman of extreme beauty. Her features were more delicate than those of other elves, as if she were carved from ivory. Even her movements were birdlike. But underneath the lithe frame, there was an undeniable strength radiating from her, as if, though bound and shackled between two soldiers, it was by her will alone that she was held. Saebariel, Warrior Queen of Shadowhaven.

"Why are you doing this?" she asked Arndorn, not even deigning to look at Sargon. Her striking golden eyes searched his face but found no trace of the friendship they had known before. A soldier backhanded her for speaking. A small cry escaped her lips, and then she was silent.

Arndorn considered his answer while Sargon eyed her openly. "You're quite a beauty, you know," Sargon said, smiling as if the obvious nature of his comment amused him. He walked up to her and caressed her cheek with the back of his hand. He had to reach up to touch her, such was her height, but he did so as if it were natural for him to do so.

"That pixie blood of yours has done you well." Her eyes snapped angrily to Arndorn, but Sargon held her chin and firmly yanked her gaze back to him. "Ah, yes, your friend here has told me much about you. Shall we see exactly how much of it was true? Open it." He shoved her toward the throne, standing stoic and elegant in the middle of the room.

Saebariel gazed around the room. Here were her beloved trees, a grove brought indoors to please her, to remind her of her home so far away. Thaniel had done this, so that she would feel welcome and could rule in a room that never knew the night sky. She felt a weight drop onto her heart as she reached out and touched the stone chair, erected from the rock bed of the mountain itself. It wasn't until this moment that she truly felt the distance between her husband and herself, and hoped he was far away, that he was safe. In that same instant, she knew she would never see him again.

Wrenching her hand back from the arm of the throne, she turned to face Sargon, chin raised proudly. "Never," she said, her voice almost a whisper. When the second slap came, it was from Sargon's own hand, and the force behind it was strong enough to echo through the cavernous room. This time, no cry escaped her, though one tear did escape down her cheek.

"There is one thing you should know about me, little queen; I don't like to be disappointed. But luckily, my new friend, Arndorn has told me much about you and your...ancestry." Sargon nodded, and the brute to her left grabbed Saebariel's arm, holding her forearm between wrist and elbow. Without hesitation, he broke it; the sound of crunching bone under metal was followed by her screams. She crumpled to the floor, whimpering.

"For such a strong woman, you really are rather frail. You really should have considered this before you decided to deny me. Tell me something," he oozed, stroking his beard, "Why exactly must a pixie hide her true nature from the elves she leads? Have the elves so biased a nature that they cannot accept you simply because you have wings? What a shame.

"Now then, shall we start with your other arm or your fingers perhaps? Don't get me wrong; I do enjoy this. It's just that I have someplace I need to be, and *you're trying my patience.*"

As a way of prodding her, Sargon's warrior reached down and crushed her left shoulder, as easily as if he were cracking ice. In agony, she screamed "No more!" Despite the pain she endured, she stood and, whimpering, faced the throne, her eyes closed.

A low song issued from her, nearly a whisper of melody rising from within. It was as if she were asking the rock to stand aside, lulling it into submission, willing it to do her bidding. Though she sobbed as she sang, the wavering melody was keenly beautiful, rising and falling in waves that wrapped around the throne and caressed the trees around them. The trees responded first, humming in accord with her song, and then finally, the throne melted away to reveal an intricately carved stairwell slithering down into the ominous dark.

"Carry her," Sargon commanded, and stepped onto the first step. As he did so, a torch lit further down the stairway, and they could see exactly how far it went.

A spiral of torches wound down through the mountain and out of sight. The procession made their way to the bottom of the cavern, hearing their footsteps dissipate into unechoed silence as they plunged deeper into the earth. When they finally reached the bottom, no torchlight was needed because the entire room was lit with a soft, blue light. The light's source, it soon became clear, was a large pool of vibrantly blue liquid that churned and bubbled, though nothing touched it. The Well of Zyn.

Sargon finally pulled from his robes the scroll that he had been keeping in his pocket. In an uneven hand, notes and diagrams regarding the Well filled the page. He read them aloud as if he were alone in his private room studying and not standing in a massive cavern beneath a recently besieged castle. "The Well will bestow upon anyone who drinks of it, their ultimate personal perfection. Be warned; not all have a perfect state awaiting them. Should you find yourself lacking, only death will be your reward."

Saebariel cried out from the crumpled heap of her limbs on the floor. "How could you?" she demanded of Arndorn. This time he answered.

"How could *you*? *Wed* a *human*? Is your memory so weak that you forgot that we were to be betrothed all those years ago? Yet Thaniel strides up on our beach, polluting it with his magicless stench, and you fall instantly into his arms. You were meant to be *mine,* my Warrior Queen. Under my guidance, the elves could have risen to heights never before seen in our culture. Instead, you tainted our race. You did this, not I. You did this the day you rejected a pure-blood elf for a disgusting human!" He spat on her then, a gesture he never would have thought himself capable. But he loved her, even now, even as he smelled the rank of the human king on her. He loved her, and it was her betrayal that doomed them all.

Saebariel looked up at Arndorn, her eyes filled with a mixture of pity and disgust. "And to think I ever called you a friend. May your heart rot long after your bones, Arndorn."

"Such fire!" exclaimed Sargon, returning from his musings over the well. "I can see what you saw in her, Arndorn, pretty and feisty. Are all elven women so heated?" He cackled then, a little too loudly for the small humor of his comment. As he did so, his laughter was echoed by a lithe female voice in the shadows. It was as if she were laughing at him, mocking him. That would not do.

"It's a shame; I should have liked to have taken you for my queen, little one. Somehow, I think the people would take this easier if you were there standing at my side. But, alas, something tells me that you would not allow that, and I have other uses for you." He stepped forward, and Arndorn appeared at his elbow, holding a large, shallow bowl, carved with birds. Owls flew across the bowl. Saebariel recognized it as an item from her personal collection. She had given it to Thaniel several years ago. She wondered how long ago Arndorn has stolen it and she had never noticed.

As Sargon neared her, she pointedly ignored him, instead locking eyes with her betrayer. "I was *never* yours Arndorn," she hissed. "You are nothing but a worm." Then she shut her eyes tight and thought hard out into the world, *I love you; protect Mylena!* She was concentrating so hard that when the dagger pierced her chest, she didn't notice it at first, the metal slicing into her heart. She opened her eyes to see Sargon pull the blade out and stab it once again into her stomach. Then the pain submerged her into a blessed blackness from which she never awoke.

"Make sure to collect it all," Sargon said, casually dropping the dagger on the floor and turning to the Well. He reached his blood-soaked hand out to touch the waters, only to be thrown backward onto his back. Huffing in irritation, he stood and regained his composure. "The shield is weakening; I can feel it. Where are the king and his brat daughter?"

A soldier newly arrived, stepped forward out of the shadows. "We searched the castle grounds, but they were nowhere to be found. My lord, they have escaped."

Rage flashed across Sargon's face, and, an instant later, it was replaced with an all-too-calm smile. He approached the basin, quickly filling with the queen's blood and knelt before it. In a tongue no one should utter, he began to chant, his fingers dangling in the blood. The words clashed with all ears who heard it, and, indeed, they did their best to blot out the sounds as best they could. When he was done, he kissed the forehead of the dead queen before he rose to his feet, thanking her for her gift.

"No matter; contingencies have been put in place." Without another word, he turned and started the ascent up to his newly claimed castle. His time would come; he only had to be patient. The shield would come down, just as soon as the king and princess were rotting in their graves.

CHAPTER TWO

Reason abandoned the soldiers as they stepped from the frozen mountain pass infested with creatures from their nightmares into the peaceful shaded glen outside the monastery. Three long years it had been since Warrek and his soldiers had seen Shadowhaven, and more than one soldier was not ashamed to fall upon the soil and kiss it in welcome. The monastery sat squat and ugly against the trees of the forest, a makeshift human structure erected 15 years ago by human hands and unaided by magic, so that it leaned to one side awkwardly. Yet for all its faults, it was the most beautiful sight they had seen in months. As elegant as the fields, towns, and villages of the Eidalore homeland were, they were hungry for the land they had created, for Shadowhaven, as good as its name.

As they neared the monastery, two lone monks approached. One was older, balding, his blue eyes milky with blindness. He leaned on the arm of a young man, rail thin under his robes, his dark hair cropped severely around his ears. The pair were praying incessantly as they approached.

"I am Warrek, captain of the guard, absent these three years from my beloved Shadowhaven. May we rest within the walls of Laud'El?" He swept his helm off his head as he spoke, bowing slightly—quite a task for someone who resembled less a man and more a mountain.

The pair of monks did not stop; indeed, they did not even acknowledge that Warrek had spoken to them. They waded through the band of fifty soldiers as if they were traversing a stream, not noticing the water was made of soldiers. As they reached the end of the column of soldiers, they continued until they reached the beginning of the pass, and there they knelt, palms clasped together, heads bent.

"Brother Abihu?" The elder monk asked, his voice richly warm and strong, but frail at the edges.

"Yes, Brother Nadab," the younger replied, in a voice less resolute than that of his companion.

"Do you see the hordes approach? Does the darkness draw in upon us?"

The younger man looked up at the walls of the mountain pass and nodded, saying, "Yes, the darkness draws close."

"Then let us pray for the safety of those within Laud'El, my brother. Let our faith be our shield." Nadab raised his hands to the sky and his prayers echoed off the ominous jagged rocks and bent trees of the pass.

The younger monk, hunched within his cowl like a man hunted, turned to warn the soldiers. "You might find it best to take refuge within Laud'El, should you want to survive the night. May the El protect you."

As he turned back to his prayers, the shadows in the pass seemed to congeal around them, moving faster than was natural. Warrek could see shapes appear out of the absolute dark, shapes with hissing, with teeth, with intent to kill. It was enough for him to know danger was coming.

"Run! To the doors!" He turned and led his soldiers toward the monastery, not stopping to inquire of the monks, and behind him he could hear their screams as the shadows enveloped them. As one, they surged toward the walls, banging on the doors, and the darkness was coming toward them.

"Open up, man! Warrek called, his voice hoarse with fear. He stood close to the doors, hearing voices within. When he had almost lost hope of survival, the doors opened, and they fell into the vestibule, chests heaving.

Behind them, a young peon dressed in armor he did not recognize slammed the door closed, and the darkness stopped hissing. "I don't understand," Warrek gasped, angry and afraid. "What is out there?"

"And why would you send those men out there to die?" asked Marcus, Warrek's sergeant at arms.

Their questions were directed toward an old man perched near the stairs at the opposite end of the vestibule. His robes were dirty and hung on his long frame limply. There was an ultimate sadness in his voice as he said in a low tone, "So that you might live, son; so that you might live."

Outside, in the dark, Abihu looked from the corpse of his friend to the dark stains pooling in his own robe. He reached his hand out to close the eyes of Nadab, blind in death just as they had been in life. As he lay dying, the face of an angel appeared before him, sad eyes and crooning voice surrounded by a radiance of light and wings. "Sleep now, young one," she said, kissing his forehead, and he closed his eyes and obeyed.

They stood there, the soldiers of Warrek's troop, staring at the door as the screams beyond wafted into a silence more frightening than the sounds that preceded it. Their greatest fears began to animate a bloody tableau along the aged panels of the door, and panic gripped their hearts in vices of razor sharp ice. Warrek's own scene included a host of those shadow fiends and his own parents, so very terrified as they huddled in a corner, awaiting a fate worse than death. He blinked away the image, corralling the fear in his gullet with a toss of his head. His battle-hardened reflexes took over, and a light switched on within him. The years of experience in warfare focused to a single fine point in his mind, lighting the way through the haze of indecision and the darkness of terror with a beam powered with decisiveness and understanding of the situation.

"Gregor," Warrek barked, his voice hard as the flagstones he stood upon, "ten soldiers guard this door; the rest come with me."

"B-but... haven't they gone?" A small voice, shaky in its self-delusion, came from within the crowd of soldiers. Warrek paused to looked them over. These were the women and men who had braved death twice to traverse the mountain pass.

These were the women and men who had stood strong while creatures from their nightmares took their comrades as supper. Another battle was the last thing they needed. As his eyes scanned the crowd, he saw the weariness drip from their brows in sweaty, fear-reeking rivulets.

"You're afraid," he said to Gregor. It was not a question. "Good. These creatures, whatever they are, are not done. Should any of you believe they have, you can go stand in those shadows outside and prove me wrong." He glanced at the monk on the stairs, read in his eyes that there was more he needed to know, and nodded his understanding. "We are in for a long night, comrades, and the quicker we take positions the longer we will last. Ten stand here; the rest come with me."

Gregor called out the names of his choice of the Queen's Guard, and the rest of the column proceeded into the monastery proper. The main building encircled a central cloister, where an herb garden and small orchard lay under the night sky. Warrek left twenty soldiers there in the courtyard, mostly archers and Fire Callers, and continued to follow the monk inside with those who were most wounded.

"What is going on here?" barked a voice from within. At the far side of the mess sat a man in scavenged mismatched armor, most likely taken from the bodies of the dead, with a napkin daintily tucked under his chin. He had a leg of mutton in one hand and a tankard in the other. In his pale gray eyes sparked the irritation of a monarch being bothered at dinner. "I demand an explanation."

Warrek motioned for his contingent to spread out throughout the room. The elves, for their part, seemed uneasy about this, despite the room's high timbered ceiling. The women did not feel comfortable indoors. They had had this same problem with their stay at Eidalore castle, surrounded by humans and so far from their forests. Strong as they were, they felt weakened if they couldn't be near the elements that gave them their power. The wounded rested at the long benches and tables, and the old monk did not bother to hide his disgust, instead wrinkling his nose and covering his mouth with his sleeve. Warrek noted the monk's reaction without condemning him for it. For a man of the El, it would be the hardest thing in the world to welcome warriors into his midst. Now he was doing it for a second time.

Without pleasantries, the monk said to Warrek, "This is Captain Harridan, commander of the forces stationed at Laud'El,, and I am Brother Timothy, the spiritual guardian of this place."

"And you are...?" Harridan sneered, not bothering to rise from his dinner.

"I am Warrek, Captain of the Queen's Guard. I pray you remember that. How many men are under your command?"

Understanding ran its course through Harridan's face, a small battle between his desires and his duty twitching along the muscles in his cheek. Duty was evidently victorious. "We are fifteen, a newly trained squad of militia formed from families sympathetic to the resistance." Harridan stood, wiping his chin, his tone suddenly deferential.

"Resistance?" Warrek asked, looking at Brother Timothy. "Could someone please explain what in hell we are talking about here?"

Brother Timothy bowed his head, folding his hands inside his sleeves. "The ways of war are no proper conversation for a man of the El," he proclaimed dismissively.

Harridan saw his moment to shine. "You must have been gone quite a while not to know the recent history of Shadowhaven," he smirked.

"We were sent to Eidalore three years ago," was Warrek's curt reply.

"Well then," Harridan began to polish his immaculate fingernails with his napkin, and then began to tell the story of that fateful night three years ago when Arndorn the Betrayer handed over Haven city and castle to the fiendish wizard Sargon. Since that time, those still loyal to the king had set up their own underground network, a militia, and communicated through codes and secrecy. With the dangers facing the monastery, Harridan and his brand new squad were sent to protect the holy men. "Only we got here rather late, it would seem."

A second monk entered the room, carrying a basin of steaming water and a basket of bandages. His wide-set dark eyes seemed strangely out of place in his moon-round face. "The shadows began eating our brothers a week ago. They have been taking two at a time, the demons."

"You've been sending two at a time," an archer Warrek recognized as Vorynne called across the room rather flippantly as she polished her hand-carved bow. It's a valid observation, thought Warrek, but he said nothing.

"What Brother Pietr means to say is that our rituals will stop for no man, monster, or demon," Brother Timothy said pompously. "We pray for the safety of our people, as their last religious refuge in this dark and blighted time. With the king gone and the queen dead, there is little hope in Shadowhaven these days, and our people—"

"Enough," Warrek interrupting with a slap of his hand on the table. "We have been traveling a long time, many of my soldiers need attention, and I, for one, am tired."

"Where are the other monks?" one of the soldiers asked nervously from his seat at one of the tables.

"We are the only two left," Pietr said sadly. "After we are gone, the Testament will have no one to understand it." His voice was oddly flat and his eyes looked beyond them to a future devoid of religion. "All will be lost without the Word of the El."

Morning came to the monastery, and the soldiers roused slowly from their bunks. Warrek himself was up at dawn, walking the grounds of the monastery, getting the lay of the land. There were three buildings on site, a barn and storage shed combined, a chapel, and the monastery cloister proper, with sleeping quarters, mess, and study rooms. To the west of the cloisters lay the graveyard, its stones newly carved and free of moss.

Beyond the graveyard lay the barn, with two plow horses and a set of cows within, and a sizeable storage of grain in the adjacent shed. The acreage of Laud'El was small, but the buildings were situated such that there were great spaces between them. Even the chapel, set back against the hill, seemed less of a boon than a liability.

Harridan found Warrek in the chapel, lost in thought. "So, I take it we're preparing to evacuate."

"Not at all. Get the soldiers to take the bags of grain from the shed. We're building walls to the east and north, between the barn, the chapel and the cloister. Get the brothers out here to move their precious book. It's best kept safe within the barracks or sommut."

"But even if we do intend to make our stand," Harridan protested, puffing up importantly, "they could appear at any moment. Those monsters attack any time of the day or night." He seemed to inflate with the status his greater breadth of experience gave him.

"Then we best get working." Warrek strode out of the chapel, pausing at the door to turn and say, "And every member of the walking wounded needs a sword."

The morning was spent constructing a barricade, building walls to fortify their position. Warrek made sure that there were two levels of ramparts, a second back against the cloister for when the first line of defense failed. With only 65 soldiers, they were going to have to fight defensively, and it was a fight he needed to win.

Knowing that the shadow creatures had flooded in from the mountain pass, he sent two lookouts to keep an eye out for any strangeness. Should they hear hissing of any sort, be it wind or water snake, they were to report it directly to him.

Around noon, the walls were finished, and the soldiers were stationed behind them. Warrek placed the archers in the graveyard to catch the brunt of the first onslaught, with orders to retreat to the second rampart when things got sticky.

"How long before they come?" he asked Harridan as they stood at their posts behind the second rampart. Harridan could only shrug, but the answer came from the two lookouts, who ran up to announce that the shadows had begun to move strangely in the pass.

The hissing began soon after that, an eerie, unearthly sound out of a child's nightmare. Like a hundred thousand snakes slithering up and down the mountain pass, the sound reverberated down to the soldiers from above, chilling their blood in their bones. Warrek's response was to send the Fire Callers out to set bonfires along the graveyard wall. If these were creatures of shadow, perhaps the fire would slow them down.

It did not. The shadows began to surge down the pass toward the graveyard wall, hissing and screaming in rage. It was difficult to get a clear understanding of exactly how they looked, so black were they. Their bodies seemed to absorb any light around them, and they moved so quickly that their outlines blurred with every movement. As they hit the wall, the Earth Wielders began their song, and the walls jumped up before them, rising ten feet into the air and forcing the monsters to go around. The minute they maneuvered around the barn the archers moved into position, and a barrage of arrows rained down from the sky. Several of the fiends fell, and more scurried out from under the shafts. As fast as they had come, they were retreating, back up into the mountain.

The shouts of victory from the fighters below rose up boisterous and unrelenting. They had fought them off and without a scratch on them. "It's not time to celebrate just yet," Warrek barked at the soldiers. "They're merely regrouping." He walked along the lines, looking over the men and women as he went. There were no bodies left outside the walls, although he could have sworn that some of the creatures had been brought down by the archers. *How can something die yet leave no corpse? Perhaps they were made out of the shadows after all.*

Brothers Timothy and Pietr broke out of the cloister at the noise, their heads held high and their gazes condescending. "Do you rejoice at this bloodshed, children?" Timothy asked, his voice dripping with ire, "I pity you. You stand within the house of the El and draw your sword as if you have never heard the words of the Testament. Need I remind you that the El condemns those who relish the use of the blade? Rather, put down your weapons and let us pray together."

At this, he knelt on the ground, his arms upraised toward the sky, intoning, "Let us pray that the El will be merciful with those who hold such bloodlust in their hearts. Pray with me, children, that you may not be punished in your final hour!" Brother Pietr knelt beside him, and, together, they began to chant the words of the Testament, written so long ago in a language only they could understand.

Warrek turned his back to the spectacle, and said to Harridan, "They are going to be a problem, aren't they?" It wasn't really a question. He called Sergeant Marcus over.

Harridan began to object. "You don't propose to stop them, do you? This is their monastery, after all; Laud'El is theirs, and they should be able to speak their minds here if nowhere else. Do this and you are no better than Sargon himself."

"Your posturing be damned," Warrek growled and turned to Marcus. "Find a nice secure place for our vocal brother there, away from danger. Bring Brother Pietr to me."

It took two elven soldiers to roust Timothy from his place in the center of the courtyard, and, as they dragged him into the cloister, he recited passages from The Testament, the strange archaic words wrenched hoarse from his fevered throat. "You will regret using violence on the land of the El!" he vowed from the doorway before he was finally pulled inside.

Brother Pietr came without such coercion. Warrek was pleased to find him more reasonable than his elder. "I understand you have some talent with healing, Brother," he said, a little more curtly than intended, "I would appreciate your help with the wounded should your stomach be strong enough for the task. I expect we shall see more than one soldier fall this day."

Brother Pietr nodded solemnly. "While I may not agree with your decision, Captain, I nevertheless am charged to help those in need. I will do what little my training will allow in service of those hurt by this terrible action." At this, he turned to face Warrek full on, his eyes intensely bright, "However, I want it be known that I heartily disagree with this choice of yours. You profane Laud'El with this warfare on holy ground. I help because I have no choice but to help, but your accounting for this will come in due time."

"No doubt, Brother, you are right. Let us hope that such an accounting will not come today, or we may all be in need of some healing." Warrek dismissed the monk, who retreated into the chapel to create a makeshift hospital, enlisting some of the newer militia to assist him.

Harridan was haughty and disapproving. "You'll come to regret that heavy-handedness of yours one day."

Warrek nodded but only said, "Regret is a luxury for the living. Now, I want you to take ten soldiers and form a gap squad. Wherever there are holes in our defenses, you will fill them. Take at least one Earth Wielder, Clodai, and one of the Fire Callers, as well as a couple archers. Go." It was obvious that Harridan had never been spoken to like this before, and it took him a few seconds before he managed to swallow his fluster and obey. He seemed the type of man who had been raised in relative wealth and luxury, one who followed the call to arms out of a desire for glory rather than a will to serve. It remained to be seen whether or not glory would be afforded him after such a gruesome day as this one. Warrek squared his shoulders and prepared for the second wave.

That second wave was fast in coming. No sooner had Harridan formed his squad than a rippling of shadow came pouring down from the hills, so fast, the Earth Wielders only had time to raise boulders from the ground to throw at the coming horde. They were too many to number, but if Warrek had been forced to put a number on them, he would have judged them at several hundred. Even in the sunlight, they seemed formed of blackened smoke, and moved so fast that as soon as he saw them in one place, they were in another place entirely. The first victims to this tide of darkness were pulled entirely into it, the flesh ripped off their bones, and the carcasses spat back out at the ranks. Those out of range of such immediate slaughter or those who held them at bay with sword and shield were exposed to a shadowy slime that burned their skin and clothes.

The fiends fought viciously, with no regard for their own safety. If one was cut down, five more would take its place. The archers and magic wielders worked hard, but just as a bow took time to restring, so the call of the magic took time to resummon, and the enemy learned of these gaps in their offense and used them to their advantage. As soon as the casters ended one song and prepared the next, the monsters would surge forward and slam the infantry with a redoubled force.

At the same time, a small group of the creatures appeared against the eastern wall, and attacked one soldier at a time there. Harridan's squad came to support the eastern wall, which had fewer soldiers on it. There were only so many of them, and too much acreage to cover.

"What are they doing?" Marcus asked, watching the eastern flank.

"They're learning from us. As we built a squad to plug holes, so they built one to find them. These are clever bastards. Expect more adaptation, and tell the squad to keep their eyes open. There's more where that came from."

True to his word, the northern attack receded and an eastern one rose up in its place. An entirely unseen force pounded the eastern wall, climbing the walls of the cloister and forcing Warrek to pull his casters and archers from the north to focus their attention on the monsters scaling the building. Again, with each enemy fallen, there was no corpse to show for their efforts, and the constant pressure at all fronts was wearing on the soldiers. They were simply spread too thin.

"Fall Back!" Warrek commanded, and the company collapsed to the second rampart, significantly narrowing their defendable area. The fiends pounded against the new wall, while a group tried as best they could to surge through the chapel. It was a lucky chance of architecture that the chapel had only one entrance and a solid stone roof. Thus, the creatures were bottlenecked at the door and easily fought off. Perhaps this was an intentional part of the design; he would have to ask Timothy after this was all over and done with.

There were four more waves of similar strategies throughout the afternoon, and then a break as the sun set, which allowed Warrek to send out his soldiers to collect the dead and rebuild their defenses. Ten of the 65 had died, defending the monastery. Of the survivors, eight soldiers, two of them archers, were wounded gravely enough to require surgery, and all were exhausted. Harridan himself had sustained a nasty gash to the neck that put him out of commission for several hours and required Marcus to step up to command his strike squad in his stead.

When the last of the sun had left the horizon, the entire company, men and elves, felt the loss of its warmth. They held the mutual knowledge that the night seemed to be the monsters' natural playground, and each of them held their breath and searched the night for signs of another attack. The Fire Callers reset their blazes, this time, across the whole of the perimeter, and Warrek set his jaw, holding onto the slim chance that they would survive the night.

Warrek saw, as he walked amongst the ranks, that the young soldiers of Harridan's command had faced their first combat with shaking swords. They were children when the battle began, soldiers in name only. But now they stood shoulder-to-shoulder with Warrek's seasoned fighters, steady of hand, though weary of eye. They had been forced to become warriors overnight. A few of them had already fallen under the tooth and claw of the enemy, and others had risen up to take their place as surely as any seasoned veteran might. They were brave soldiers, to a man, though some were not yet old enough to sport a beard.

When the next wave hit, it was slow in coming, but built up speed as a sailing yacht might in high winds. They surged with invisible claws and teeth, hissing their rage into the night, crashing upon the ramparts like the waves of the ocean, and just as numerous. And just like waves of the sea, they would recede only the strike again with equal power in another spot.

"How many times have they come tonight, do you think?" Warrek heard one lad ask of his mate, tossing his sandy hair as it drooped across the space where his left eye had been earlier. "Eight or nine, I can't be sure," the other replied, their whispers hollow in the darkness. "I think I was asleep for at least two of them." Sleep was indeed taking the troops between fights; sleep was the second enemy, more seductive and harder to fend off. Warrek even let Harridan and Marcus doze against the grain bags of the second rampart for a half an hour or so before he woke them.

"You shouldn't have let me doze off like that," Harridan scolded, sounding grateful rather than irritated. He rubbed his eyes and ran a hand through his now-tousled brown hair. Marcus jolted awake beside him, "I only closed my eyes for a moment, honest," he murmured as he went to rouse the soldiers.

The sun rose over the monastery and found the soldiers standing exhausted at their posts. More than a few heads lolled, until Warrek stepped up to speak to them. "I know you are tired and hungry and scared. Well, the truth of it is, I don't care. We have a job to do, and we will do it. Why? Because our king commands it. He is still out there somewhere, and, until I hear otherwise, my orders still stand. What are my orders? you may ask. The same as yours, to protect the innocent, to protect Shadowhaven. Now, we don't know what these bastards are or where they came from, but we know they can be killed, and we know that we are the only line of defense. Perhaps we will die here today; perhaps we will live. But, either way, let us fight with our consciences clear, knowing that we did our best to hold Shadowhaven up to its name.

"There is a reason we live in a land called such a thing, and another reason still that we fight creatures from the darkness. We are a symbol of what this kingdom stands for, brothers and sisters, and if we fail, that symbolism can only extend to mean that the kingdom itself will fail. I know we have heard that the kingdom has fallen, but I say as long as we believe in what we have built here, then Shadowhaven is still alive. As long as we fight, she lives."

Instantly, the energy of the troops changed. They stood a little straighter against the ramparts, shook the sleep out of their eyes, and looked almost eagerly toward the mountain pass. So when the hissing and screams arose again to taunt them, the elven soldiers among them met the chaotic noise with a battle song in their native tongue. The chant's rhythm wrapped each and every soldier, elven or human, female or male, in a patriotic pride that steeled them for the next wave that hit them.

This time, Warrek had prepared something extra. As soon as the onslaught began, he had Marcus call the retreat, and they pulled back to the second barricade. Only, this time, he had his Air Weavers behind the wall, and they immediately began their weather-calling song. As they did, a thunderstorm crackled the sky with static, and the monsters were struck down by multiple bolts of lightning. As the smoke cleared, only smoking puddles of slime remained. They had killed them all.

This victory brought no celebration, for the contingent had been taught that one success in this battle was often short-lived. Again, they collected the dead—another seven bodies—and prepared themselves for the next assault.

But that assault never came. They waited for one hour, two, and then three. "Where can they be?" Harridan asked, irritated. The irritation boiled over in him, and he screamed out at the hills, "What are you waiting for? Come on then, come and get us!"

"Don't ask for what you don't want," Warrek sighed, leaning against the barricade. "You just might get it."

Marcus came to give the report, "They've gone, Captain. The scouts report the pass is empty."

"Gone?" Harridan was stupefied. "Where could the demons have gone to?"

As if in answer, the mountain pass filled with dark, shadowy shapes. As many as they had killed, and thousands more. They lurked there, their reptilian bodies crouched against the rocks, silently watching the soldiers below. Warrek felt his heart stop to look at them. *There are just so damn many of them*, he heard a small voice inside his head say. Beside him, Harridan began to laugh a quiet, nervous twitter that devolved into a guffaw. "I had to ask," he said when he caught his breath again. "I had to ask."

The chorus began then, the mixture of hissing and screaming they knew so well after a day of hearing it. Only, this time, the tone changed, and it became a howling, like that a snake would make if they were given the lungs of a wolf. The howl rose to a collective pitch, thousands of voices in unison, and then promptly died away. In the minutes of silence that followed, no one moved, not soldier nor monster. They just stood and looked at one another, across the expanse between mountain ridge and monastery courtyard. No one could quite believe what was happening. It was as if time had stopped, and held all there in a piece of eternity as surreal as anything they had seen that day. And then suddenly, the monsters turned, and, as one, they all disappeared over the ridge. They were gone as silently as they had come, and if it weren't for the carnage they had left behind, some would have had a difficult time believing they were ever there at all.

"What just happened?" Harridan asked, disbelieving his own eyes enough to rub them.

Warrek thought about it a moment, and then smiled mirthlessly at the mountain pass. "They're leaving us alone. Something tells me we've just been given a stay of execution."

"Whatever for?"

"For bravery."

The sun sat fat and yellow in the sky, and the monks were at their prayers. The soldiers who remained were tending each other's wounds, breathing the new day's air as if it were a new experience. No one knew why the creatures had suddenly broken off, and no one wanted to voice their deepest worry, that they would soon return.

When the prayers were over, Brother Timothy came to see Warrek. The priests had conferred and decided that the Laud'El could no longer protect the Testament.

"We must leave this place, and journey back to Eidalore to our brethren in the north. Only with greater numbers can we hope to fulfill our holy charge." Timothy folded his hands within his sleeves, his watery blue eyes scanning the warrior's face, gauging Warrek's reaction.

Warrek wasn't fond of being manipulated. "And what charge would that be, Father?"

"Why, to protect the Holy Writings, of course." Timothy stated it as if there could be no other commission for a man to be given.

"We require protection on our journey. I would like to take a small contingent of your —"

"And travel south, of course; I understand." Warrek stood up and proceeded to make his way to the infirmary. Internally, he counted the seconds: one...two...three...

"But Captain!" Three. He smiled as the priest approached, obviously ruffled. "The southern lands are captive, the people in slavery. There is naught but danger to the south."

"Sounds to me like people who would need some hope and prayer, I should think," Warrek replied, not slowing his step.

"The book is too precious to send into Shadowhaven. It will be destroyed." The monk's voice was filled with genuine worry. It was clear that if he had to choose the peace and happiness of the people of Shadowhaven or the book, he would choose the book in a second, without hesitation or a second thought.

"You are free to travel where you like, but my soldiers are going south. South is where Thaniel is, and, above and beyond being our king and leader, he's my friend and the man who saved my life on more than one occasion. Being that I am the man who saved your life only last night, that means you are indebted to me. I am going to find Thaniel, and I suggest you come with me." Here he stopped and turned to face the priest. "However, if you do not think that journey safe enough for your book, you can go back to Eidalore. Alone."

Timothy considered his options, and the struggle played visibly across his face. It appeared that in the struggle between traveling with the soldiers south into danger, and traveling north alone into danger, what little shred of honor he had left in him won out. Or it could be that it wasn't much of a choice at all. In any case, he replied, "As you say, I am indebted to you. Were it not for the bravery of you and your soldiers, the Holy Writings would have been lost last night to those fiends. Let it not be said that the men of the El are not also men of their words. Not only will I accompany you, I am privy to knowledge that will help in this journey. I know of a man who can tell us the location of our leader, if our leader is still alive. However, rumors of his death fly fast in this blighted time, so I would not hold out much hope."

"I don't need hope, Father; I have you."

Warrek gave his soldiers a week to rest and recuperate under the protection of the monastery's roof. He saw no peace within them, though, and no matter how much sleep they seemed to get, their eyes were still haunted by the gruesome fight and loss of their comrades. Even the stoic elves seemed restless, and spent much of their time in the burned-out orchard, staring up at the sky.

So when he called his band of thirty warriors to assemble, there was more than just a little eagerness in their step as they formed ranks. They were grateful to do something, anything. With a breakfast in their bellies and their swords on their hips, they were bright and alert, every one of them, even if not all of them could stand without assistance. The priests, however, were not as jaunty, but that could very well have been from the massive burden of the tome they carried between them. As per the rituals of their order, Timothy and Pietr blessed the monastery and the road before them, and bid farewell to Laud'El with singing. Behind them, the elven women reflexively began to lift their own voices in tribute. Brother Timothy silenced them with a scathing stare. Evidently, he felt their pagan worship unworthy of his God. In the gray morning fog, the small group left their sanctuary behind and made their way southwest, into the swamps.

She was always sensitive; everyone could tell that about her. But her sensitivity went beyond understanding the feelings of others. She knew things before they happened, could sense the natures of arguments and defuse them even before they began. From the time that Joppa was a little girl, playing in the fields with her brothers, she would always know when the rain was coming or when her mother had cut her hand preparing the noon meal. The twins, Joppa and Abihu, created secret languages and spoke for weeks in their gibberish tongue, felt each other's pain from great distances, laughed at jokes the other had never spoken aloud. Thus, when her brother finally answered the call of the El, it was the hardest day of her life. That was, until a week and a half ago.

Joppa, ever the daughter of the soil, was out with her older brothers, enjoying the end of a long day, working the grain harvest. The air smelled of rain and dirt and traces of the swamp that bordered their land. It was her custom to spend the time walking back to the house talking to the plants and animals around her, connecting with the lives of the world. There was only so much you could learn listening to human voices. At times, the lesser understood citizens of this world were more intuitive and certainly more interesting conversationalists.

This particular evening, a cold breeze rolled down from the mountains, rustling the trees and bushes as it went, gaining momentum as is sped down from the rocky peaks. The frigid air reached Joppa as she stood in the field, knocking her to her knees with one arctic blast, more like a hammer than a wind. She was wrapped in a cold so profound it choked her, and when she was finally able to catch her breath, she began to scream. A great wailing and howling boiled from within her so totally she lost all sense of its boundaries. She did not stop screaming for two days.

Locked in the dark of her room, supposedly for her safety but mostly for theirs, Joppa paced until the boards did nothing but creak in anticipation of her footsteps. She had grown up in this room, shared it with her brother until the day he traveled to be with the brethren. There were so many memories here they saturated the very walls like whitewash. She remembered her childhood in a series of vibrant flashes, like the stained-glass windows in a cathedral transported here to her room. The more she recalled images, the more fractured they appeared to become, until she wasn't exactly sure she was seeing anything at all but blocks of bright colors.

One image is of the harvest when she was young. There she is standing in a field of golden grain, the tops of the stalks brushing against her shoulders. She is six. She is watching her father pull the oxen, watching the great beasts snort and toss their massive heads as the whip comes down on their backs. Don't hurt the cows, Daddy; they're helping you. She reaches out to pet the plants around her. The heads of grain tickling her palms. She sees a field mouse darting between the rows of stalks and begins to give chase and then...

Another image appears of Abihu receiving his first lesson in the Language of the El, sitting at the feet of the traveling priest, eyes wide and heart aflame. He was eight. His older brothers thought him crazy, and even his father looked at him askew, as if not quite sure what to make of his interest. Only his sister Joppa understood, and sat down by the fire next to him, and held his hand as he listened to the priest tell stories about the Miracles and the Heroes in the Testament...

Then the harvest memory continues. She falls, scraping her knee on a rock's jagged edge. For a moment, she doesn't notice, so intent on the mouse is she. The mouse, seeing its advantage, dashes away out of sight. She cries loudly with the great heaving sobs of the young, whimpering as she limps back to the house. But her father is there to give her a plum and plants a kiss on the scrape. He sings her a song her mother used to sing, only his voice is low and scratchy and not nearly as pretty as Mommy's was. He always knows what to do in order to make her feel better. It is almost as if he heard...

The calling of the El, he felt the pull of the Order long before he even realized he had decided to leave home. The day he told Joppa, she was smiling and sobbing at the same time, and he felt like he was betraying her most of all. But he also knew that she understood, deep down, that this was what he had to do. He could no more deny the call than his father could ignore the fate of the crops on a frost-ridden evening. Hadn't they since childhood woken in the middle of the night to walk among the crops in the freezing cold with buckets of smoldering coals, smoking the frost away from the precious grain? Wasn't his heart's ambition, his drive to serve his fellowman, equally as vital? He was setting out to tend the crops of Shadowhaven, to smoke the frost away from the tender shoots of mankind, yet his father's eyes were nothing but cold to him. He spoke as if his son were committing some great crime. Couldn't he understand that...

The room spun, feeling both cavernous and confining by turns. For days, Joppa couldn't distinguish whose memories she relived. One moment, she was lying by the hearth listening to her brothers talk about the day's activities, and the next moment threw her into a prayer service filled with faces she did not recognize. Were they her brother's thoughts or her own? Day and night, she labored with two minds in her one skull, fighting to find her own identity at the same time. By the end of a week, she could no longer tell the difference between the two, but she had given up trying and didn't care much about it anyway.

Once a day, a member of her family would bring her food. They tried their best to communicate with her. It was as if they came to see if she had finally healed herself of the illness that plagued her. Abihu would have found it amusing that they would expect a sickness to go away without treatment, and his comments to that effect sent her into fits of giggles. Joppa just wanted to be let out into the fresh air to work the fields with her brothers, to feel the damp soil squish between her toes.

This morning, her brother Aebrin brought her a bowl of broth. He was the youngest of her elder brothers, around seventeen, with their father's dark eyes and brooding expression. Despite his looks, he was, nevertheless, a sensitive person and had stated more than once his objection to seeing his sister made a prisoner in her own room. It was he who had smuggled in the drawing tablet and pencils to her the first day. The tablet had immediate taken flight out the window, but the pencils she used to write her essays and sermons on the walls. She was down to the last one.

"I've come to see you, Joppa," Aebrin announced a little too loudly as he unlocked the door. "Now, don't throw the chair this time; you know how it angers the other furniture."

Joppa was sitting in the windowsill, looking out at the fields, her eyes constantly scanning the rows and rows of golden grain. "The cock gets to crow and the boys get to tend the fields, but can Joppa go out to worship in the sunshine? Oh no, the dark is the place for her, even though the days grow short and the light grows more and more skittish. It hardly ever comes to play in Joppa's window now. No, the light is as skittish as Father. 'Lock her away,' he says. 'The dark is the place for her.'" Then she jumped down from the sill and began scribbling on one of the few blank places on the wall, her penmanship rough and simple like a child's.

"Now when did you learn to do that? Was you stealin' books from the Callisters' farm when we weren't lookin'?" Aebrin set down the bowl of broth on her little wooden table and took a turn about the room, surveying the hieroglyphic records that wrapped the room from ceiling to floor. "Don't see no books, though. Strange sickness that struck you, Love. I can hardly understand it." There was concern in his eyes and in his hands, which twisted nervously, the fingers turning into knots.

"Anything is understandable if you take the time to observe," Joppa replied icily, snatching her bowl from the table and retreating to the windowsill. "Once, you had little knowledge of what it was like to be a jail keeper. How well you have learned. You've turned into an excellent warden. Father must be so proud." She slurped down her soup loudly as if she hoped to annoy him as much as possible. Aebrin was hurt.

"Aw, come now, Joppa, don't be like that. We was always pals, wasn't we? You remember when I would take you on my back and you would ride like I was a pony? Remember that? They was good times we had. I did my best to be good brother to you like Abihu was..." He trailed off awkwardly, rubbing the back of his neck.

"Of course, I remember; are you insane?" The question hung in the air in front of her, and she stared at it, tilting her head like a confused dog. "Scratch that; never mind..." She paused. "I believe this belongs to you," she said, chucking the bowl at him. He ducked as it flew by his head, and turned, managing to catch the crockery before it exploded against the door.

Aebrin sighed sorrowfully, evidently making the decision that today was not the day to press the matter. He left the room with the bowl, shutting the door behind him and relocking it with a rusty snap. Joppa waited until his footsteps faded down the staircase, and then pulled out a spoon that she had secreted in her hair and put the finishing touches to her masterpiece, a hole in the window frame large enough to stick her hand through. She had been digging at the wood all week when she wasn't interrupted by visitors or caught by the urge to write. It was rough work, digging with spoons or whatever random implements she happen to steal from her family, and she made sure to make a small prayer of contrition to the El for every theft. The little scrap of blue curtain her mother had tacked to the window when Joppa was a girl had covered the opening whenever someone came to pay her a call. She tossed aside the cloth with little ceremony, and set to her task.

After an hour of steady digging, she broke through. Reached through the opening, Joppa tugged with all her might at the nail that held the window fastened closed. The motion, although strange to most hands, was one Joppa was used to, having performed just such a task numerous times out in the field with her brothers. If she could pull weeds from the ground with all their persistent root systems, with their need to grip the earth for their very life, then she could do this. Which had the greater tenacity, the weed or the nail? Or Joppa?

It was Joppa who won out. To her delight, the nail was shorter than it looked, and the wood of the frame was already beaten by weather and time. After two hours of persistent pulling, she was able to wrench the nail free. She had spent much time at her perch, observing the comings and goings of her family below, and now they were all at evening meal. Before she opened the window, she collected the two items most precious to her in the world: her pencil and a doll Abihu had made for her out of scraps of cloth found around the farm. Then she bounced up to her windowsill, pushed open the one thing keeping her penned up, and rolled down the roof, landing softly on the cool, damp earth. For a moment, she let it squish between her toes, smiling to herself.

Mustn't be late, oh there is so little time! Told me to be there at dawn, and that was more than a week ago. Though patience be a quality I must cultivate, I cannot abide being held from what I must do. How will I ever explain to Brother Timothy what has happened here? The anger in my father's eyes when he read the letter, the disdain in his voice. The arguments that followed and the hateful, raging words. Oh, Brother Timothy shall give me the strongest talking to, allow me to read my penance from the Testament, standing, all night long, and then I will surely be given service in the kitchens. How I hate doing dishes! That is if I am allowed to take my place amongst the brethren at all. Patience, Abihu, remember patience. As the Testament says, "One must first make the journey before he knows the end of it."

North then, and be quick about it. It's into the swamps I must go, trudging through the water, as the El has bade me do. Don't mind the muck, or the smells; it'll be the creatures that you must worry about. Sleep in the trees, they say; sleep in the trees. Once I get through the swamps, Laud'El can be found, nestled before the mountain pass. To the East. Follow the rising of the moon, the letter said. "Its light will show you the way, just as the Light of the El guides our very lives." If I hurry, I can reach the monastery by dinner tomorrow.

The evening was cool and breezy, as if autumn were entertaining winter for the evening and wished to hear him sing. Joppa ran across the fields, resisting the urge to howl at the moon as it rose on its invisible string, pulled above the eastern horizon. There was too much work to do, though, and she had to travel fast if she wanted to make sure she reached her destination before the conscriptions were closed. What good was a calling, if you heeded it all too late?

If any one of her brothers had been looking out the window just then, they would have seen a dark-haired beauty dashing through the rows of grain, hair unbound and arms flailing, heading northeast towards the Swamps of Keracor.

## CHAPTER THREE

The dream came again that night, Illuminata Castle rising from the mountainside it was built from, a forest canopy of stone rather than simply a building. Strong, graceful arches and walls that mimicked the waves of the sea. Seeing it now as it would never be again choked her, yet something within her bid her on. She walked along the mountainside caressed by the salty sea air. The doors she found open and the grounds likewise vacant, so she made her way into the foyer. Inside, she turned up the western staircase through the massive grand entrance hall, winding up to the royal apartments, down corridors lined with gardenias and roses and little willow trees. Every branch and leaf glowed bright green as if living under the bright sun rather than within the Shadowhaven seat of power. Every plant thrived within the castle while under the care of Saebariel.

At the end of the hallway, a pair of grand doors led to the queen's chambers; their massive wooden handles forming the head of a great horned owl. Turning left, she entered a small stairway leading up to her own set of rooms. Drifting along the corridor, she could hear music playing in the drawing room, a sweet, peaceful melody that would never grace the castle halls again. Her bedroom was filled with lilies and narcissus, ever white and ever blooming. In fact, everything within the room glowed with the whiteness of freshly fallen snow. She stepped into the flower-scented bedroom; her hands touched the imprint of her head upon the pillow, fingered her pale gauze and lace nightgown, laid out like a spider's web across the bed, trailed down the finely carved posts, and plucked at the bed curtains made of a white, filmy gauze. She turned at last to the dressing table at the far end of the room, a section of the room she had, until now, intentionally kept behind her.

There stood a mirror, one of the few human-made elements in the room, finely carved from a single piece of silver and glorious in its craftsmanship. Many an hour had she spent inspecting her appearance in the glass. As she stood in front of it now, the reflection revealed a girl of seventeen with hair the color of a blazing sunset and eyes as golden as autumn leaves. In the wide upturn of her eyes and the high cheekbones, her elven blood was clear, although her ears had no points at all. She reached up to remind herself of their roundness, a result of her father's human blood. She ran her fingers through her thick, red curls, and her hand came away clutching a clump of hair. Horrified, she looked at her reflection in disbelief. As she stared, all her hair fell away, strands floating down in a rain of fiery tendrils, landing in a pile at her feet. As they lay there, she watched in horror as they turned into writhing black snakes that coiled around her ankles, hissing menacingly. Crying out, she ran from the mirror to seeking refuge at the window.

There stood a figure of a woman, hidden in shadow, her eyes gazing out at sea. She spoke to the stranger, but she would not respond. As she approached, the woman neither turned nor acknowledged her presence. She just stood there, staring at the sea. All around her, the flowers withered, and the bright sunlight hid behind dark ominous clouds that rolled in from the ocean with incredible speed. Only when the clouds reached the castle gates did the figure turn, and she saw finally the ultimate sadness that welled from her eyes. They were dark eyes that accused and scorned and blamed, eyes that saw every black thought scratched in her heart, eyes that knew what she really was.

Mylena awoke then, sitting up in bed, her breath caught in her throat, and she sat in the darkness of early morning, shivering despite the warmth of her blankets. At once, as she always did when she had this dream, she grabbed at her head, grateful to find she still had hair. It was still there, dyed black, braided, and coiled around her neck, much like the snakes in her dream. The fear dissipating a bit, she wrinkled her nose at the dark plait and tossed it over her shoulder.

She hopped out of bed, slipped on her clothes by touch, and wrapped herself in a shawl to ward off the chill. Mylena moved by rote, as if she were still dreaming, fingering the tousled bed clothes and touching the simple pine wardrobe that served as her only storage. She went to the fire then, stoking the coals back to life, and adding more fodder for them to chew on. She swung a kettle of water over the newly risen fire to boil, and moved on through the house with her head still tingling. She trailed a hand down the sturdy farmer's table and touched each plate and cup laid out upon it as she wandered dreamily through the place she now called home. This is reality, not that crazy fantasy of a castle. This is the place of security, of warmth, of family.

Sighing, she reached a heavy red curtain, a divider between the sleeping quarters of their home and the shop where her father did business. One would never have thought a man of his position would take to working as a lowly herbalist. But here he was, finishing up his third year as the local expert on all things medicinal. Strangely enough, for a people so keen on nature, the elven citizens of Shadowhaven had never bothered to know the deeper lore of the plants they favored. It was almost as if they respected their privacy. Instead, they would come to the shop whenever they needed anything, and had begun to turn to her father—now calling himself Vidius—for more than remedies. He was now a local doctor of sorts.

Mylena wiped down the tall table they used as a counter and workspace, and then moved on to dusting the bottles and vials that lined the shelves. There were nearly a hundred of them. Some of the remedies were from the forests around Kir'Unwin, as the elves called this place. Several of the fungi and roots she dug herself, after learning the proper procedures from her father. Many of them came from far-off lands, countries she only knew through the tradesman who wandered the roads, selling the supplies they needed.

Once she had finished her organizing of the shop, she paused, turning to survey her surroundings. This was home, and this home was filled with a good life. A warmth filled her, spreading across her chest and shoulders. It was a hard life certainly, and one she hated nearly every day, but she was learning that life was more than what fancy dresses you wore, what hairstyles you sported, what parties you attended. Life was hard, full of difficult tasks and even more difficult choices. Life, for most of the people in this kingdom, was digging out what little sustenance they could from the harsh, dry dirt. It was a struggle she was just learning something about. It was a struggle that made her finally feel alive.

Returning to the fire, she carefully poured some tea into two of the three clay tankards they owned, cut a hunk of bread from the previous day's loaf, and made her way to the far end of the one-room cottage to wake her father.

"It's morning Dad; time to rise," she whispered softly, nudging him with her elbow since she had no hands free. The steam from the tankards of tea tickled her nose.

"Is it a good morning?" came the sleepy reply as he turned over. Her father was a handsome man with dark hair and light brown eyes in his late 40s, a man old for his years. Three years ago, they had run for their lives, through swords and maces churning a sea of pain that had left him wounded and ailing in ways he never would recover from. His legs, in particular, were badly injured from their sad adventures, and he had a great deal of trouble walking, and an even greater amount of pain.

Mylena handed him one of the tankards of tea and the hunk of bread as he sat up in bed, and pulled the blankets up to expose his legs. From the foot of the bed, she brought out a mortar full of a green creamy mixture, and, as she talked to her father, she rubbed the balm on his legs, starting at his knees and working towards his ankles. More than once, he winced under her touch, and she did her best to work more tenderly while still applying the necessary pressure.

"It's a morning. The sun is out, the fog is lifting, and the walnut shells are running low. How are your legs feeling this morning?" As her hands ran up and down the leg bone, she could feel the knotted cords of scar tissue that webbed the skin. She knew the scars went much deeper, into the muscles and tendons below the skin. That was what the balm was for, to see to it that the scar tissue didn't lock up his muscles entirely. But it had to be applied once a day. If she forgot one day, her father would have to spend the day in bed, resting through the pain.

Just as every morning, her father was quick to change the subject. He had never been good talking about his weaknesses, and, although she knew the pain was substantial, he did his best to never discuss it. "Is there anything else that we risk running out of, Muirinn?" She was Muirinn now, she reminded herself, just as she had to every time the name was used. She was Muirinn and he was Vidius and so they would be for as long as they were in hiding. Her father made a point to use the name several times throughout the morning hours while they were still alone together in the cottage. He knew it helped her to remember her persona before she had to wear her new identity with the villagers.

"I will draw up a list. There are a few mushrooms I will need to gather in the next few days, and I believe there is at least one root, Root of Blackthorn I think, that we will need to buy when next the traveling merchant comes to Kir'Unwin. But most pressing is the walnut shortage. I shall have to go out and pick some today." She finished with the balm, placing the mortar back at the foot of the bed, and helped her father dress.

"Good, good," he said in a way that told her he hadn't heard a word she said, "When you are out, be a dear and send the boy Chiave to see me. That child has so much to learn, and with you gone, I could use the help."

"Of course, Father," Mylena replied, and took her tankard of tea out to the front steps of their cottage. There, she sat, watching the tendrils of fog wander through the streets of the village and brushing out her long, dark mane. She remembered her dream again, and pulled the brush away from the mass of curls to make sure none of her hair was indeed falling away. But no, it was still there but in a shade of black she still was not used to after all these months in hiding.

Kir'Unwin was an elven settlement, inasmuch as elves settled themselves in any place at all. The place had been chosen for their clan because of the spring found gurgling along the edge of the forest. The first thing the elves did when they arrived was build a fountain atop the bubbling water, and from the fountain, they dug a waterway for a stream. The stream wound through the village on its way into the forest, and even looped behind Mylena's home. It was strange to think that every building in the settlement had grown from the ground. Much about the elven magic still confused her, but she knew the Earth Wielder who had coaxed the buildings from the stone beneath the ground. At this, she paused in the braiding of her hair to blush down at her lap. Yes, she knew the Stone Weaver, but mostly, she knew his son.

As she finished her braid and secured it with a leather thong, she stood up from the steps. Holding the steaming tankard in her two hands, she toasted the morning and said quietly to herself, "I am Muirinn Vidiuson, the herbalist's daughter. I am Muirinn and I am home." She downed her tea in one fluid motion, and then retired inside to begin her day.

Kanefionn Stoneweaver, called Fionn by those who knew him, was both a romantic and a warrior wrapped up in the same person. Having been the only child born to Rentyl Stoneweaver and his wife Vorynne, he had been raised from the time he was young in the soldier profession of his mother, once they realized no daughter would be born to them. Though not common, such things did happen in Shadowhaven amongst the elves, and there was more than one male warrior in the clan. Fionn was proud of his training, and grateful his mother saw past his gender and welcomed him into the warrior fold. He was still young, though skilled enough as an archer to best the women warriors stationed at Kir'Unwin, so Fionn remained at Kir'Unwin until the call to complete his training came.

He was grateful for this because, without his time at home, he would not have met her. Muirinn, the herbalist's daughter, a creature in every way his opposite. Where he was tall and pale, she was short and dark. Where he was an elf who spent most of his time in his own head, she wore her every thought openly on her face. He was quiet; she was larger than life. Until they came to the village, he had only seen a handful of people with such dark hair. It was what first drew Fionn to her, and it was the fire in those golden eyes of hers that held him fast to the spot. Fionn had more than once caught himself sitting on the low wall in front of his home watching the path to see if she was walking it. Just as he was doing right now, he realized, tossing a stone across the pathway into the orchard.

Fionn raised his arm and was just about to toss his second stone when Muirinn appeared around the corner of one of the buildings, carrying a large hand-woven basket. She looked preoccupied, but when she reached where he sat, she stopped, looked up at him and smiled lightly. "Why, hello, young warrior. I see you are out enjoying the fall weather. However, it appears you have some issue with the stones of the earth today. Could it be some jealousy for all the time your father spends with them? Tell me truthfully, Kanefionn. Are you enacting revenge on the stones? Tsk, tsk, that shade of green does not become you." She was smirking then, her golden eyes twinkling with mischief.

Fionn immediately dropped the stone, feeling the heat of embarrassment flare in his cheeks. He stood up a little too quickly, nervously tossing his head to get a stray hair out of his eyes. "I hate it when you call me that," he mumbled, awkwardly trying to rub the blush from the back of his neck.

"I know," Muirinn replied mercilessly.

An uncomfortable silence stretched out between them, as Fionn fidgeted underneath her gaze. He unsheathed his sword and began to sharpen it reflexively with his whetstone. After a while, she said, "I am off to pick walnuts. My father asks that Chiave join him this morning for some further instruction. Do you know if he is available?" Without replying, Fionn dashed inside and pulled his sleepy brother from his bed.

"Up you! The herbalist wants to see you." He unceremoniously kicked the ball of blankets on Chiave's pallet.

"And you want to see the herbalist's daughter," Chiave taunted, despite being half asleep. Though there were many advantages to having a brother, even a foundling one such as Chiave, most times, it was merely irritating to have him around. It would do him good to spend some time with the herbalist. Maybe it would teach him a little sense. And yes, he was right about the other thing too, Fionn begrudgingly admitted. The trip to retrieve Chiave would give him an excuse to make sure he followed Muirinn home.

Fionn returned outside to see that Muirinn had continued on her way to the orchard. Briskly, he trotted up the path to meet her, catching her as she reached the fence that encircled the stand of walnut trees. Muirinn smiled at him, but did not say anything more, only started expertly twisting the ripened fruit from the lower branches of the trees. She dropped each green pod into her basket never looking, never missing. Standing on her tiptoes, she looked more like a statue than a person, and it was quite a while that Fionn stood staring, until he shook himself out of it with more than a little effort.

"I can help if you like," Fionn offered, taking up the basket.

"Oh, I always do," Muirinn said lightly. For a while, they worked in silence. Sometimes, Muirinn climbed the trees in order to reach the fruit in the higher parts of the trees. After a bit, she called down to him, "Fionn, what is your gift?"

"Gift?" Fionn asked, caught off guard. He had been too busy staring at her as she plucked nuts off the trees.

"Yes, each elf I've met has some magic talent. I wonder even if your brother might not have some bit of a magical leaning somewhere within him. Where do your talents lie?"

Fionn thought about it a moment, then set the basket down and knelt, one hand outstretched before him. A low humming started from within his throat, and he closed his eyes and allowed the song to open his mouth. He could feel what he sought rise from the ground, and his deep baritone warbling coaxed it up until it broke free of its restraints. When the song trailed into silence and he opened his eyes, a small geyser of water was bouncing up between his fingertips. Cupping his hand, he filled it with some of the fruits of his labor, and took a drink.

"Marvelous!" Muirinn gasped, clapping her hands together lightly. She dropped from the tree to kneel beside Fionn and trail her fingers in the magical fountain he had created, her face filled with wonder.

"It isn't the most practical talent on the battlefield, for the most part. So I am honing my skills as an archer and swordsman." This last he said a little defensively, setting his jaw as if waiting for criticism. Fionn was an elf who felt his warrior pride strongly, even if he was too young to fully understand that pride. Although he waited for the biting comments of the quick sarcastic nature that were so common with Muirinn, none came.

"It's a wonderful skill to have, being able to quench your thirst whenever you need to." Muirinn smiled openly up at him.

It was one of the first times he had seen unguarded delight illuminate her eyes, and he loved how shockingly golden they were, even in the shade of the walnut trees. He had a sudden urge to kiss her there, over the fountain he had summoned from the earth. In order to cover up this urge, he changed the subject to his mother.

Fionn laughed nervously. "Yes, I inherited the aptitude from my mother. She too is a Water Caller."

"Do you miss her greatly?" Muirinn asked, standing to resume their work.

"Yes, I miss her strength; I miss her voice. I think it is always this way when she is on assignment. She has been gone these five years, and I miss her every day. Isn't that always the way, though? I think every child misses their mother."

There was a snap in her eyes and a cloud passed over her face; Fionn knew instantly that he had said something wrong. He wracked his brain for what it might be. Assignments? No, mothers. Muirinn lived alone with her father. Wherever her mother was…it wasn't here.

"I'm sorry," he said, softly, and went to put a hand on her shoulder. She shivered under his touch and looked up at him with her eyes welling with sadness.

"You're right," she said, her voice almost a whisper, "every child misses their mother."

When Muirinn's basket was full, Fionn toted it for her back to her shop and home. He felt absolutely horrible, as if his stomach were filled with gravel, but there was nothing he could do. She walked in brooding silence the entire way home, not even answering him when he asked questions. Lost in thought regarding whatever ill memories their conversation had triggered, Muirinn walked as a woman not seeing her path. Fionn worried if he had harmed their friendship in some irreparable manner. He couldn't bear it if that were true.

As they arrived at the herbalist's shop, Muirinn took her basket from him and disappeared behind the door without a word. A moment later, Chiave emerged, his sandy blond hair tousled and his face smudged with dirt. It was how he normally looked, come to think of it. He took one look at Fionn, and nodded solemnly in that knowing way a fifteen-year-old boy should never be able to do.

"Women are a race we will never truly understand," he said a little too wisely for his years. He put a comforting hand on his brother's shoulder, since Fionn was too tall to wrap an arm around.

Fionn looked at the closed door of the cottage and then sighed. "You know nothing," he growled at Chiave, but allowed the boy to lead him home.

Home at last in her own private sanctuary, Mylena found her father dozing by the fire, his head bouncing lightly on his chest. She draped her shawl across his neck and chest like a small blanket to ward off the chill. Mylena selected a worn-out bucket from the corner and settled herself in front of the fire, the bucket at her right hand, the basket at her left. She then set to shucking walnuts, allowing the rhythm of the task to lull her into reverie. As she divided the meats from the shells and reserved each for their own special purpose, she thought about her mother, the great Warrior Queen. It was, at its core, an impossible standard to live up to. Saebariel had been raised to fight and to lead her brave people, and had fearlessly followed the yearnings of her heart when she married Thaniel. What they built together was nothing short of miraculous, one stable kingdom from two opposing factions. Only the power of their love kept the kingdom together.

But, in the end, there was nothing to protect Saebariel from the evils that befell her. Although the details of her last moments were still a mystery, refugees from Haven City had told of Arndorn's treachery, and Mylena's father explained to her that her mother was most likely dead. Judging from how this

Sargon worked, it seemed the most likely result, considering the strong will Saebariel was known for.

Mylena took the bucket of shells and retreated into the shop area of the cottage, where she transferred them by handfuls to the mortar, pressing until her palms were indented with the imprint of the pestle. The powder she returned to the bucket, where she mixed it with water she had carried in the day before. It was a ritual she had done many times before, creating a dye of surprising tenacity considering the simplicity of its ingredients. This concoction she took out to the where the stream behind their home met the forest's edge, and then she strode confidently into the seclusion of the forest, seeking cover for her next task. Stripping off her corset and shirt she sat in the underbrush of the forest, her pale skin dappled with fingertips of light searching through the forest canopy. With practiced hands, working from years of experience, she drenched her hair in the dark liquid.

It was as if she were reaffirming Muirinn's place in her life, this act of covering up the color of her hair. As she worked, she could feel the princess slide deeper under the mask of the peasant, the mask she wore to keep herself safe. But no matter how often she dyed her hair, the red was still there at the core, waiting for her to get lax, to forget to keep up the ruse. No matter how she tried to bury her origins, her haughty attitudes would surface at the most inappropriate moments, and the gaps in her knowledge of everyday things were frighteningly numerous and threatened to expose their secret on a daily basis. Shaking her head in rueful reflection, Mylena recalled the three weeks it took her to learn how to dress herself. At the same time, she had to struggle with learning how to cook food that would not choke them with its horrid taste. Well, she was finally getting past that one, thankfully.

The dye applied, Mylena rinsed her hair in the icy cold waters of the stream, the frigid temperature making her skin prickle. If anyone were to happen by the stream as it wound its way through the forest, they would have seen the dark cloud of inky water float away, the shadow of a memory of the Princess of Shadowhaven. With the ritual completed for another month, Mylena dressed and went home to her life as a peasant, her wet hair a black wreath of snakes winding around her shoulders in the chill autumn air.

High atop Illuminata Castle, the fires blazed once more in the queen's chambers. In the years since the coup, much about the castle had changed. The plants had long ago turned to dust, and it had been years since the trees in the throne room sported any leaves. Those who stayed in the city did so under compulsion, and those who served in the castle often did so under duress, sometimes without the use of their eyes or their tongue.

The nights seemed colder than they did under the old regime, the wind more chilling as is whipped the mountainside the castle stood on. It was as if nature itself were commenting on the state of affairs. As if the elements would care who sat within the castle. There was little change to the area. It's not as if Sargon had completely razed the city. He only mostly razed it.

Sargon was fond of a good blaze, the rippling heat a reminder of his childhood in an arid land so far away, so he had every fireplace in the queen's chambers stoked every hour of the day and night. Despite all the months of occupation, those who worked in the castle called the rooms by their original names. Some might have considered it a small act of rebellion against their new lord. Others might have replied that old habits die hard.

Yes, there were many changes to the castle since Sargon's arrival, the least of which was an apparatus erected in the queen's bedroom. A set of chains hung from the ceiling in front of the windows that overlooked the valley and forests beyond the castle. These were mirrored by a similar set and shackles bolted to the floor. In front of the manacles, there stood a golden basin, engraved with a Great Horned Owl, its interior caked black with ill intentions. This evening, a young elven girl was attached to the apparatus, and between sobs, she wriggled against her restraints with all the strength of her youth.

She was a pretty thing, but then, they all were pretty. It was a common enough trait amongst the elves. This one was a third-generation soldier, and oh, how Mommy must have been proud. Not so proud now, though, that she wet herself and cried like an infant. He did so enjoy this part.

"Please, m'Lord, I beg of you," she pleaded, her voice hoarse from crying. "My life is so small, but it is all I have. Please don't take it from me." So, she had been informed about her circumstances. The little ones in the castle must be talking.

Sargon slid his dagger from its sheath and idly scratched his cheek with it. "But your life is so important to me, my girl," he said, smiling. "From you, will flow a hundred great experiments. You will be the mother's fluid that my magic will be birthed in. You are exceedingly important. You should know that," he said, nodding earnestly. Then he slit her throat as simply as if he were cleaning the blade on her neck instead of using it to slice open her flesh.

The rich, bright red ooze of her life force flowed into the basin, and Sargon stood back to admire his work. He enjoyed it so much, he wouldn't allow his minions to take the blood for him. It was so much more satisfying this way, almost like meditation.

His servants, only a clap away, came when he called, first to dress him in his robes of ceremony and then to retrieve the corpse and carry his things down to the throne room. Down before the throne was another elven girl, this one older, chained to the dais. When she saw him coming, she clambered up and began to sing the stairway open. So useful, having these elves around. Speaking of which.

"Bring me Arndorn," he commanded as he entered the stairway to the Well cavern. Even at the top of the stairs, he could feel the power of the water calling him from below, beckoning him to come and drink. Had not that horrid Thaniel bound the waters in that shield, he would already have tasted their ultimate power. The time walking the stairwell down to the cavern floor gave him the chance to consider all the things he would be able to accomplish once the Well of Zyn was his. First, he would wipe this godforsaken realm from the land,

and no one would know Shadowhaven ever existed. That would be his last gift to Thaniel. It was a shame the man wouldn't be alive to see everything he created turned to dust.

Finally, he was standing before the pool, looking at the glowing mass of churning blue liquid, not unlike one might eye a lover. With a flick of the wrist, he bade the servant carrying his items forward, and the little worm scurried forth to leave the basin and tome at his feet. Sargon reached down and bathed his hands in the still-warm blood, chanting under his breath a spell he knew better than his own name. As his fingers began to glow in the dark depths of the basin, he lifted his hands out of the basin and held them out to the shield. Where the blood touched the magical boundary, it sizzled and smoked, smearing down the invisible wall. Sargon watched with satisfaction as the magic he wrought attempted to eat away at the force field, bubbling along its surface. Yes, work my lovely, eat your fill, and leave me room enough to squeeze through. You drink first, and then so shall I.

But something changed and the blood stopped smoking. Perhaps he had lost his concentration, perhaps it was a mistake in the spell. He reached out to hold his precious spell to the boundary, and was flung across the room like a sack of flour. Stunned by the fall but used to its effects, Sargon stood up, howling in rage. He had waited far too long. He should already have the Well's power; he could see it, he could taste it, he could hear it calling to him in his dreams.

Enough of this foolishness. Sargon spun around and ran back to the basin of blood, shoving his hands back beneath the surface of the liquid. He chanted a spell of a different kind, his eyes rolling into the back of his head, his head lolling to the side of his neck. With his consciousness he sought a thing repellant to his very nature, a thing that revolted and thrilled him all at once. The mind he touched pulsed with dark energy, a darkness he himself knew all too well. I weary of this game, he told it, once he had received acknowledgement; kill them both, the king and princess, and quickly. I no longer wish them brought to me, I want them dead, yesterday. Do you understand? Hunt them down, but don't just capture them, slaughter them.

The reply came slowly as if pulled from far away, We understand. No capture, only slaughter. The connection broke; it appeared the Ombrid were setting to their task immediately. As his senses returned to him, Sargon congratulated his younger self for taking the time to seek out such a strong, unstoppable race, and for enslaving them.

As his sight returned to him, he stood up to take one last look at the Well of Zyn but, instead, came face-to-face with the ghost of Saebariel.

The "request" came for Arndorn in the middle of the night, waking him from a beautiful dream of indiscriminant make-up. In the dream, he was a god amongst his people, but he wasn't sure how he had gotten to that power, and he very much wanted to slide back into sleep to find out. But the sniveling servant would not let him be and insisted that he join Sargon down at the Well of Zyn. As if somehow his presence down in that dingy dank cavern in the middle of the night would make all the difference.

Arndorn arose and dressed and then kicked the servant for having the audacity to awaken him. It made him feel slightly better, despite being summoned like a dog whenever Sargon was in the mood, to order someone around. The night was a chilly one, and, as he wrapped himself in his robes, he thought a torch might be in order, so he plucked one from the wall on his way down to the throne room. There, the doorkeeper was snoozing on the dais, so he kicked her too for good measure, and she hurried to sing open the stairway for him.

He had learned not to grumble in the presence of the slaves, and he had Sargon's manservant following at his heels a little too closely the entire way. Cruelty to those of lesser status than you was one thing. Indeed, it was practically expected of one who worked closely with Sargon. But to show the least amount of dissent with their master would be dangerous, since these slaves worked within hearing distance of the Master. No sense in losing his head, not when he was steps away from getting everything he ever desired. Well, everything except her, of course, but that couldn't be helped. His fingers twitched, reaching for a phantom strand of hair, brushing it away from an imaginary cheek.

The faint glow from the pool at the bottom of the cavern wasn't nearly strong enough to light his way, so Arndorn was grateful he had thought to bring a torch. Then again, he was always thinking ahead; that was what got him where he was today. He had planned the takeover virtually on his own, had sought Sargon out, had taken his time, and ten years of planning had paid off. Look at him now, steps away from the seat of power.

It wasn't until he reached the middle section of the winding stair that he heard Sargon speaking, and a few flights further that he could understand the words. The Master was conversing as if someone were in the cavern with him, and animatedly so. Arndorn dared not move any further toward the cavern floor lest Sargon spot the torchlight, so he stood frozen on the stairs, listening to the Master argue with thin air. The servant paused only inches behind, and he could feel the cretin's breath on his neck. Shooing him with a toss of his shoulder, Arndorn bent an ear trying to make out what he heard.

"Who do you think you are, coming into my palace without invitation? Do you have any idea who I am?" Sargon was pacing in front of a corner of the cavern just out of range of Arndorn's vision, but the wildness of his gestures was obvious, the blood still dripping from his fingers splattering in thin arcs as he waved his arms. Arndorn found the waste of a normally precious material interesting, but, at the same time, he felt repulsion that Sargon would use blood to emulate the magic that naturally flowed through Arndorn's veins. Either Sargon had been interrupted in the middle of his ritual by something or he was losing his grip on reality. Knowing the lateness of the hour and the extremes to which Sargon was prone, Arndorn expected the first, but hoped for the second.

"I am Sargon the Terrible," he announced as if there needed to be an introduction, "Master of the Ombrid and destructor of worlds. There is no one who can defeat me." A little pompous, Arndorn thought. Perhaps he was preparing for a speech. "I wield the very darkness as my weapon, and the shadows of the night jump at my very command." The very darkness? Arndorn highly doubted that. Yes, the strange grey-skinned army he commanded was full of savage deviants, but he would hardly call them the makings of the very darkness. Still, Sargon was a man prone to hyperbole.

"I demand you tell me who you are. Who is it I am sending my minions out to destroy?" Sargon seethed, his voice cracking with rage. Whatever he heard sent him into a fit of enraged howling. It was as if he were being insulted by the very stones around him, by the Well of Zyn itself.

Arndorn, standing stock still on the stairway, began to allow a seed of hope to sprout within his heart. He had long considered the possibility of Sargon's madness, but until this moment had never seen evidence of its existence. Now he was listening to the man as he argued with thin air, and, moreover, he was losing the argument. Arndorn smiled to himself, the smirk stretched upon his face by the torchlight. He was no longer regretting his rising in the middle of the night to travel down to the cavern. He reminded himself to reward the manservant later, perhaps when he was Arndorn's own valet. Yes, he liked that thought. He liked that very much, indeed. Under the cover of shadow, he allowed the smirk to spread into a grin, but only for a moment. Sargon was still ranting down below, and he didn't want to miss a syllable. It was essential he witness every word. How else was he to build a case against the Master?

"I demand as the one who killed 'the queen of this place.'" Arndorn's heart skipped a beat at this. It was true, Sargon had killed Saebariel on this very spot, and a small part of him realized his culpability in that heinous act. He had hated her for betraying him, but his love still burned, even three years after her death. In that instant of realization, for the first time, of his true feelings laid bare, Arndorn made a promise to Saebariel, sleeping in the graveyard on the mountainside. He vowed to avenge her death, to punish the monster who had robbed the world of her beauty. He was brought back to the present, to the current situation by Sargon's haughty proclamation, "It is by my own authority that I speak, and no other." His fingers twitched once more.

"Hah! What can you do against me and my horde of shadow demons? So come; I dare you." Sargon laughed then, a high maniacal laugh that left little doubt as to his lack of sanity. This was a crazy man barking at a moon that shone only in his mind. He seemed obsessed with trying to convince the Well of the depth of his powers. Perhaps he was trying to prove his worthiness to the pool of power before him. Perhaps he was trying to convince himself. Whatever the case, Arndorn was doubtful he would ever be sure. He merely absorbed the damning evidence, listening as Sargon continued, "The magic I cast is built of darkness itself, and I will watch as you and your little winged friends melt in the shadow of your own destruction. Please hurry; I hunger for your blood."

Evidently, more threats needed to be made. The emphasis on exactly how much destruction the listener would face needed to be made clear. "They will eat your eyes from your sockets, and then you will rule over only the maggots in your skull." Sargon was smiling now, he was in his element once more. Intimidation was his favorite side dish. Arndorn had seen this tactic before, and it had worked to great success a myriad times over the years. However, he suspected it worked better on opponents who actually existed.

"You don't leave until I say you can leave! Come back here, answer me! I will show you the meaning of importance! COME BACK HERE!" Sargon's bellowing echoed off the walls, and even made Arndorn jump a bit. It seemed that Sargon's debate with the Well or whatever his crazed mind conjured up was over, however, because he was silent for quite a while. As Arndorn listened, Sargon attempted to regain his composure and continue where his spell left off, but he kept losing his place in the chanting, and ended screaming oaths into the darkness. Arndorn considered, for a moment, obeying his charge to attend Sargon in the cavern so that he might wallow a bit in the Master's madness, but it seemed unwise. Instead, he reversed his footsteps, plowed past the cowering servant on the stairs, and began the long climb toward the throne room.

Every step seemed a step toward his own victory. As he traveled up the winding stairway, he formulated a plan, a plan that would remove the madman from power and install Arndorn in his place. It would be much simpler now that Sargon was unfit to lead. The people of Shadowhaven would see that all Sargon wanted was the Well, and, now that he couldn't have it, he was devolving into a witless screaming child. Even if he did manage to get to the waters, the legends stated that some would drink and die. Would that not include a man who had taken leave of his senses? Would it not be better that someone sane, an elf, drink and absorb the power of his ancestors? Surely, the powers would prefer to reside in a vessel of elven make.

The more he thought about it, the better it seemed to him. He would be saving his people from sure destruction, since Sargon would no doubt execute them all once his prize was obtained. Arndorn would do no such thing. He loved his people, well the elven peoples. Any executions would focus on the human taint in the Shadowhaven population. As he reached the stairway's top landing and stepped through the doorway, he felt a swelling of benevolence fill his torso and spread into his limbs. The warmth was a stark contrast to the cold temperature of the throne room. As he made his way back to his room, he felt compelled to kiss the sleeping head of the doorkeeper he had previously kicked. She too was a citizen of the new Shadowhaven. And in a land of light, there was no place for bickering, for hatred, and definitely no place for a madman like Sargon. As Arndorn dropped his robes to the floor and climbed back into his bed, it seemed as if his dream of godhood was not as far off as he had previously thought.

It was mid-afternoon when Warrek and his small band arrived at their destination. Brother Timothy would not tell them anything about exactly who they were meeting, only that whoever it was held the key to unlocking the king's location—if he were alive at all.

Warrek was beginning to wonder. He still had ultimate faith in his friend's resourcefulness. Thaniel had gotten out of scrapes before. But never before was he in such a huge amount of danger. Long ago, when they started this crazy plan to create a new type of government, Warrek had sat him down over a pint and talked it all out.

"You realize what you're doing. Not only are you consorting with the enemy but you're also handing your people over to her. Elves do not live with humans; that's just not how it's done."

"I do," Thaniel had smiled wryly, intentionally missing the point. "And I know what you're saying, old friend; I do. But the truth of the matter is that I am only a good leader amongst my lads. The survey team, we were a family, and it is always easier to tell your family what to do. But Saebariel has been raised to lead thousands, and she does it better than I ever could. I want to make this work, but I can't without you, Warrek. She's strong, but the people need to know that we are strong too, that we are accepting her leadership as equals. I know that, you know that, but they don't."

He was right. Thaniel, ever the planner and the researcher, had an inventive mind filled with curiosity and spark, but he would often forget the people needed to eat. He was an academic, whereas his wife was a warrior. She knew how to keep all those in Shadowhaven happily coexisting. It was a masterful balancing act, and one she had successfully been impressing Warrek with for twenty years, until the bastard Sargon had ruined everything and killed her. Warrek would pay him back for that, sooner than anyone might expect.

The route they took traveled through the heart of one of the most dismal parts of Shadowhaven, the swamps of Keracor. Whoever Keracor happened to be, Warrek wasn't exactly sure, but he must have been a lunatic to want to own a wretched stink-hole like this. Putrid mud boiled up from the earth and oily trees slumped low over the water. It took the group two days of slogging through the muck to reach dry land, and when they smelled fresh air, they nearly passed out with the power of it.

Where the swamp ended, a farm of medium size began. It was spread low over the rolling hills, and its fields had recently been harvested of their wheat, which stood in great rolls along the middle of the fields. The very existence of the newly built farmhouse with its warm stone façade and smoking chimney made Warrek homesick for his childhood days on a farm so very far away. Brother Timothy broke him from his musings.

"Joram is a good man, a man of faith," the monk said by way of introduction, "and he guards his secrets well. We shall have to be extremely cautious with him. If we do not tread lightly this day, there will be blood spilt on all sides."

Warrek nodded his understanding and ordered his soldiers to fall back to the edge of the fields to wait. He and the two monks continued on alone to the farmhouse. As they approached five figures came out of the gloom, three with bows drawn, arrows notched and pointed at the newcomers. Brother Timothy seemed prepared for this.

"Though the shadows be strong, the light within in stronger," he spoke out loudly enough so that he could be sure they heard him. Warrek watched the approaching group of men for signs of understanding. None seemed to be found.

Brother Timothy continued, his voice loud, but calm, "I come in the name of the Union, in the binding of the halves, I come seeking the Nest, and bring with me one who knows the power of our cause."

"The Nest cannot be found except by its maker," a gravelly voice replied, and an older farmer with dark hair and eyes stepped forward, his sword still drawn. Warrek noted it was an Eidalore military issue weapon, and realized he recognized Joram from younger more carefree days. The men behind him were young, but each resembled Joram in their stature and eyes. His sons were handsome, brave boys, the lot of them.

"But should a fledgling fall, one must know where to return the infant," Brother Timothy said and smiled. "Otherwise, the shadow will have won."

Joram laughed and clasped Timothy's forearm. "How long has it been, Brother? Two years? That is far too long to stay apart."

"It was for the good of the cause and the safety of the secret. But yes, I agree, it has been far too long." Brother Timothy seemed to forget his companions for a time, but then, bringing himself back to the task at hand, introduced them. "This is my apprentice Brother Pietr, and Captain Warrek of the King's Guard. We have come seeking the Owl."

"Of course you have. Now, call yer soldiers in, Captain, and have them bunk in the barn. We haven't room for them in the house." Joram's eyes twinkled with long-submerged humor.

"How long did you know?" asked Warrek, his curiosity getting the better of his natural stoicism.

"My sons saw you in the swamp yesterday, and heard you leaving it this afternoon. For a stealth party you sure make a lotta noise. Come on in and we'll get you something to eat." Warrek made a mental note of the farmer's sons' talents for future reference. Such keen observation might be useful to him. The two monks followed Joram into the house, while the farmer's sons eyed him with interest. It was clear they had had little exposure to soldiers. Warrek signaled his squad to approach and sent them to bunk in the barn with the promise of food later. They seemed ultimately grateful to rest and to be away from the stench of the bog. With the troops relaxing in the hay of the barn, Warrek entered the house, hoping against hope that they would find the information they needed.

Joram set Aebrin to feeding their guests and sat down beside the younger monk at the table to better gauge their intentions. As he did so, that wall of a man, Captain Warrek, bowed through the doorframe to stand just inside the threshold. At least a head taller than any of them seated in the room, Warrek's dark eyes peered out from under a hooded brow, unreadable yet understanding all he saw. A webwork of scars crisscrossed the left side of his face, crawling down from his hairline to slither off somewhere below the neckline of his tunic. This was a man who had seen much pain and suffering in his life, and expected more to come.

After a moment's pause, Joram continued. "The information I hold is only to be given out in greatest peril, and under certain conditions."

"I understand," Brother Timothy said brusquely as if he really didn't. What sort of hurry could a man like that be in? "May I speak plainly, friend Joram?" Joram nodded that he could continue. "Laud'El was attacked a few short days ago. The creatures came out of the darkness, as if they were demons created from shadows. I regret to tell you that your son Abihu was one of their victims. All my brothers save Pietr were lost in the slaughter."

Joram slumped slightly in his seat as though the slight hope he had been harboring in his heart that his son was still alive had left him, but he did not react angrily or interrupt Brother Timothy as he continued.

"And, had it not been for the bravery of Captain Warrek and his subordinates, I would not be sitting with you today. I understand that we come, asking for something that you have been sworn not to give. I understand that, although times are particularly hard now, they have been hard for quite some time, and I understand you would see no need for our small tragedy to change your mind. I understand that I am traveling with our most holy relic," he continued, pointing to the bulging pack that Brother Pietr labored to shoulder, "and that it needs to be taken to the one person who will know where it can be safely hidden. There is much I understand. The question remains, do you understand?"

"I have yet to forgive you for taking my son, Timothy," Joram said, surprised at the bitterness of his own voice. This was not what he had intended to say, yet he couldn't hold it back. "Yes, Abihu was dedicated to the El, and aren't we all in our small way? You took him from us, and now he is dead. How can I trust you with my most sacred information when I could not trust you with my boy?" These were not the regulations for oathkeeping. This was not how it was supposed to be done. But his heart had been aching for weeks now, and damn the regulations.

"You can't trust him," Captain Warrek said, just as suddenly. He moved away from the door, his massive arms still crossed stoically along his broad chest. "Clearly, the man is here to protect his precious book. That is his only priority." Brother Timothy looked affronted, and Brother Pietr looked murderous. "I too am dedicated to protecting something even more precious than a heap of paper and leather. I have sworn my life to protect Thaniel and Saebariel. Well, I have failed in half of that oath, but I will not see the second half fail as well, simply because you have a grudge against the self-centered cleric. If you want to punish him, so be it. But I will get that location from you, and I will find my king. It is only a matter of how you choose to relent." The threat in his words was clear, although his tone was even.

The stew offered them was a man's doing, a simple meat and potatoes dish with no frills. Warrek could tell that they had no woman in the house. It was, therefore, surprising that Brother Timothy asked after the meal as they sat by the fire, "And where is Joppa? Is that bright daughter of yours off creating another artistic masterpiece?" The pipe smoke wafting through the room made their faces indistinct, as if Warrek were seeing them through squinted eyes in the firelight.

Joram's face dropped, and an etching of sadness spread across it. Without a word, he stood up and flicked his hand as if swatting a fly, motioning them to follow him up the stairs. At the top of the landing, he turned left around the banister and opened a door. With lace curtains and handmade linens, the room they stepped into was obviously a girl's. But the girl had written over every inch of wall space in a scrawling, childlike hand. Warrek couldn't read what was written, and when he stepped closer, he could see why. This was unlike any human language he had encountered.

"A few weeks ago, Joppa started to act...strange," came Joram's haunted voice from the doorway. "She was ranting, feverish, insisting that Abihu had left this world. The two were close, being twins, y'see." Joram stopped to trail his hand across her table, a vase of withered flowers and a comb lay there, slightly dusty. "Then three days ago, she broke out of here and ran away. So now I've lost two children, thanks to you." This time, there was no bitterness in his voice, only sad resignation.

Brother Timothy barely heard him. He was studying the wall writings with fascination. "I don't understand, Joram. How did she learn the language of the El? These are scriptures from the Testament." He pressed one finger to a line of text, reading aloud, "'The council of the wise shall be your constant companion.'" To Warrek, the words looked more like wavy lines than text.

"That's not my question," Joram said softly, almost to himself. "What I'd like to know is how she learned to read and write at all." His voice cracked, and tears rolled out of his eyes. "And where is my girl going, now that she's out wandering in the world?"

Morning on the farm always came early, starting before the sun rose. Each day, one of his sons would rouse Joram and they would begin the labors required to keep a farm alive. This morning, it was an uncomfortable silence that woke him instead. He dressed quickly, pulling his tunic down over a belly knotted with unease. Years of working that land had given him a strong appreciation for his first instinct, and his instinct was telling him something was very, very wrong.

Joram arrived in his kitchen to find the entire house empty, and only quiet rested in the barn now, revealing that the soldiers were gone. It didn't take him long to realize that his sons were gone as well, that the roving band of soldiers had taken the last of his family away. He sat down on the front steps of his home and looked out at the fields vacant of grain. I wonder, he thought to himself, what shall I do now? And Joram began to ponder how he would survive the first winter he had spent alone in thirty years.

Warrek and his soldiers prepared to move out, edging along the swamp eastward. Only then would Brother Timothy speak to him about what he had learned from Joram.

"Your soldiers must not follow where Brother Pietr and I have been called. I suggest you go north and rally an army to siege Haven City and return it to our control."

"You suggest? You were called? Damn it, man, speak plainly!" Warrek fumed despite being within earshot of his men. "Are you telling me we came all this way for nothing?"

"You came all this way to protect me. I had to settle my grievance with Joram before I was able to do the El's work. One cannot travel into danger with a weighted conscience. But where we travel you will only draw attention to the king's location. You will get your king killed, Captain, if you follow. Do you understand me?"

"What you mean is, this journey had nothing to do with Thaniel; it was all about appeasing your guilty heart. I pity the spiritual health of a nation that has you as their guide! Did you know the king's whereabouts the entire time?"

Brother Timothy bristled a bit, but replied, "I did. He is hidden in plain sight amongst the villagers in a settlement along the forest's edge. I will not tell you where, for fear you follow foolishly and slaughter our last hopes for salvation. I may be manipulative, Captain, but I am not a fool. Should we reach King Thaniel, he will, no doubt, have instructions for us. Return to Laud'El, and I will bring them to you safely and without endangering his life. You may not like what I say, but I can see you recognize wisdom when you hear it."

"It is true that I despise your methods; and were you not a man of the El, I would kill you here and take your place. Say any more, and I just might. But as you say, a troop of soldiers will cause more attention where none is needed. Take your book to Thaniel, but upon your god, I bind you to return with news of his intentions for us. Now get out of my sight. I don't want to see you again until you have answers from Thaniel." He thumped Timothy hard in the chest with the flat of his meaty palm and repeated the gesture so the monk would understand his point.

"I understand and am so bound, Captain. I will return to Laud'El within the week with news of the king's intent. Brother Pietr, let us go. The journey is long, and the daylight short."

The two monks turned their horses east and lumbered off into the forest. When they could no longer be seen, Warrek gave the order for his band to head east, back to the monastery. He saw their surprise but gave them no satisfying answer to quench their curiosity. He was still resisting the impulse to run after the monk and beat Thaniel's location out of him. Once they entered the swamp for a second time, he welcomed the stench as it went far to made his dark mood a reality.

## CHAPTER FOUR

Second only to the spring planting, the fall was Shadowhaven's busiest season, largely due to the Festival of the Elements. Each clan celebrated the holiday differently, but the same basic tenants were observed by all. The autumn months were always when those in military service would return home, and, together, they and their families would celebrate the gifts their blood had bestowed upon them. It was more than simply an exaltation of all elves, it was a time to be thankful for elements in the earth that every magic user drew upon to produce their extraordinary abilities.

For the Unwin clan, this meant a night of feasting, of dancing under the moon, and of exhibitions of magical might within the peaceful village. The preparations began days before, and Mylena and her father did their part by dripping dozens of candles for lighting the village center for the dancing. Although it was time consuming, Mylena liked the feeling that she was accomplishing something, that she was contributing in some small way to the festival. Each year, she made candles, and, each year, she lit one for her mother, alone, under the huge autumn moon.

The young boy Chiave came to assist in the messy process of candle creation. Having him around to haul the used water out to the stream and refill the buckets was very useful, and it was nice to have a child around. He saw everything with a brightness in his eyes that made Mylena yearn for her younger years.

While they worked, soaking pieces of string in resin and dipping them repeatedly in the heated buckets of wax, Thaniel, in his guise as Vidius, would engage Chiave in debates and discussions. It appeared that Mylena wasn't the only one fond of the boy, but she knew that from her father's frequent requests for the young one's company. Thaniel was training him, almost like an apprentice, and Mylena felt a twinge of jealousy at his devoting such attention to Chiave. But, strangely enough, she also felt proud to see how well the child was catching on. When he first started visiting her father shortly after they arrived, he was fascinated with the few books they had with them, and with her father's jotting of notes in his journal. Chiave, it would seem, did not know written language, despite being of at least partial human lineage.

Mylena was shocked, but Thaniel took it in stride. "The elves are a people of oral histories, daughter. They have writings, but most of those are runic in origin and used primarily to aid them in those magical tasks that are done often. Think of them like a recipe for cooking, if you will." From that point on, Chiave was in the shop at least once a week, spending most of his time learning not only reading and letters but also her father's strangely secretive shorthand that he used in his research. She didn't mind, since it gave her time to collect herbs or shop or do one of a hundred tasks she was not able to do when she was tied behind an herbalist's counter bandaging wounds and selling remedies. He had come to be part of the family, a situation made all the more complicated by Mylena's delicate relationship with his brother.

Nevertheless, the child intrigued her. From what she could gather, he had lived with the Unwin clan all his life, even to the point of taking the name of the family who raised him. But he looked nothing like an elf. His broad freckled face and bright green eyes under a mane of untamable sandy blond hair couldn't be less like the physical description of an elf if his skin were blue and his hair eternally on fire. There was something so innately awkward about Chiave, although his movements were graceful and he never forgot something once he heard it. Although part of the clan, he was ever outside of it; thus, he jumped at the chance to spend some time with the only humans he had ever known.

Chiave was also inordinately observant for a lad his age. That very morning as he repetitively dipped the candles between wax and water, he nonchalantly asked Mylena, "Why do you dye your hair? I think you'd look better in your natural color. Black is too harsh for you."

Mylena and her father exchanged shocked looks. They had both heard the question. He snapped his fingers and she scurried across the room. "When did you tell him?" Thaniel demanded.

"I didn't; I swear, Father, on my life!" Mylena was desperate he understand she was doing her utmost to keep their secrets hidden. After searching her eyes for a long, tense moment, he nodded slowly.

"Chiave," Mylena asked a little too casually, returning to her candle dipping, "how did you know that?"

"I'm not sure exactly. I just seem to, well, know. Sometimes it's like that with me. There are things I just know, but I don't know how. I'm sorry if it bothers you. I don't want to make you uncomfortable; I just was curious is all." Worry crinkled the freckles across Chiave's nose, darkening his skin as if the emotion were literally painted upon him.

"Oh no, I'm not bothered, but I am curious," Mylena replied, smiling warmly. She put an arm around his shoulders to confirm there weren't any hard feelings. "There's a good reason I want to be mysterious about my hair, only I can't tell you. Do you understand that you can't mention what you know to anyone? Will you do that for me?" She looked into his eyes searching to see if he was loyal enough at fifteen to be able to keep the secret. He was.

Smiling at her, he said, "Oh yes, I understand. Being a secret assassin makes keeping your hair color disguised of vital importance." He was joking now, making them all feel comfortable with his easy manners. Mylena envied him for that too. It was silly that she envied this child of fifteen. But there was so much about him that put one at ease, so much praise he received from a father who gave her so very little. It was as if every time Thaniel saw her smile, he remembered her mother, and the sadness was opened anew. The more she tried to draw near to him, the further he pulled away, and she realized now as she watched Thaniel joking with Chiave, that the relationship between her and her father would never change.

The Festival of the Elements opened up its third night, as Mylena recalled, as it always did, with the fire birds and the stone dancers. The clan was a small one, and only had a few with the talents to create the great winged creatures, but the effect was nonetheless spectacular as plumes of fire and smoke became massive winged birds that circled the village and lit up the night sky.

Next came Rentyl Stoneweaver and Chiave, who coaxed three little mannequins of stone from the ground and bade them dance. The jig was a merry one, and many of the village children followed along, giggling, as they weaved in and out of the crowd in the village center. Mylena did not see Fionn with them, but felt sure he was somewhere nearby, lurking in the shadows. He was not the type to enjoy gatherings, yet he felt compelled to join the celebration with the rest of his clan. And then she saw him, standing apart with a small group of clansmen, together humming a low song that reverberated off the earth, their hands outstretched before them. When the great serpentine shapes burst from the ground, many cried out, but then clapped and cheered as the water snakes slithered along the ground close enough for spectators to trail their hands into the spines of the massive beasts.

It wasn't until after the feasting began that the Air Callers began their high lyrical song, stationed at points all around the crowd. Small clouds formed above the places where they stood. Out of the cloud tiny bolts of lightning slashed the night air, only instead of disappearing, they began to swirl in the air like funnels, twisting about the sky in little tornadoes of light. From somewhere within their midst, Rentyl stepped forward, and, with ceremonial solemnity, raised his hands to quiet the crowds. He stepped up upon the fountain so that he stood a head taller than even the tallest of the warriors, and, in a voice used to song, he began to recite the tale of the Beginning.

"Out of the darkness of the land, the pixies were born. Their love of the light made them steadfast friends of the land, and they ruled over it in wisdom and harmony. Their kingdom spread throughout the land we know as Shadowhaven far to the North beyond even Eidalore itself. All were happy in the land of the Pixies. There was peace and prosperity for all.

Many moons passed, and there was nothing but happiness within the Light of the pixies, until the wooden boats pushed up out of the sea and landed on our shores. They called themselves humans, and the humans were fierce and cruel and wanted the land for themselves. The King of the Pixies, Great Ione, saw the evil in the hearts of the men, and struck out to protect his realm. He waged war against the human armies, alone flying full into the battlefield to arise victorious.

Having vanquished all his foes, King Ione made the humans a solemn vow; if they would stay north of the mountains, the pixies would relocate to the south, and each race would have their own land. To sign this agreement with the king of the humans, Ione took their shape. But the son of their king was a human of hard heart, and he struck Ione down with a blow of his sword.

King Ione collapsed to the ground, slain with a weapon of iron. Where he fell, his blood flowed into a river, and the river traveled south along the mountains, through the pass, until it came to rest in a pool. From out of the pool, came a new people, tall of stature, who could speak to the elements and work with the magic that surrounded them.

We are those people, we have risen from the blood of our pixie ancestors, and, tonight, we celebrate the elements that bind us to this land. Hail Ione, Father of the elves!"

A chorus of "Hail Ione!" rang out, echoing into the forest, the voices sometimes singing, sometimes shouting, so that bright bolts of lightning and columns of fire burst out all around Mylena. Although her face wore a smile, the creation myth of the elves always troubled her. Mention of the pixies reminded her of her mother, and a sadness shrouded her shoulders and kept her silent.

As the evening died down, Mylena felt the chill of the stars settle along her spine and longed for home. She walked slowly, the reality around her blending into a dream, a dream where she walked along the parapets of Haven Castle, the moonlight sifting through her red tresses. As she floated, nearly weightless, along the walls painted in silver light, she felt drawn to the balcony outside her bedroom.

Mylena drifted upward on a column of warm air, alighting gently in front of the open doors leading into the interior of her sleeping chamber. There stood the figure, tall and imposing, wrapped in shadow. Only her eyes were visible, glowing with the sadness of a hundred years. The figure looked upon her in her freedom of flight, a look of derision in her pale eyes. The gaze seemed to accuse, "How dare you fly free when so many others die in captivity?" She could not understand, but she saw the figure try to speak. No, she would not understand, did not want to hear what she had to say, refused to let the voice into her head. She couldn't face what she had to say. So she turned, and flew east over the castle, toward Kir'Unwin, toward the reality she knew now, away from the pain of her past...

"Muirinn?" She heard him at first, not seeing when Fionn came up walking alongside her. She smiled lightly at him, trying to clear her mind of the strange waking dream.

"Did you enjoy the display?" he asked softly, his voice barely audible above the humming in her ears. Was it a song? She didn't recognize the tune.

"The display?" Mylena asked, snapping back to the present. "Ah, yes, the snakes were wonderful. It reminded me of your geyser in the orchard, only, of course, more reptilian. However did you think of such a thing?"

"Somus the Water Singer, he came up with the idea," Mylena heard him say, although the song still rolled around in her head. If only she could place it. Was it a spell perhaps? It sounded like an elven spellsong. "He had seen water snakes in the ocean when he was younger, and thought the clan might enjoy seeing them too. I merely leant them my voice."

Voice, yes that was it. "Fionn," Mylena asked, unsure how to phrase it, "how do you know the spellsongs? Did someone teach you to sing the water out of the ground?" She stopped walking and looked up at him. Her gaze must have been a trifle too insistent because he took a step back from her, surprise etched on his features.

Blinking, he looked down at her, angling his head so that he watched her out of one eye. He did that when he was trying to see meanings beyond the words she spoke. As if he could hear the truth not spoken underneath what she said. She loved it when he did that.

"Well, I suppose it's a combination of things really. I hear the water singing. No that's not exactly true. I hear the magic within the water singing, and I respond."

"Do you hear it all the time? I should think that would get vexing, never having silence in your head. I wouldn't be able to think," she said. *I can't think right now, not with this endless song wrapping around my brain.*

"I don't hear it all the time, only when I am near the water. And even then, well, my training has taught me to control the magic, to block it out. When I was a boy, I heard it always, but it isn't bad to have the magic sing to you without ceasing. It's more like always having a friend, always being with someone, or knowing they are just around the corner. Comforting would be a better word."

"Would you teach me, Fionn, to block out the song?" Mylena asked, feeling frantic and fragile all at once. She needed to know how to control this spellsong, but, more importantly, she needed to know how to make it stop.

"I can try. But tell me, Muirinn, are you hearing spellsong? I did not think that was something that humans could—" Fionn broke off suddenly and burst into a run. They were near her cottage, and his elven eyes could see better in the dark than hers. Suddenly afraid, Mylena ran after him, coming to a halt outside her own front door.

A man lay slumped against the door, dressed in robes of the clerical order, his arms wrapped around a large square pack. Fionn knelt and felt the throb of life in his jugular, and turned to say, "He's alive, though just barely. This man has been attacked by a horrible magic, I can smell it on him." Mylena wrinkled her nose at the stench rolling off the man, and Fionn realized that she smelled it too. Another mystery for another time.

The man lifted his head at the sound of Fionn's voice, and, in a shaky whisper, said, "I am Brother Pietr. I am looking for the Owl of Shadowhaven." And then he passed out. Mylena felt the adrenaline rush through her veins at the sound of the secret phrase. Together, she and Fionn brought the man indoors and she laid him on her bed.

"Fionn, get my father. This man needs my constant attention. Please, fetch him quickly." Not even bothering to turn as she heard the front door close, she stripped the man down to his underclothes to survey his wounds. A great blackness spread across his chest, and there were deep gouges on his arms and face. He had been running frantically and had fallen once, as was evidenced by massive bruising on his legs. She washed the blood from his limbs, but there was a dark, sticky substance that she could not remove. It seemed to absorb the light in the room like cloth absorbed water. The more she scrubbed at it, the more it resisted.

It was a little while before Fionn returned with her father. Thaniel limped in with the use of his staff, then, leaning heavily on Fionn's arm, slowly lowered himself into a chair beside the bed. There was more than alarm in his eyes; there was recognition and an understanding that scared Mylena. He had seen this before.

"I am here, Brother. You sought the Owl of Shadowhaven, and you have found him. What would you have of me?" Thaniel's face was grim and etched with shadows as he looked down on the monk.

The young man fluttered his eyes open, looking up into Thaniel's face. When he saw him, it was as if a light turned on somewhere within him, and he smiled despite his obvious pain. "My lord, I have traveled so far to find you! There are many who would gladly have been here in my place, your

Captain Warrek for one, but I was the one chosen by the El to reach you."

Thaniel waved away the praise as if it were a buzzing fly. "Yes, yes, but how came you to be in such a state, boy? Who are you and what is your business with me?"

"My name is Pietr, and I am a brother of the Clerical Order stationed at Laud'El. I have been there these seven years, tending the ill and working with those in need, under the direction of Brother Timothy. It is a good life; one I am proud to live. I do good works in the service of the El.

"Several weeks ago, demons began attacking from the mountain passes, and put to sleep all our brethren save Timothy and I. It was a dark time, and we would have been consumed by it as well, if not for the blessing of Captain Warrek and his soldiers. They fought off the darkness that threatened to swallow us, and we were grateful. Brother Timothy realized that Laud'El was no longer a safe place for the Holy Scriptures, so, in his wisdom, decided we should bring it to you."

He coughed then, and his breathing continued to come in long, deep gasps as if he were drowning. Mylena recognized the breathing of one whose lungs were filling with liquid. "The greatest of sadness claws at my throat, but my oaths to the El require me to continue my tale. While in the forest, Brother Timothy and I were attacked by the same demonic hordes that nearly overwhelmed Laud'El. Dear Brother Timothy did not survive the attack, but, before he slipped into the Eternal Sleep, he told me where I might find you, and bound me to deliver the Testament. Though wounded myself, I continued on, ever mindful of my charge." Another cough, and Pietr closed his eyes, needing to rest.

"You have the book?" Thaniel asked quietly, his voice almost soothing considering the import of the conversation. Pietr nodded and with a shaky hand indicated his pack, which Mylena had left near the open shop curtain. She retrieved it for him, not a small effort considering its weight, and opened it to reveal a huge leather-bound book, its pages trimmed in gold leaf. Her father eagerly took it out of her hands, laying it on his lap without opening it. "Then you have done your duty. Is there anyone I can speak to on your behalf, son?"

"No thank you, my Lord," Pietr was almost whispering now, so great was the effort to speak, "I leave this world as I entered it, alone and unafraid. I am an orphan from Eidalore, but I call Shadowhaven home." With those words his breathing slowed, then stopped, and he was gone.

Thaniel took a moment to cover the boy in a blanket, and then turned to Fionn, who had stood the entire time in the shadows, watching. "I know these creatures, and you see what they are capable of. The Ombrid have tasted his blood and have his scent on their tongues. They will be coming here soon." He looked at his daughter, and smiled sadly, holding her cheek in his hand. "Take her someplace safe, far from Kir'Unwin. Take her to the Eye," he said to Fionn, "You must go now and travel fast, for they will be hunting for you and do not sleep as men do. She must be protected at all cost. At all cost, do you understand me, boy? There is no time to explain, they are coming; I can smell it on the wind."

"But father," Mylena protested, disbelieving her own ears and eyes. "I can't leave you. If something is coming, we need to stand together or—"

"No! You will obey me, girl, as I am your father. Go now and do not stop until daybreak. Go!" Thaniel pushed her away, forcefully enough that her cheekbone ached from the force of it. Mylena stood, hurt outside and in, unsure of what to do. It was Fionn's hand on her wrist that made the decision for her. She looked up questioningly into his eyes, and the determination she found there bolstered her enough to do as her father commanded. She wrapped herself in her cloak, covered her hair with a cloth, and bound her traveling pouch to her belt. Mylena turned and embraced her father, never knowing when she would see him again. He said nothing in return but only stared at the fire, his expression unreadable.

Fionn guided her along the stream to his home, where he slipped in silently to grab his bow, his cloak, and a traveling kit of his own. "Do you know where we are going?" Mylena whispered as they made their way out of town. Fionn only nodded and kept going, heading north into the forest. Just before they lost sight of the village, Mylena stopped and turned, trying to burn a memory of her peaceful days at Kir'Unwin in her mind. A part of her knew with utmost certainty they would be the last calm days of her life.

# BOOK TWO

Listen to the melody grow strong.
Its power echoes far both day and night.
Entwine the magic's essence to your song.

Though the road you travel wanders long
And twists and turns upon you in your plight,
Listen to the melody grow strong.

Within your beating heart, the rhythm sounds so wrong.
Until surrender comes, wrapped in its arms you might
Entwine the magic's essence to your song.

For some, the battle raging does prolong
The search for wisdom hidden in plain sight.
Listen to the melody grow strong.

I pray you'll hear its meaning 'fore ere long.
Reach for the truth; make not your grip so tight.
Entwine the magic's essence to your song.

The power that lay dormant for so long
Now bristles with its ever blinding light.
Listen to the melody grow strong.

Entwine the magic's essence to your song.

—Spellsong lesson, traditional

## CHAPTER FIVE

Ritual incense still lingered in the air as Thaniel made his way along the pathways of Kir'Unwin, guided only by the moonlight and his memory of the place. He was grateful for the gift of his staff, created by Rentyl Stoneweaver when they first arrived in the village. He had gotten so reliant on making his way around the world on his daughter's arm that he wasn't used to working under his own power.

He approached the first intricately carved door and rapped on it vehemently with the butt of his staff. Through the series of oval gaps in the stone front of the house that served as windows, he saw a shape approach, his face silhouetted by candlelight.

A dark haired man opened the door. David Brehmer was one of the many Eidalorians who helped build this new world of theirs. He and his wife Nissa had been traveling minstrels in their former life, but were weavers of fine textiles in this one.

"Pack up Nissa and the loom, David. It's time."

Confused turned to understanding in David's eyes; he nodded, and, without a word, closed the door, going to rouse his sleeping wife. No doubt, it would be the last sleep she would have for a long while to come. Thaniel hoped she was dreaming of music.

So it went, door after door, first confusion then understanding, then action. While he strove to save the 200 families that comprised Kir'Unwin, he wondered at how long it would take without the aid of his daughter.

His daughter...as he knocked on doors rousing elves and men from their sleep, he thought of the pain in Mylena's eyes as he pushed her out the door into the cold, unfeeling night. There was so much he had withheld from her as a father, and as a king. For so bright a child, she really knew nothing about her own origins, about what he had done to protect his people. He cursed himself now for not explaining. If he survived all of this, he would tell her everything. No matter how difficult it might be for her, she needed to know exactly how important she really was.

But for now, he must be content with working to warn the people who had protected him for so long. Mylena had her mother's strength; she would be able to fend for herself. With a chill in his heart, Thaniel prayed that it be so. He banged on doors and called out into the still, silent night, waking every elder and asking them to convene at Rentyl's home. There, he told them about what was coming, about the stand Warrek had made against them, and about all he knew of the creatures.

The elves were surprised, but, in their stoic strength, they quickly adapted to the new situation. It was decided that the village would pack up early and move to the wintering grounds, their next planned settlement in their nomadic travels. A young community by elven standards, it had been only 100 years since they settled by the little stream at the edge of the forest, but, at some point, the time comes to move on; it always does. It was just that that time had come much sooner than they had all expected.

To protect the elderly and young, a small contingent would stay behind to fend off the invading monsters. It would be a dangerous mission. Among them would be the few warriors stationed in the village, and those magic callers who were considered brave enough to risk their lives for their people, and expendable enough that the village could survive without them. Rentyl was among them, as was Somus, and a slim, reedy Fire Caller named Galenthail. The last in the group was Thaniel himself.

"But Vidius," Rentyl objected, "How can you even think of staying to fight? There is so much at stake...your life is too important." It was obvious Rentyl was at odds with himself. He had sworn to keep Thaniel's secret, but, at the same time, he felt he had to speak his mind at this very important juncture.

Thaniel rose shakily from his chair to stand and face the group of elves. "Do you challenge my right to command my own fate, Stoneweaver? If so, you know little of me or my resolve." The words rang out into the closed space, filled with all the bitterness and bile that Thaniel felt flowing in his veins. Fury was too calm a word for what he felt, but no matter how he tried to calm his indignation, it came surging forth from within, a never-ending supply.

Rentyl raised his hands defensively. "No, Lord, I never suggested you cannot choose your own actions. I only express...concern...over the possibility of losing you."

"What you do not understand, friend, is that they are here for me. No matter what I do, no matter how far I run, they will find me. I would rather make my stand here, protecting those who have sheltered me for so long. There is no more running, no more hiding." Suddenly, he was standing at his full height, the hunch of his alchemist guise shrugged off like a cloak. He tossed his chin up and glared around him fiercely, from under his hooded brow his brown eyes blazed like sparks of fanned embers. In that moment, Vidius was gone, and only the king remained.

"Your majesty," they murmured, and fell to their knees, each overwhelmed to a man.

That morning, as the sun rose, every man, woman, and child save the honor guard packed up their lives. It was with surprising haste that they uprooted themselves, considering how long they had lived there, some residing in Kir'Unwin their entire lives. By the time the sun rode high in the sky, the caravan was already moving, and, an hour later, the village was little more than a collection of empty buildings, their footsteps echoing in the eerie silence and they walked through them, searching for stragglers.

In Galenthail's home, he warmed mead for the men and women of the Honor Guard, "So what can we expect?" he asked as he held the tankards over the flame burning in mid-air with no stove to hold nor fuel to feed it. The heat seemed not to affect him at all, as if he felt most at home within the extreme temperature.

"They are called the Ombrid," Thaniel began. "Where they originated from, few are sure. But they are creatures made of shadow, so are most difficult to see or fight, and even harder to kill. Killing them can be done, but it requires more power than we have at our disposal. You will hear them first. It will sound as if the air around you were crackling and hissing, and then the shadows around you will begin to take shape. So keep your eyes and ears open, and give them everything you have. Be ready to face your worst fears." He saw a flash of fear flicker across the archers' faces. These girls, although well trained, were young and had lived in relative seclusion assigned to the village. But he didn't have the time to coddle them. They were chosen for their bravery, and if they couldn't handle it, they would die.

Thaniel left the group as they planned their defenses and returned to his cottage to retrieve his armor and weapons. It took him a moment to collect his thoughts before he entered. He stood there, his palm pressed against the door, allowing the memories to wash over him. Here was where he last spoke to Mylena, here was where brave Brother Pietr had taken his last breath. With a sigh, he shouldered into the shop and past the curtain into the living quarters beyond. The place seemed foreign to him without the life Mylena infused into it. She had started out a horrible cook and housekeeper, but she was fiercely devoted to learning to survive, and had become quite the herbalist in her own right. With a shake of his head, he forced the musings from his mind and went to the cupboard for his armor locker. Only when he opened the door, it screamed.

Chiave was sitting on the floor of the cupboard atop the armor locker, his hands flung across his face in terror. Thaniel felt the fury rise within him as he yanked the boy out of the cupboard by his shirt front. "What in the name of Eidalore are you doing here, boy? Are you some new kind of fool? Speak! Explain yourself before I beat it out of you."

Chiave cowered again for a moment before he said "I know I was supposed to go with the rest of the village, but I thought about what you asked of those who stayed behind. You asked for bravery, and that I have."

"I don't doubt your bravery, I doubt your sanity," Thaniel growled as he collapsed into a chair.

"And I have no connections to this world, the second requirement. You asked that the Honor Guard be expendable. Who could be less important than an orphaned child?"

"My boy, you are more important than all of us combined," Thaniel replied cryptically, and, as he did so, he pulled the Testament onto his lap and opened it. Taking a quill from the table, he began to write in the margins of the sacred text as he spoke. "Imagine, if you will, a large priceless jewel. If you owned this jewel, would you wear this precious gem around your neck everywhere you went, show it off to all who know its value?" He finished his writing, placed a piece of cloth in the book to mark the place, and closed it with a thump.

Chiave thought seriously a moment, then said, "No, I think I would hide it away someplace safe. What is the good of a jewel if it's stolen the first time you wear it."

Thaniel nodded, smiling, "You were always a bright lad. Well, Chiave, you are my jewel, and I hid you in the safest place I could think of. Now do you understand?" He stood, not waiting for an answer, instead pulling the foot locker from the cupboard and opening it. Within lay a king's armor and sword, glinting with carvings of a Great Horned Owl. "Now, help me with these. I've never gotten the hang of being able to dress in armor by myself."

Chiave's eyes were wide and squinty by turns as he tried to wrap his mind around the revelations of his origin and the true nature of the man standing before him. Thaniel resisted the urge to smile. After a moment, however, the spell was broken, and he rushed to help Thaniel strap himself into the plates of armor. When they were done, he stepped back and surveyed their work, saying something that completely surprised them both: "I will miss Vidius."

"As will I," Thaniel replied, sighing; and he meant it. There was something tragic about putting away the kindly guise of the herbalist. It was as if he had torn himself away from his younger self, from the days he spent with his dear Saebariel, from the foundation of Shadowhaven and all that it meant to him. As he strapped the greatsword of his office to his back, he felt the researcher within him fading away until he was no longer recognizable.

"I bind you, Chiave Thanielson, to guard the Testament with your life. Go and take this book to Captain Warrek at Laud'El. He will help you take it further east to someone who can help save Shadowhaven. The way is fraught with danger, but he will protect you. My instructions should be clear, and I know you are the one who must do this. There is so much I should have told you, but there is no time now. Go, my boy, our fate lies in your hands now." He clasped the boy roughly to his armor-clad chest, and then in a moment of ultimate déjà-vu pushed his younger child out into the cold, cruel world without an explanation.

Thaniel returned to the center of the village, striding tall despite the weight on his heart. He did not regret dying, that was something he had been expecting for years now. No, the regret that clutched at his heart and threatened to choke him until he lost consciousness lay closer to leaving his children to the wolves. He was certain there was no one else he could trust, but there was little hope that either child would succeed. So today, as the warriors of Kir'Unwin assembled and prepared to fight to the death to protect their families, Thaniel prepared by saying goodbye to the kingdom he had built alongside his elven bride. As sure as his sword was sharp, he knew they could not succeed in the face of such evil.

It was the hissing that brought him back to reality, the familiar call of this most heinous of foes, the Ombrid. The research he had done on them flashed in his mind, the writing on the pages indistinct, and for not the first time, did he wish he had his research library and volumes of journals at hand.

"Be ready, warriors!" he called, drawing his sword, its golden hilt glinting with import of impending bloodshed in the afternoon light. The shadows around him began to cackle with menace, and then without further warning the Ombrid were there, slashing with their claws, biting with their fangs, hundreds when only five would have been deadly. The archers reacted swiftly, and, as the mass of demons blotted out the sun, the heads of the arrows glinted like small stars in the instant darkness. Beside him, he heard Somus singing his water-calling magic down at the ground and he hoped greatly that these brave elves and men beside him would survive.

Chiave trudged through the forest, grumbling each step of the way. "Who is he to tell me what to do? Did he raise me? No. How can he just tell me who I am, give me a family, run off to die, and then expect me to do nothing?"

It wasn't fair. He had spent his whole life feeling separate from the members of the Unwin clan, so obviously different, so hideously human. No matter what he tried to do, he always got the feeling that Kanefionn was humoring him more than anything else. He called Chiave brother, but he could tell there was a reservation behind any of the affection his mother and father displayed. No, not his mother and father, his what? Handlers? Was he a pet then, pawned off when he got too annoying to take care of?

Vidius…Thaniel had called him his jewel, something so precious he had to hide it. Is that why he was never told who he was? Why wouldn't they trust him to know his actual parentage? What could be so very dangerous about knowing he was a prince?

He was a prince, dammit! He wouldn't be ordered around by a man who didn't even want him around! He was beholden to no man.

Fueled by his rage, Chiave spun on his heel, and began the long march back to Kir'Unwin. He had been walking for several hours, following the orders of his so-called father. He wasn't even certain Thaniel had been telling the truth, or if he had just heard what he wanted to hear. He needed to know. He needed to understand why. Why hadn't they wanted to be with him? Why had they left him alone in the hands of strangers? Didn't they love him?

For so few, they fought long and hard as the afternoon wore down to a fine nub. Galenthail was the first to fall, exploding as he died in a fireball that consumed his attackers. Next was Somus, who died washing away their enemies with waves of water summoned from deep within the ground. Rentyl watched as the darkness continued to roll up to them. No matter how many walls he raised or how many of the monsters he encased in stone, another myriad were waiting to take their place. It was as if they were conjured from the very shadows around him. Although the thought was preposterous, it still weighted his heart with something awfully close to fear.

He heard the screaming before he noticed what was happening. Despite the walls he had raised, the Ombrid had found a way to break through the stone. Perhaps it was determination, perhaps it was their ungodly strength. Whatever it was, the creatures were on Thaniel before anyone could do anything. They swarmed him like locusts, dozens of them, piling atop him until nothing more of him could be seen. They fought their way to him, the remaining few, and tore the creatures from their king as best they could. Rentyl was not so much amazed at their fervor, but that they were indeed making a dent in the mass of bodies. Perhaps in their haste to get at their prey, the Ombrid had begun to attack one another.

And then, a stillness pressed upon everything, and the creatures retreated from whence they had come, leaving no corpses behind as proof of the battle. Rentyl rushed to Thaniel's side as fast as his wounded body would limp, but he wasn't the first to reach the monarch. A boy with sandy-blond hair dusted with dirt and leaves and a deeply freckled face streaked with tears seemed to appear out of nowhere. He was just there, kneeling beside Thaniel.

"You didn't leave," Thaniel whispered before Rentyl had a chance to even register the shock of seeing Chiave there in the midst of all this bloodshed.

The boy shifted so that Thaniel's head rested on his lap, and there were tears in his eyes. "No one orders me around. I'm a prince of Shadowhaven," he sniffled petulantly.

"I'm glad. It means I get to see you," Thaniel said softly, for his voice would go no louder. He reached up a bloody hand to brush Chiave's cheek. "I am proud to have known you even this brief time, my son. All those wasted years we could have been together. But I have hurt those closest to me for reasons I cannot say. Only know that your mother loved you so very much, as did I. It's been a privilege I could scarce have hoped for, to see the man you will become."

"It's not fair," Chiave cried. "I just found out you're my father, and now you're going. What will I do now?"

"What you've promised to do. Save my Shadowhaven, Chiave Thanielson. Save us all." With a long sigh, Thaniel settled back and did not breathe again.

Though the sun was low in the sky and the day relatively warm, Mylena stopped and shivered underneath her cloak. Something told her that her world had changed, that she would never be the same. Her heart ached like it never had before, and she felt an icy chill settle in the pit of her stomach. Fionn noticed her pause and turned back to see if something was the matter. A low moaning wail escaped Mylena's lips, and she collapsed on the ground, crying, great sobs welling up from within. He comforted her as best he could, but could do nothing as the tears and grief consumed her.

After an hour or so, Mylena stood up, blotted her eyes, saying "He's been killed, I can feel it. He's dead, and we have to continue quickly. They are coming." Together, they continued on in silence. Had anyone stopped to look at the indentation in the grass where Mylena had sat, they would have seen the fire spark where her tears had touched the ground. They would have wondered at the miracle of the small fire that burned intensely hot for several hours, consuming nothing around it.

Wandering the swamps, the girl Joppa stopped her rambling to stare up at the sky. "Why did you do this?" She asked of seemingly no one in particular. "Do you not know what he means to us? There is but one thread now that hangs between us and utter desolation. I may still believe in you, but I do not believe you always act wisely." She took a great handful of mud and hurled it at the sky, and she seemed completely insulted when it came raining back down upon her.

"Will it be like that? Are you going to mock all of us, or just me?" She punched at the sky, and then returned to her wandering, despite having been in that spot many times before, despite all common sense, she retraced her steps and promised to herself she would never more pray to the El.

Rentyl watched as Chiave, the son he had raised for fifteen years, wept over the body of his true father, and, oddly enough, he felt proud that the child could feel so deeply. After a while, he gently pulled the child off the corpse, and he and the two remaining archers buried the dead on a small rise above the village so the morning sun would shine upon their cairns. Before Thaniel was entombed, Chiave pulled the greatsword from his grasp though he was barely able to lift it. No one stopped him, as it was his right to claim a memento of his father.

"Chiave, child," Rentyl said as the evening seeped into night, "we are setting off to join the caravan. I see no need to risk the chance the Ombrid might return. Will you join us?" It was the first time Rentyl could remember asking the boy's opinion, but something told him that Chiave's fragile state would brook no command after what had happened.

Chiave looked from him to his pack, which lay in the dust where Thaniel had lay, to the cairn atop the hill, where the king's helmet rested glinting dully atop the stones. "I have promised to undertake a journey, and so I must go my own separate way. Perhaps we will see each other again, Master Stoneweaver. He clasped forearms with Rentyl as a man might. Indeed, Rentyl wondered if perhaps this were not his first step toward becoming a man.

"Take my name with you on your journey, Chiave. You may find it of use to cover your identity a while longer. You have seen what you are up against. These creatures will come after you too should they find out who you are."

"Then let us hope they do not," Chiave replied, as he bound the greatsword to his back. He picked up the pack, the lump of an unspoken question rising in his throat.

"Father—Rentyl, do you know why they left me here?" the words rushed out of him in one hurried breath, since he was certain his courage would fail him if he spoke any slower.

Rentyl sighed and reached as if to take him by the shoulder, then dropped his hand slowly to his side. "I know, but Vorynne and I swore an oath when we accepted you into our home, an oath to keep secret all our lives. Sometimes, knowledge can be as deadly as a sword," he finished, his eyes drifting to the implement of war strapped to his adopted son's back.

Chiave waited to see if he would say anything more, but it appeared that Rentyl was as good as his word. Silence he had promised, and paternal feeling or no, silence was all he had to give him. Turning his back on the village of Unwin, Chiave lumbered into the forest, barely able to walk under the weight of all he carried.

When Warrek had arrived at Laud'El and announced that he needed a contingent of brave soldiers, Harridan had volunteered at once. He had spent too long sitting on his arse waiting around for the Captain to return and could no more stand the idea of sloth in himself than in his soldiers, not after having stood alongside Warrek as he commanded them to such an amazing victory. How could he go back to his chess games and fox hunting when he knew so much else was out there? When he knew the strength awakened in his own heart?

He had been ordered to choose a band of soldiers and take them to Eidalore, where he would somehow convince the king to send an army to retake the capital. What he didn't realize was exactly what he and his troop were getting into. He was too young to know the wilds of the mountain passes north of Shadowhaven, and only a handful of those with him had experience with the creatures therein. His first encounter with the Jaarg left him winded as he and his soldiers ran from the deadly pack of wolfmen. He wasn't sure exactly how such animals were even possible, but he soon realized that he and his warriors were no match for the beasts.

They took shelter in a cave on the mountainside, high enough from the valley floor that he thought they might be safe. The soldiers collapsed within the expansive cavern, sheltered from the wind, the snow, and the Jaarg.

"We will rest here and continue our journey after we are better prepared. Perhaps there is a strategy for dealing with these challenges we have not thought of," Harridan announced optimistically. He was hoping that, by some miracle, the Jaarg would have moved on, or even better, an elven soldier would have thought of some marvelous way to deal with these furry devils. No such luck, though, and, as he drifted off to sleep, it was with the knowledge that he would have to face the enemy in the morning. Well, perhaps something would occur to him once he had a good rest.

No sooner did he nod off, though, then Harridan heard whispering in the far side of the cave. Irritated he roused himself in time to see one of his soldiers about to impale herself on her own sword. "STOP!" he screamed, just in time, and the elven woman looked down in shock at the blade pointed at her heart and dropped it, backing away. Although the archer collapsed against the rock wall of the cave, the whispering continued. Soon, Harridan saw why.

A group of cave sirens, floating eerily above the cave floor, were whispering their temptations to the soldiers. Their beauty radiated a soft light and their voices were soothing and melodious. No sooner had the first victim been saved than another warrior rose sleepily to wander toward the back of the cave. Harridan acted fast.

"Arise! Wake up! We're heading out, be quick about it! We are under attack!" His voice echoed throughout the cavern, and while he saw his troop wake and begin to pack up hastily, the cave sirens hissed and spit in his direction. Harridan was depriving them of their dinner. He made sure that all his people were out in the snow away from the sirens' influence before he himself exited the cave. As he stepped into the cold, wind-tousled night, he realized there would be no rest for them until they reached Eidalore.

At supper that evening, Sargon dined on duckling in a red wine cream sauce. In a rare mood of generosity, he had invited Arndorn there to eat with him, rather than stand in wait for when Sargon might think of something he required. The meat was succulent and tender, just the way he preferred it. He was pleased to see that Arndorn was an elegant eater. He despised those who inhaled their food.

Halfway through the meal a soldier entered the dining room, bowing his lavender-haired head low, with a message for Sargon. He took it off the tray and opened it with a nod of dismissal to the messenger. As he read through the letter he smiled, and the more he read, the deeper his smile became. "The king is dead; long live the king," he said, nearly giggling. His eyes glinted darkly in the firelight as he raised his glass, toasting himself, "LONG LIVE THE KING!"

Sargon had never really cared much for royalty, even as he considered his aspirations for world domination. He wanted the power, he lusted for it, he craved it the way others wanted women, wine, or food. Ever since he was a child, sitting on the steps of his father's hovel, dissecting live animals with his father's seam ripper, he knew that the control of people didn't interest him. His interest lay in their pain, in watching their pain. In causing their pain.

As much as control was important to him, he could care less about the movements of armies or the food supplies of Haven City. Even now the people below him scrounged for food for the first time in their existence, and far from bothering him, it amused him. It was his goal, after all, to see all beings writhe in pain, as he did on those hovel steps all those years ago. His mother, before she succumbed to a sudden illness, had told him to always give the gifts he received, to be generous with what he had. Well, Sargon intended to give even better than he received.

It was for that reason that he never bothered with the title of king or emperor, never bothered with renaming this hunk of earth. None of it would be around long enough to build any kind of society. Once the Well of Zyn was his, he would grind everything around him into dust, starting with those disgusting elves.

The wine slid around his mouth like a ribbon of sweet silk, and he held it on his tongue a moment before he swallowed. The elves of Shadowhaven were excellent craftsmen, and they bottled the best wine he ever tasted. For a moment he considered sparing a few of the most gifted to serve him. It would be a shame to lose the best wine he had encountered in all his days. As he thought and ran his tongue across his teeth, his gaze settled on Arndorn. Certainly, Arndorn had proven himself a capable lackey, one worthy of service. There was nothing that Sargon had asked for that Arndorn had not provided, up to and including serving up his beloved for his master's cause. There was a lovely streak of betrayal in the elf that brought a smile to Sargon's face. They were alike, he and the elf. They knew the taste of power and hungered for more.

Sargon rose from the table and walked down the long room to where Arndorn sat. Cocking his head to one side, he smiled.

"You've been working for me for quite a while, haven't you Arndorn?" He asked, his voice silky smooth, his yellow teeth showing between his smiling lips.

"Yes, Master. I have served you for over a decade, though it is only recently I was given the privilege of serving in your presence." Smooth, that one. Arndorn always knew exactly the right things to say.

"And you would do anything I asked of you?" Sargon watched him out of the side of his eyes, his eyebrow rising quizzically.

"Anything, Master," Arndorn said, rising as he wiped his perfectly clean mouth with an equally immaculate napkin. "What is it you ask of me?" He folded his long-fingered hands in front of him, the picture of servitude. The Betrayer of Shadowhaven looked to Sargon for direction.

Sargon's hands shot out, wrapping around Arndorn's neck. He squeezed with strength augmented by the magic that flowed through his veins. As the elf struggled, Sargon only tightened his grip, until, at last, Arndorn sank to the floor, dead. Sargon stepped over the body of Arndorn the Betrayer and left the room, tossing a comment over his shoulder as he went:

"Your services are no longer required."

## CHAPTER SIX

Failed as he had to navigate properly, Chiave spent a few days wandering the forests of Shadowhaven before he managed to find his way out. Although he had lived his life in relative seclusion, his elven parents had taught him to survive with relatively few provisions. What they had not taught him was physical strength. The elves were the sort of people who simple were strong by nature. He supposed it never occurred to them to train his body as well as his mind. Chiave was laboring under the weight of the book and the sword, barely able to move, yet, somehow, he traveled on. There was something within him, an unseen presence, an unheard voice, that told him this was possibly the most important thing he would do in his life.

In truth, there hadn't been much going on in his life other than his studies. He was a young man who no one really took seriously. What little talents he had shown with wielding stone had surprised Rentyl, but had not encouraged him to train the boy. Chiave was left to learn the stone summoning songs by listening to what Rentyl sang and mimicking the words. It was hard work for him, and work made even more difficult from its need to be done in secret. At night, when his family slept, Chiave would creep out into the orchard and raise small stone walls from the ground. None of them looked as elegant as those Rentyl could coax from the ground, but it was a start, and he had so wanted to please his father.

Father. Chiave stepped from the cover of the forest into a marshy wasteland thinking of the man he had buried just a few short days before. Vidius had been his great, venerable teacher, but, in the end, the man he had looked to as the champion of truth turned out to be lying to Chiave the way they all were. The man who had taught him to read the human language, taught him to listen to the history of the world as a way of determining the future actions of men and elves, that man had been a warrior and a king and a father—his father.

Every time Chiave tried to think about it, his head hurt. When the tears came, he wasn't sure if they were for the man who died, for Thaniel, or for himself, for all the years he lost that could have been spent with his parents. Yes, Rentyl and Vorynne raised him, and did so lovingly, with affection and warmth yet... Yet they were play acting for his benefit, protecting him from who he really was. They were surrogates for a king and queen that what? Couldn't be bothered to raise a second child? That hated his gender because he was not a girl? There bubbled up within him a frustration he had never felt before. Normally he was a calm boy, even a bit too timid at times. Now he felt rage, indignation, pain. Why didn't they want him? Certainly there was room in that great huge castle for one small boy?

Hot tears stung his face as he waded through the thick mud. It just wasn't fair, that was the plain and simple truth of it. But his newly budding wisdom told him somewhere underneath his tantrum that there was much about the world that wasn't fair. His mother and father had sent him away to protect him, and now they were dead, so it would seem their caution was within reasonable limits. Even as he railed in anguish at the parents who had sent him away, his keening was tempered by the sense he saw in what they did. Still, the mystery surrounding his existence deepened, and the more he tried to grab at it, the more it slipped through his fingers until he feared he would not be able to understand any part of it if he tried too hard.

Preferring his rage to his reason, Chiave allowed his frustration to boil up within him, and he began kicking at anything within reach of his foot, rocks and sticks included. A log lying on a small island in the murk posed as an excellent target for his pent up anger and the heel of his boot. But when his kick connected with the dirt-encrusted thing, he heard not the crack of splintering the wood, but a moan of a decidedly more vertebrate sort. Chiave jumped back as best he could being sandwiched as he was between a huge book and a massive greatsword. The log began to move, and unrolled itself to reveal a girl, her dark hair matted with mud and leaves.

"You would think that the world would conjure up something a bit less freckled to torture me with," she said and attempted to go back to sleep. Chiave stood rooted in shock, so completely frozen it seemed likely he himself would become a tree, unsure at first what we was seeing, doubting it was real. "You oughtn't have kicked a log like that. What did logs ever do to you?" The girl grumbled as she settled back into place, and instantly he knew it was real, this vision he was seeing of the log girl in the swamp.

"What are you doing here?" he asked, setting down his pack on a sandbar.

"Getting kicked," she sat up, pouting. She looked to be a few years younger than he, with startlingly wide-set dark eyes set in her pale, mud-covered face. Idly, she began piling stones next to her, one on top of another. Instantly, her complete attention focused on the moss-covered pebbles. It was as if she had entirely forgotten Chiave was there. She lay down, flat on her stomach, creating squares of stones, completely fascinated with her creations. "Build to last, we raise the walls to keep in the prayers," she whispered, giggling softly to herself.

Chiave wasn't sure where the compulsion came from, but he suddenly needed to sit down in front of her, to sing the wielding song so few had heard pass his lips. Realizing this girl was completely strange, or perhaps because she was a complete stranger, he softly began his secret stone calling song. Wiggling his fingers next to her three stone squares, he rose small buildings of stone next to them, identical to hers, but smooth, with rounded tops for roofs. It was the first time he had called stone in front of someone else, and, although he was feeling a nervousness in his stomach, the delight in her eyes made it all melt away. He felt safe here, as strange as that was, in the middle of a swamp with a deranged girl he did not know.

The girl looked up at him, her face the picture of happiness. "You rebuilt the monastery. Brother Timothy will be so proud. It was Abihu's job, but you made it stronger, and with song!" She clapped her hands, jumping up to dance her joy right there on the sandbar, spinning with her arms flung wide, she tilted her face to the tree-shrouded sky and grinned. Chiave looked up at her, entranced in this moment, until he remembered what was really happening. He had found a girl in the swamp, a girl who had been sleeping on the ground, and who appeared too distracted to look after herself. He decided to bring a little reality back to this very dreamlike moment.

Even as he made the decision he was sad to ruin everything, but in the end he asked:

"Are you Abihu? My name is Chiave," he said, reaching out an introductory hand to shake. She looked down at his hand, as she spun, stopping her dance to look at it more closely. She pulled at it with her own, turning it over this way and that, fascinated.

"Sometimes Abihu, but mostly Joppa. Magic in the hands, magic in the blood. The Chiave is special. Not like Joppa is special though. Joppa sees things. She feels them." She looked up at him, her dark eyes intense. She seemed to read everything about him in one look, and Chiave didn't like the feeling at all. She lifted his fingers to her lips and bit him.

"Ouch!" Chiave pulled his hand away, fingers smarting. "You're hungry; I have food, but I am NOT food." He pulled from his pack a small collection of fruits he had gathered in his days in the forest. Without hesitation, Joppa grabbed them up and shoved them one after another into her mouth. She was ravenous, apparently, and probably hadn't eaten anything but leaves and sticks for days.

"How long have you been out here?" he asked, watching in amazement as she inhaled the food.

Joppa seemed to have forgotten he was there, because she looked up, blinking at him, cocked her head to one side and said, "The magic fingers speak. Surprising. I wonder if they know where the water ends? Ask them. Ask them where the waters end."

Chiave squatted there for a while in silence as the girl ate her way through his food. It was obvious that she had been out in the elements for quite some time, and by the drawn look of her face, it might have been several weeks since she had had a good meal. He couldn't leave her here, and since his mission was too important to simply give up in order to search for her home, he made the decision to bring her along with him. First things first, though; she looked frozen solid. He slipped off the harness of the greatsword and lay it on the ground next to his pack. Suddenly his shoulders seemed light, tingling from the sudden lack of weight on his tendons and muscles. He felt off-balance. He removed his coat and wrapped it around Joppa's shoulders.

The girl seemed please by this, and eagerly shoved her arms into the sleeves. "I get to be the soldier now," she giggled to herself, admiring her reflection in the muddy waters of the swamp. "If I get to be the soldier," she said triumphantly, "I am missing my weapon. Give me my sword, and I shall spare your life, worm." She was grinning now, clearly replaying some sort of childhood game in her head. Joppa didn't wait for Chiave to react. She hefted the sword in her arms, carrying it like a baby, and plunged into the water, heading off in a random direction.

"Hey!" He called after her, hastily slinging his pack on his back. "You're going the wrong way!"

At this, she stopped, turned, and, in a voice more regal than any ruler could hope to use, she commanded, "Well then, lead on, I haven't got the time to waste while you fiddle around with your maps and directions. We have a journey to complete." And with that, she saluted him.

Chiave couldn't help but shake his head at the ludicrous nature of the situation. It was madness enough that he was traveling alone, carrying a book and sword to meet El knew who in some monastery to carry out the last dying wish of a father he barely knew. But now, he had a companion who, by the look of things, had about as much a grip on reality as he had on his lineage.

"Here, let me carry that," Chiave said, relenting. He tried to pry the sword from Joppa's arms, only to find she was unusually strong for a human girl her size. She simply wouldn't let it go.

"A soldier is nothing without her sword," she proclaimed, clearly enjoying this.

"Then at least wear it properly. You're getting it filthy." Chiave slung the strap along her back, and, although it looked quite silly on her, he imagined he hadn't looked that much better when he wore it. At least now, his burdens were shared, and he was grateful for that.

Now that he had Joppa to keep him company—in reality she was more ordering him around than anything else in her never-ending game of soldier—Chiave's journey seemed to move much quicker. He set himself with the afternoon sun on his right and slogged through the water, careful to keep his pack dry. He had wrapped the book in oilskin before he left, but he wasn't going to take chances that something might seep through.

Joppa noticed his carefulness and commented, "The baby mustn't like getting wet," pointing to his pack.

"No," he replied, playing along, "babies don't like water. It makes them cry." Joppa nodded at this, suddenly solemn, and for a while continued along without speaking. The silence was strangely comforting to Chiave, and he spent the time considering his situation in life.

By evening, they were stepping out into the dry plains, the mountains looming before them in the distance. Chiave was awed by the majesty of it all, having spent most of his existence wrapped in the secure darkness of the forest's edge. Knowing that the monastery was close by even though he couldn't see it, Chiave had the feeling that his world was suddenly a hundred times larger than he imagined it before. The mountains are old, ancient, existing long before even the elves, and would remain long after they were gone. What can I hope to do to affect a world so set in its ways? He thought to himself.

"Small stones," Joppa said suddenly, as if continuing a conversation with his thoughts. "The mountain is just a collection of small stones. One stone can bring the entire mountain down or keep it from falling." She looked up at him, her expression blank, "You are one small stone, but an important one. You will either shore up the mountain, or bring it down. The difference is, you are a stone that has yet to choose which path it will walk."

Chiave thought about this, not clearly able to put a finger on what she meant. He was surprised too that she seemed to be able to read his thoughts. He knew that elves were magical, but they aligned themselves with the spirits of the elements of the earth. What spirit would allow one to read the thoughts of others? So much about his life was a puzzle in recent days. He hoped that one day, he would be able to sort it all out.

When the last of the light leaked from the sky, the monastery finally came up on the horizon, a squat set of buildings that reminded him of something. Chiave wasn't able to place it until they were closer, and then he realized that this looked exactly like the small set of buildings he had made for Joppa back in the swamp. She had been building a model of this place. In truth, the compound looked less like a monastery and more like a barracks on the edge of a battlefield. Grain sacks built makeshift barricades along the eastern expanse between the monastery proper and a small chapel behind it. The buildings looked as if they had been pelted repeatedly with flame and claw. Whatever happened here, it was far from the peaceful nature of its design and original intended use—to keep the prayers in.

Once she caught sight of the buildings, Joppa broke into a trot despite the weight of the sword strapped to her back. When they reached the complex, she did not go to the front door as expected, but circled around to the west side of the building where a graveyard squatted, elven walls raised around it as tall as a man. Within its protective stone barrier, the graveyard was filled with recently dug graves, and it was to one of these that Joppa collapsed upon, weeping. As Chiave approached, he noticed that this grave like the others had no gravestone. The dead would be forever interred with no name, no doubt a result of the great tragedy that had recently ravaged this place.

Joppa dropped to all fours, tears streaming down her face, her hands grabbing handfuls of grave dirt. Her voice, which started as an inaudible moan, rose until it was a great wail that echoed off the walls of the graveyard, bouncing into the mountain pass beyond. The call was one of ultimate grief, and ululated with pain Chiave didn't think was possible in someone who was not being physically tortured. Her wailing ended like it began, dwindling down to a moan. Chiave stood there slightly apart from her, giving her the space she needed while still being close enough to support her.

"I came, like you said," she said through her weeping. "I brought another pair of hands, magical ones. The harvest will be easier this year, now that we are all together. Abihu, wake up, we have work to do!" She pounded against the dirt, her little fists making small dents where the blows landed. She squeezed her eyes closed, and let the tears leak from underneath clenched lids. "Brother, wake up," she begged.

The understanding hit Chiave like a tidal wave, and he had to lean against the wall with the power of it all. Joppa, the little waif, lay sprawled now against the grave of her brother in the darkness, her madness the mantle of her grief. He went to her then, the waves of her sadness washing over him, and pulled her from the dirt. It was as if she were finally realizing that Abihu was truly gone, and Chiave did not want her to endure that loss alone.

Joppa slumped heavily in his arms, the grave dirt from her brother's final resting place dribbling from her limp fingers.

"He's not waking up," she shuddered against Chiave as he raised her to her feet. She looked up into his eyes, her face a mask of sorrow. "Why can I still hear him? If I am to be mad, why must I also remember he no longer breathes? Chiave, I can still hear him screaming as if I was there. How can the El be so very cruel? Chiave, I'm cold. I'm so very cold."

The night around Mylena and Fionn was never quite the same after they began their flight toward the east. The forest took on a cloak of menace when the sun set, and Fionn had the feeling that it wasn't just their imaginations keeping pace with them as they ran. The first few days were alright, went along without much happening. But even during the nights when they made camp and Mylena appeared out of the brush with fruits and mushrooms to cook for a meal, Fionn hadn't exactly felt able to relax. Who knew what was lurking in the bushes around them? He hadn't spent much time in the deep forest, but he could guess that there was a contingent of nasty monsters eager for eating unsuspecting travelers when they let their guard down.

It was for that reason that he slept in short shifts, and always with his sword in his hand. This particular night the moon had set behind the trees many hours before, and Mylena was already curled in her cloak by the fire. Fionn stoked the fire with the heel of his boot, thinking about the events in his life that had led to this moment. He had been trained as a warrior, yet was left at home when his mother went off to join the Queen's Guard. Why did she leave him at home? Fionn had been told that he was too young, but he was certain that wasn't it, because there were warriors taken for combat much younger than him. No, it had to be something else.

Perhaps it was his mother's insistence that he protect Chiave. The foundling child was human, and, as a human, was victim to his weaknesses. For one thing, he aged incredibly quickly in comparison to an elven child. Fionn himself had taken many years more to mature when compared to the brief childhood Chiave experienced. And Chiave was never able to understand the basics of swordplay. Fionn's mother had long ago given up attempting to teach Chiave how to defend himself, which, in itself, was strange, when connected to the fact that Fionn was charged with protecting the boy. Hopefully, Chiave had gotten away safe with the rest of the village. Whatever had done those horrible things to that priest was still out there somewhere, and Fionn hoped fervently that it wouldn't find his brother.

As if he had conjured the nightmare by just thinking about it, the night around Fionn began to hiss. Instinctively he drew his sword and crouched low beside the fire to silently wake Mylena. She stirred slowly, and then when she saw him holding a hand over her mouth, she jolted awake. Her golden eyes flew open wide with fear as he gestured around him, cocking his head to listen. The hissing rose in pitch around them as Fionn removed his hand from Mylena's mouth, and together they rose to their feet back to back, still without speaking. Try as he might, he was unable to pinpoint the direction the voices where coming from, so had to conclude they were surrounded. Silently, he cursed himself for allowing the fire to burn throughout the night. They had created a beacon for the monsters to follow, and now they were trapped.

The first of them appeared to the south, hissing and snapping its jaws just on the edge of the firelight. Mylena cried out as another three appeared to her left. Fionn guessed there were half a dozen in total, perhaps a few more staying out of sight. A tiny hunting party compared to the enormous army that had overwhelmed Laud'El, but still enough to ensure that the two of them would not make it through the night alive. As smoothly as he could, he crouched down to the earth, attempting to hum some water from the ground, but there seemed to be no aquifer beneath them. Besides his sword, he had his bow and a full quiver of arrows, but in such close quarters, they would be useless. They were going to die.

The creatures seemed to realize this as well, so they braved exposure in the light to taunt their prey. As they stepped into the firelight, Fionn could see that they were humanoid, although they did not stand as men did. Hunched over, they hung their heads and swayed a bit like snakes might. In fact everything about these monsters was reptilian, even the green-black shimmer of their skin. Yes, it was skin, not shadows he saw, which explained how they could be fought.

No matter what he thought of, it wouldn't be enough to stop these creatures. What did he have besides a sword and his bow? Only a scared girl who quivered behind him. She wouldn't be any use. His magic was gone, his ability locked away with the spirits of the water that was too far for him to reach. Fionn racked his brain for something, anything that would keep them alive long enough to get away from these monsters. Would the fire do it? He kicked coals and fiery logs at the nearest creature. Although he ducked and backed away, it looked more surprised than hurt by the flames. Damn.

"I can't do anything," Fionn said, finally breaking the silence. "I'm sorry, Muirinn. This is not the way I wanted us to spend our last moments together. Forgive me." He closed his eyes and prepared for the end to come.

"You are an elven warrior. You do NOT simply curl up and die! We have come so far, too far to simply give up after everything." Muirinn's voice was surprisingly strong despite the way she trembled. Fionn wanted to think that something might happen, that he would think of something that would be their salvation, but, instead, he just stood there.

The creatures evidently decided they had had enough of taunting their prey and began to lunge toward them, their teeth gnashing. Muirinn cried out as one began to scratch at her, slashing with one clawed hand and then watching her wriggle away. It seemed to be enjoying itself, and if it could have laughed, Fionn imagined it would have.

Suddenly out of nowhere he heard a song burst forth behind him. He couldn't tell exactly where it was coming from, but it sounded like a variation of the spell songs he had been working with. The sounds were indistinct and difficult to understand, as if he had never learned them, but from behind him, a white light began to glow so bright it hurt his eyes. He turned to see Muirinn radiating light from within her. It was she who was singing, her eyes closed and her mouth thrown open with her head thrown back, as if she were calling out into the night. The light flowed from her face and hands, radiating from her fingertips. It burst forth, growing in intensity the more she sang. The light seemed to be seeking something, and, as Fionn watched entranced, he realized exactly what it searched for. The light was looking for the creatures.

The creatures, repulsed by the light, shrank back and then began to run away, completely retreating. The light didn't stop at the edge of the clearing, though, but followed them into the forest, seeking them as a hound would seek a fox. The light burst through the trees, through the bushes, and as it reached the first of the creatures, the monster exploded into a ball of light. All six were eventually found, and destroyed in small explosions that looked like tiny suns. And then the light was gone, switched off as one might snuff out a candle.

Muirinn collapsed into a heap on the ground, her hands shaking and her eyes glowing with residual light. "What happened?" she asked as Fionn went to her, holding her as she shivered against his shoulder. She looked up at him with her glowing eyes. "What happened?" she repeated and then passed out.

Chiave led Joppa out of the graveyard, holding her up by leaning her against him. He considered leaving without confronting the soldiers inside, but he knew that she needed food and rest, and he needed to unload himself of the burden of the testament. So he rapped on the door of the monastery, his heart heavy, and his companion barely conscious. Immediately, the door opened and an arrow knocked for flight was leveled at his head. Chiave had expected this, however, and, without flinching, managed to say in a fairly steady voice, "My name is Chiave Stoneweaver. I come bearing a message for Captain Warrek." Immediately, the bow was lowered, and the figure in the doorway wreathed in light stepped forward.

"Chiave? Son?" she said, and, as she came closer, he recognized her.

"Mother?" he said, disbelieving even as he felt her wrap her arms around him. It was incredible to see her here of all places. It seemed to make sense though, and, as she embraced him and brought him inside, he considered that this would be as likely a place for her to be as any. She was, after all, a member of the Queen's Guard, and her last letter had mentioned traveling north. But that had been several years ago, and they had not heard from her since the overthrow of the kingdom. Before he could allow himself to reminisce, however, he had a few things to attend to. He shrugged out of her embrace, saying, "Take me to Captain Warrek."

Vorynne looked at him, concern in her eyes. She was obviously surprised to see him there, and definitely surprised to see this new commanding side of him. But she complied and took him to a makeshift war room deep within the monastery where Captain Warrek sat surrounded by books. He was a massive man, his shoulders so broad, they barely fit in the tunic he wore, and his neck pulsed with veins over his collar. He was sipping a glass of brandy when they entered and set it down immediately, his eyes traveling from Chiave to Joppa standing behind him, and finally rested on the leather-wrapped hilt of the sword that peaked out over her shoulder.

He rose from a chair too small for him and, despite her protests, lifted the greatsword from its resting place between Joppa's shoulders. He crouched and lay the blade across his knees, examining every inch. "No, it cannot be," he said to himself, a great grief in his voice. He turned the steel over in his hands, the weapon glinting gold in the firelight. "Thaniel, my friend..." His voice trailed off, as it was choked by emotion. He turned then to face Chiave, painful questions etched on his face along with his battle scars, old and new.

"The monsters followed the priest," Chiave began without preamble, "the one with the book, to Kir'Unwin. He was staying there, hiding amongst us as an herbalist—and as my teacher. He had been with us three years. So when the word came that the monsters were coming, he stayed behind while the villagers left. He stayed behind so they could live—" It seemed enough, and Warrek ran a hand along the blade while holding the other up to silence Chiave. He slumped into his chair once more, staring at the sword in brooding silence.

Locked in his grief, Warrek seemed unable to break out, so Chiave helped him. He sat Joppa down in a chair against the wall, and shrugged off his pack, pulling out the massive book wrapped in oilskin and laying it in front of Warrek. As if performing a grand ritual, Chiave unwrapped the book and opened it to the page marked by the little scrap of cloth. There, visibly clear in the firelight, were the words written along the margins in Thaniel's strong hand.

"Thaniel sent me here with this book to ask you to protect me," Chiave said. "He is sending me east. There is someone who needs to see this book, and I cannot get there alone."

Warrek lifted his eyes from the sword to the book and the words scrawled there, marring the perfectly scribed pages with their blocky text. It was easy to tell he couldn't believe what he heard, but he was no fool. After reading the text written therein, he finally met Chiave's eyes, then nodded.

"Vorynne, the children are under your charge. See that they are bathed, fed, and given a place to sleep. What is your name, son?" Warrek stood, once again the military leader, no longer a man mourning his friend.

"I am Chiave Stoneweaver." Warrek's eyes flicked between Vorynne and Chiave, a hint of curiosity alight in their gray depths.

"This gets more interesting by the minute. Oy!" He called two human soldiers in from the corridor. "This book shall be under your watch day and night. It is now the most important thing in this building, and one of you must be guarding it at all times. Do you understand me?" The two soldiers nodded and took up posts at both edges of the desk. Warrek looked at them, giving them a sidelong glance, then said, "We're going to have to find a place for that thing until we leave."

"We?" Chiave asked.

"Yes, boy, I'm going with you," Warrek said, sitting back down at his desk.

Vorynne motioned to Chiave that it was time to leave and strode out into the corridor. As Chiave led Joppa from the room, she turned and tried to make her way to the book. The two soldiers stood in her way. "It's a crime," she steamed, suddenly furious, "keeping a man from the scriptures he's dedicated his life to. You'll regret this," she said and finally allowed Chiave to lead her from the room.

Vorynne led them down to a washroom where pools of heated water stood along the walls, worked no doubt through the magic of the elven soldiers as there was no basin holding the water in. Chiave left the room to give his mother and Joppa some privacy, but as soon as he did so, Joppa began to wail. She absolutely refused to be separated from him. He, therefore, found a chair and sat within the room with his back turned as she was bathed.

Never a great one for maternal instincts, Vorynne, nevertheless, worked at her duty thoroughly, washing the mud, sticks, and leaves from Joppa completely, if a bit roughly. More than once, he heard Joppa whimper under the strength of Vorynne's enthusiastic scrubbing. Chiave smiled to himself, remembering times he had been subjected to just such an overly thorough cleaning.

When she was finished, Joppa presented herself before him, wrapped in a drying cloth and smelling of bath salts. Chiave smiled. "So that is what you look like." Joppa giggled back, and then bounced back behind him to get dressed. Vorynne had found two sets of smaller soldier's garb for them both, and dressed Joppa as Chiave bathed himself in the hot, steaming water. It felt good to get clean after many days, trudging through forest and swamp. He slipped beneath the water and blew bubbles like he used to when he was a child swimming in the stream with Fionn. Chiave was loathe to leave the water, and, when he finally did, it was to find a freshly laid out set of clothes for him. He dressed and wandered out to find Joppa lured out into the corridor by Vorynne to give him a bit of privacy. She had been bribed with figs, and was stuffing them one at a time into her mouth, following Vorynne who dangled them in front of her the way one might tempt a beast of burden with a carrot. It seemed to be working until Chiave snatched the last one and took a huge bite of the sweet, juicy fruit. Joppa frowned, smiled, pouted, and grinned in turns.

"I am truly the soldier now," she announced, turning around so that Chiave could see her leather armor. She looks so strange, so skinny as she is, like a child wearing a specially created costume for a play instead of a girl about to set out on a dangerous journey, Chiave thought. Of course, it was the first time he saw her without her cloak of mud and leaves, so perhaps he was reacting to that, but, either way, it appeared to him as if he were standing with a stranger.

"No more strange than you," she said, seemingly replying once again to his thoughts. She grabbed hold of his hands and ran toward the end of the corridor, dragging him along. As they reached the corner, he could smell food cooking, marvelous smells that made his mouth water, and his stomach groan. He looked back to see Vorynne smiling at him, nodding permission for him to turn the corner. And then she was out of sight, and Joppa was pulling him into the mess hall, into a room that made his head spin with all the delicious smells.

Mylena could feel Fionn's wariness around her now, it hung on him like an odor, and there was nothing she could do to stop it. No matter how hard she tried, she couldn't remember the incident he described, so she didn't even bother trying to explain it. There was caution in his eyes like never before, and she did not like it at all.

After five more days of travel, they reached the edge of the forest. Stepping out into open space was harrowing for a while, as she wasn't used to the expanses of the eastern plains, but, as she followed Fionn in their northeasterly course, she came to luxuriate in the openness and the rhythmic rolling of golden grasses as they whispered in the afternoon breeze. They could see for miles here, which meant that no monster could sneak up on them, which meant there was no chance to change into a column of light and scare her friend half to death. She was concerned that he might never truly feel comfortable around her again, and she desperately wanted him to feel comfortable around her.

For Mylena, Fionn was a comfort and a security, she felt safe just having him around. Maybe it was because he was the one constant thing in a world of turbulent change. Whatever it was, she felt better, knowing he was there to look after her. She still had to face the strangeness of what she was able to do, but she did not have to face it alone.

Toward the end of the seventh day, the plains wrinkled into foothills, and, together, they climbed up into the hills toward some unknown destination. Mylena didn't inquire exactly where they were going, and she got the feeling that after her little display, Fionn wouldn't have divulged where they were going even if she had asked. It seemed to be a sacred spot of some sort, and it was certainly difficult enough to reach. Once the hills turned mountainous, they followed a winding trail that wound around the ever steepening peaks, wrapping their cloaks around them to protect them from the late fall frigid air, made colder by the stiff mountain breeze as it swept along recently fallen snow. The cold chilled them to the bone, yet they continued stubbornly on, neither one wanting to admit to the other that they need the warmth of a fire to melt the ice in their bones.

In the late afternoon, they reached the top of the trail and stood at the edge of what Mylena realized, from it's shape and plume of geothermal steam, was a great volcanic bowl. Within the bowl, a small oasis lay of sorts, nestled deep within the earth, a small circle of green made all the more verdant by the white snow surrounding it. Within the center of the circle was a small cobalt-blue lake of steaming water. The path they were taking slithered down along the wall and into this basin, ending at the oasis.

"It's beautiful," Mylena said, and she meant it. To her, it looked like a huge eye staring up wonderingly at the sky.

"Welcome to the Eye of the World," Fionn said, although he didn't quite sound as if he meant it. Nevertheless, he took her hand and led her down the path, and, together, they descended into the Eye.

When they reached the oasis itself, Mylena bathed her hands and face in a bubbling spring, warm with volcanic heat, that fed the lake and set about making a fire. When she came back from collecting firewood, she saw Fionn had made a set of pallets out of the oily leaves of a fruit tree she could not identify. From the same tree, he had collected enough fruit for several meals.

"There aren't any mushrooms around here, I'm afraid. We will see about fishing tomorrow when the sun rises above the basin wall." Something about the way he said it made Mylena excruciatingly sad, and she could no longer bear the forced silence, the strain between them.

"I am sorry. I don't know what happened, but I frightened you, and that is the last thing I want." She took his hand, holding it to her heart. "Please forgive me."

The look in his eyes was strange, as if he weren't quite seeing her, despite the fact that he looked right at her. "You're human," he said, and traced the edge of her round ear, still with that distracted far-away look in his eyes. "Yet you call the magic. How is that possible?" She held her fingers to his lips, shushing him, and then, finally, it appeared that he saw her.

She kissed him then, feeling the warmth of his lips contrasted with the coolness of the air around him. After a moment, his stiffness melted and he returned the kiss, embracing her. It seemed an eternity of bliss that wrapped them in that moment. The oasis seemed to begin with them and extend throughout the entire basin. The heat of the kiss promised to melt the snow off the very mountaintops.

Around them, an entire field of golden butterflies erupted into existence, the whispers of a thousand flapping wings dancing on the cool evening breeze. The two of them looked around them astonished; Mylena reached out her hand and a butterfly alighted there, its glowing wings fluttering and then opening and closing in time with her heartbeat.

"We live in a magic time, Kanefionn Stoneweaver. Who is to say that it is not you who create these marvels?" She shook her hand and the butterfly flew off to be with its brethren. "Or perhaps it is this place?" She smiled up at him affectionately, reaching up to caress his cheek. Mylena looked out at what had spawned around them, and oddly, she felt no twinge of worry. Her very happiness had been made real, and it made her smile to think of it. That night, they slept underneath a cloud of glowing butterflies, resting deeply for the first time since they had left Kir'Unwin.

## CHAPTER SEVEN

"Is there any way I can truly trust her?" Fionn stood on the shores of the small lake, watching the clouds reflected in the water. Within the water, darted fish of a color he had no experience with, but they had been eating them for over a week now, and they had had no ill effects. He could, therefore, assume that there was no poison in the creatures.

A low humming began deep in his throat, and he stretched his hand over the water. The water began to ripple underneath where he waved his hand, and then it began to part. Fionn's song grew louder, and the water solidified around the fish, allowing him to pluck them out of the water without the need of net or hook. He filled the basket he had with him with fish, and then finished his song. The waters of the lake rushed back in to fill in the spaces his magic had created, soon settling down to their original glassy state. Lifting the basket of wriggling fish, he turned and made his way to the camp he shared with Muirinn.

Muirinn. He still couldn't tell what exactly she was. She was a woman full of secrets, some secrets withheld from herself as well. There was great power within her, that was evident, but she herself didn't seem interested in figuring out exactly what her boundaries were. Anytime he brought up strange events that happened before they arrived at the oasis, she waved them away. For her, there was no existence outside the Eye of the World.

To a certain extent, he understood. Their week there had certainly been peaceful, nigh paradisiacal. There was enough food, no one was chasing them, and he could spend his evenings holding Muirinn and watching the stars. For them, time had stopped, and a part of him wondered if that wasn't her doing as well.

But as he reached the camp, reality burst into their little haven. Muirinn was looking, not at him, but at something along the wall of the basin. Following her gaze, Fionn was able to see figures making their way along the path.

"Kir'Unwin has arrived," he said simply, and set to cleaning the fish.

"What do you mean?" Muirinn asked, concern evident in her voice. She crouched down by him so that she could look up into his eyes to gauge his meaning.

Fionn looked at her, trying to understand her concern. Did she not want others to intrude on this place? But who could own a place?

"The clan left the forest's edge soon after us, it would seem. Migration came early. We usually stay in a place for several hundred years. It would appear that something occurred to make them wish to leave sooner."

"You knew this would happen?" she asked, slightly disturbed.

"Yes, I came here, knowing that our people would follow. If you are to be protected, is it not better that your clan do so rather than simply one man? My people selected this as a settling ground long before you and I were born."

Muirinn locked her expression down such that Fionn wasn't sure exactly how she might have answered the question. Having completed the dirty task of removing the insides from fish, he sung a small geyser up from the ground as he had done in the orchard all those days ago, and washed his hands in the stream of warm water. Then he went out to meet the travelers and welcome them to their new home. He left Muirinn behind mostly so she could get used to the idea of others coming to live there. He really wasn't sure what had gotten into that girl. The more he knew about her, the more he cared for her, but then she would show some hint of strangeness, and he would realize exactly how different they were from one another.

When he reached the point where the path from the summit leveled out into the basin, Fionn met the forerunners of the caravan. It was exciting to see his people again and even more so to see his father leading the expedition.

"Well met, Fionn," Rentyl said from atop his steed. From the look of him, Fionn's father had been through some great hardships since they last saw each other.

"Hail, Father," Fionn replied, smiling. "Where is Chiave?" He looked back toward the rest of the caravan to search for his brother.

"The boy has a journey of his own," Rentyl said simply, sadness in his eyes and voice.

"There is a tale behind your words; I can hear it," Fionn said, his smile fading. The fact that Chiave, his charge and his responsibility, was not amongst the travelers worried him. Something had gone on. Suddenly, Fionn recalled the attack of the shadow creatures back in the forest. Those monsters had been coming to the village. He cursed himself silently for forgetting the danger he and Muirinn had run from. "Tell me."

Rentyl sighed, and with great effort dismounted to stand before his son. The sadness laying in his blue eyes pointed to a newly cut scar, snaking bright red and hideous from the corner of his eye down towards his ear and disappeared into his hair. There was more of a story here than Fionn had previously thought. His father had been in battle.

Rentyl began his tale where Fionn last heard it, with his own leaving. "Once you had fled with your commission," Rentyl said, his eyes darting down to the valley floor for but an instant, "Vidius came to warn Kir'Unwin that monsters were coming. It was a hundred years too soon, but we knew at once the time had come to move the village, so we collected our items and, in most cases, our families, and they began the trek here.

"A few stayed behind to slow the progress of the enemies, including Vidius himself," Fionn thought it strange that an infirm apothecary would stay and fight, but he decided to reserve that line of questioning for another time. He listened as his father continued, a growing sense of unease nestled between his breastplate and his skin.

"The demons came, made from the darkness that surrounded us, turning day to night. I cannot say that we fought valiantly, for a valiant victory can only be had by those who have been victorious. But we fought, and a few of our small number fell, among them Vidius. A brave soul he was, he fought with the heart of an elf, but, in the end, the fiends were there only to take him from us, and we could not stop them. I am sorry, Son, but we could not stop them." Suddenly, Fionn got the feeling that the sorrow in his father's eyes still had more meat to chew on. He felt certain that the true tragedy was still to come.

With a choked heart, he asked, "But Chiave...?" Why was his father talking about the death of the herbalist when he had asked about his brother? Had the boy been one of those who had fallen in the fray, and, if so, why by the El had Rentyl allowed him to fight? Did he have no fatherly instincts? Did he not know that Vorynne had charged Fionn with the task of taking care of the boy? What had possessed him to think the child had so little value? Sure he was young and bumbling and so very human, but he was still a member of the family.

Fionn's fury grew, bubbling inside him until indignation surged through every inch of his body. He was angry that the boy had been killed, that he had been forced to fail in his oath without even being able to do something about it. The entire situation was so damned unfair it turned his stomach sour and wrapped his heart in an unearthly chill.

From somewhere outside the radius of heat and anger consuming him, Fionn felt a hand on his shoulder, and turned to see his father with compassion and understanding in his eyes. "The boy is fine," Rentyl said simply, and waited a moment while Fionn composed himself. "It is true, Chiave hid away in the village so that he could fight, but he was not allowed to do so. I still have little understanding of what transpired between him and Vidius, but the child came to sit with the herbalist in his last moments, and then set out on a journey. It appears he has a commission of his own now. I would not worry about him, Fionn; he's a resourceful child. I feel certain that we will see him again."

The icy hand slowly unclenched around Fionn's heart. He turned to look down into the valley, watching the smoke of the cooking fire waft up into the cold, cloudless sky. Suddenly, the last week he had spent with her felt little more than a dream. Somewhere within him was the knowledge that it couldn't last, but he had buried that so deep inside himself that he had forgotten there was a world outside the Eye and outside of Muirinn's eyes.

As if following his thoughts along with his gaze, his father said behind him, "They will be coming for her, those monsters. They killed Galenthail, and you know how hardy he was. It is only a matter of time before they track her down. She will never be safe."

"She must be told what has happened, and it will be easier if this happens without others around. I ask that you wait a moment before continuing down to the valley floor. It should come from me."

When Fionn arrived back at the campsite, Mylena was busying herself in preparation of their simple midday meal. She had picked the fruit herself especially, wanting to maintain as much normalcy and continue their small routines as long as she could. She may not have agreed with Fionn's choice of hiding places, but she was no fool. Mylena knew this wouldn't last, and if their little paradise was being intruded upon, they might as well enjoy their last few moments together.

The small salad she made was a mixture of some of the fruits growing on the trees around the oasis. Despite the cold of the season and the snow capping the ridge of the cauldron walls, these plants appeared nearly tropical in their bounty, and it was a lovely thing to try new tastes she had never experienced. The look on Fionn's face as he arrived told her that her little trick of fooling herself into believing the world could not intrude on their happiness was failing miserably. Fruit or no, there was the weight of the world pressing firmly on his shoulders, brought no doubt by his father and the rest of his clan. Why couldn't they leave him alone? Why wouldn't they allow him to be happy, even in this small thing? Could nothing in her life be good and happy and pure?

"Muirinn....," he began, and to her ears the name had begun to sound more like a pet endearment than a false mask she wore to hide her identity. She fancied herself a peasant girl, an herbalist's daughter, who had been swept off to a magical land of bounty and beauty by a handsome elf. He called her Muirinn, his Muirinn, and they lived in the Eye of the World surrounded by love and peace.

She refused to allow his family to burden him with their prejudices. If he was to be sad because of their beliefs, than she would be doubly happy to make up for his sadness. She smiled as he approached, and flung her arms around his neck, not minding how sticky her fingers were from preparing the fruit.

Fionn would not be deterred from his seriousness, however, and, with the great strength of his race, pulled her arms from his neck. He held her hands in front of him and looked down at them as if studying some ancient text to learn its meaning. Mylena watched as he stood there, hunched, lost in thought, and tried one last time to break the mood.

"With so many coming, we certainly will have our hands full making dinner. Would you be a love and go out to collect a little more fruit? We wouldn't want to be bad hosts, now would we?" The light tone in her voice reflected in her eyes, and she leaned up so that he was forced to look her in the eyes, breaking his train of thought.

"They came for him at Kir'Unwin," he said bluntly, and Mylena felt the happiness seep out of her through her feet and into the ground. "There was a battle, and though few fought off the many, he fell under the weight of their attack. Muirinn, your father is gone." His eyes were filled with apology, as if somehow it was his fault that her father was dead.

Everything within her felt numb, as if all sensation had simply ceased. And then it started at the pit of her stomach, a small darkness no bigger than a pin point. It spread slowly as she looked into Fionn's eyes, until it was the size of a fist, then spread into her chest and shoulders and finally clawed its ways into her eyes. She didn't cry then, but the darkness streamed out of her, the pain of realizing that she had already mourned her father that day back in the forest. She had known then that she was alone in the world.

She did not cry, but the sky did. A great black cloud formed above her, and a torrent of rain opened over the oasis, despite the calm temperate nature of the day. The rain started suddenly and drenched Mylena and Fionn in seconds, and as she sank to the ground, the rain only intensified. Lightning crackled and split the sky, their ears ringing from the repeating peals of thunder.

Mylena closed her eyes for the moment, feeling nothing but the chill of the rain on her skin, the water rolling down her shoulders and back. When she finally opened her eyes, she thought for a moment that the rain was somehow black because she sat in a pool of inky blackness that stained the grasses around her. After a moment of disbelief, she looked up at the sky and saw nothing but pure, clear water pouring from the sky. Then her eyes met Fionn's, and she saw his face flooded with disbelief and a small amount of horror. It was then she realized what the black liquid was.

Reaching up into her hair, she pulled back her hands to find them covered in black stain. It was as if her nightmare of losing her hair had suddenly come true. Only the reality meant she was losing the dye in her hair, losing her protective disguise in the face of her personal tragedy. Sure enough, the tresses she pulled into sight were red, not black, glinting dully as the rainwater dripped off them. It had been so long since she had seen her natural hair color, she wondered at it as if she too were seeing something new. Alarmed, she looked up at Fionn, and the darkness within her receded enough so that the rain lessened to a light mist, and then evaporated as quickly as it came, leaving the sky clear of clouds.

"Who are you?" Fionn asked in disbelief. He had taken several steps back defensively, and he looked upon her as if she were a monster instead of the girl he had cared so much about.

The change in feeling in someone she had grown so close to brought everything into focus for Mylena. She stood, rain-soaked, her clothing dark with black dye, her drenched hair an unmistakable shade of red. *I am Muirinn*, her heart screamed, *a village girl who wants nothing more than a village life*. But even her heart knew that dream was over. Throwing her head back as she used to do oh so long ago in a gesture of regal authority, she said, "I am Mylena Saebariela, Princess of Shadowhaven, daughter to Saebariel and Thaniel."

It had been several days since Chiave's band of protectors left the known lands of Shadowhaven's boundaries and began to cross the Plains of the Beyond. None of them had ventured this far; indeed, no citizen of Shadowhaven had explored their expanses and lived to map their boundaries. Expeditions had been sent numerous times, but none of them had come back alive. Captain Warrek had learned over the years that there were simply some assignments that you gave out fully knowing that the soldiers would not return. Exploration of the Plains of the Beyond was just such an assignment.

Thus the mood turned somber when they stepped into the golden grasses of the Plains. Each member of his squad knew exactly the odds they faced. Chiave, the young boy with the extraordinary commission, and the insane waif Joppa, they had no idea, and did not have the sense to read the moods of their companions. Joppa had taken to haunting the book, bothering the guards who carried the Testament, insisting that she get access to the book. Poor thing. Warrek suspected it had something to do with her brother and his death, but could not be certain. All he knew was that his soldiers were tired of toting around children on a fool's errand.

He could not tell them what the book had said, what was written in the margins of the holy text in Thaniel's blocky script. He couldn't share their mission because, in the end, it simply wasn't his information to give. Chiave had been commissioned by Thaniel, and the boy had either the loyalty or the stubbornness to insist that they head into unknown and dangerous territory in search of ...well, what they sought was too strange to even think about.

Just last night, Warrek had been pulled into a conference in the tent of one of his archers. Inside, five of the best of his soldiers were conferencing and wanted to talk to him.

"What are we doing trekking all over El's green earth with children in tow?" Gregor came to the meat of it without much fuss. He was always a straight shooter, and Warrek appreciated that about him.

"The boy has been commissioned to bring the book to a person of importance. That is all I can say about it. He has authority from those who matter in our realm, and that is enough for me. It should be enough for you too, as these are your orders." Warrek leveled an even gaze at each of the dissenters in the tent. "Do you have problems with your orders?" He made sure to leave a note of danger in the question so that they would know how to answer.

"No, Captain," an archer said, very quickly even for an elf. She knew better than to try to flout his authority. "It is only that I question the necessity of having the girl with us. She brings nothing but distraction and irritation. Chiave is a brave soul, a member of the Kir'Unwin clan, and I have every respect for his mother. I only ask that we send the girl away. She is ill in the head and needs treatment, not danger."

"You make a valid point, Bellamy," Warrek acknowledged, standing himself, "but you forget that it is not I who leads this expedition; it is the boy. Speak to Chiave should you wish to discuss Joppa's utility. You might be surprised at his wisdom."

The group looked at one another, none brave enough to go and speak to the boy. Warrek sighed and left the tent, making for the campfire where the young people sat with Vorynne enjoying their supper. He squared his shoulders and sat down beside Chiave on a log that served as a makeshift bench before the warmth of the flames.

"Evening, Chiave," he began, feeling the group of dissenters standing behind him outside the ring of firelight. It was amazing to him exactly how cowardly brave men and women could be in the face of very simple challenges. Give them an ogre to fight, and they would do it without hesitation. Ask them to talk to a boy about leaving his friend behind, and they shivered like willow trees in a breeze created by their own fear.

Not being the sort to resort to flowery speeches, Warrek got straight to the point. "There are concerns amongst some of my soldiers that Joppa may not be fit for travel. Perhaps it would be best to send her back home so that she can receive the proper care." He watched Chiave contemplate his proposition.

While Chiave was thinking, Joppa herself chimed in. "Of course I am not fit for travel. Have you seen a girl who could fit in a travel case? Nonsense. Honestly, for warriors, you sometimes say the oddest things." She went back to her food, crooning lightly to the plate in her lap.

Chiave watched her as she serenaded her food and then, after a moment, gave his reply. "If we are to abandon all those who need help simply because it is inconvenient, then we have lost ourselves along with our realm and should accept Sargon's rule without issue. The girl stays because I have need of her and she needs me. If your soldiers have a problem with that, I suggest they rethink the generosity of spirit that created this great nation twenty-four years ago. If she goes, so do I and the Testament." Without another word, he returned to his meal, and Warrek left them in peace to join the group of dissenters in the shadows.

"There, you have your answer. Without her, you'll be without him, without the book, and without a future. Is that enough of a reason to keep her around? Now, how much of an ass does that make you?" Warrek asked, and shouldered past the group into the night. This would not be the last of this, he could tell, but at least they had seen the strength of Chiave's resolve for themselves.

The Plains themselves were of little challenge, and by the middle of the fifth day, the squad was beginning to relax a bit as they traversed the rolling hills of waving grass. The simple truth of it was that, without danger, the soldiers had the opportunity to unroll the great walls of tension in their muscles caused by the events of the last few weeks. They had seen their comrades die at the hands of an unimaginable foe. They had wandered the land only to discover their errand fruitless, and, in the end, the priests were dead and King Thaniel was dead, so that left the realm without spiritual or royal guidance. So much had changed in their lives in so short a time, Warrek was grateful they had a respite from the constant warring to get their bearings again.

So many had died in such a short time. It didn't seem possible that the world they had created, the utopia built around the love shown between Saebariel and Thaniel, had crumbled without a fight, sighing into oblivion without a whimper. He had thought that his people were better than that. He had thought that the elves and humans of Shadowhaven had been stronger than most, certainly more tolerant than most. They had had so many hardships creating their world, it was difficult for him to understand a situation where they wouldn't fight to keep it. It was as if without the ruling family, they had no focus. Without the queen and king, there was nothing worth fighting for.

Could Shadowhaven survive without its monarchs? It is true, the nation began with their marriage, but what Thaniel and Saebariel had created was so much bigger than them. Warrek considered it an ideal place where research and knowledge could be performed openly and without secrecy. It was a place where anyone could be accepted regardless of race or background. It was a new world, and it didn't matter who you were when you arrived; once there, a citizen of Shadowhaven could become exactly what his or her potential would allow.

Why then had there been no uproar when Sargon came in and corrupted their dream with his lust for power? Why couldn't the people see that their power lay not in some archaic Well but in their hearts, in what they had built, in Shadowhaven itself? What would it take for them to stand up and take ownership of their destiny once more? Warrek chewed on this thought as the band stopped to camp for the night.

A scout rocked Warrek from his deliberations. The girl was young, but smart, and had proven herself in battle more than once in the brief period she had joined on. "What is it Alarvel?" Warrek asked, still half-pondering his dilemma.

"Smoke, Captain, on the eastern horizon. Lots of it." She led him to his mount, a sturdy black steed that had seen him through years of battles and trials and El knows what else, and together they rode toward the east. Apprehension grew in his belly as Warrek caught sight of what Alarvel had mentioned. There was indeed smoke, a thick cloud of yellow, blighting the sky. It looked as if whatever it was had been burning for quite some time, and there was a sickly sulfurous smell in the air. The hackles on the back of Warrek's neck rose as if in animal instinct, and he sensed that such a sight could be nothing but bad news for the group.

The two of them, Warrek and Alarvel, rode east until the edge of the plain dropped sharply away. Standing there on the edge of the cliffs, Warrek could see why there was so much smoke in the air.

"It appears," he said to his companion as he looked out beyond the cliffs, "that there is a very good reason why no explorer returned to extend our maps." Then, without another word, he turned his horse around and rode the long distance back to his soldiers. In his heart, he knew that the journey Chiave was on would definitely require the protection of all his soldiers, and that their peaceful respite on the Plains of the Beyond was suddenly and irrevocably over.

## CHAPTER EIGHT

Because of its very nature, morning in the soldier's camp was always the most difficult time of the day. For the soldiers, it meant rising and stretching limbs scarred with war wounds, preparing meals, and packing up camp. For Chiave, it meant meditation on his task.

I can do this. I must do this. There was so much happening that he didn't understand. He was just a boy, nearly sixteen, and he had seen so little of the world. He knew his clan, his village, and only recently realized that neither were really his in the technical sense. Everything he had connected to, everything that he was, was an illusion. His real parents were dead. His brother, who was not his brother, was off protecting his sister, who he only recently realized he was related to.

And then there was the promise he made Thaniel, his father. This huge book must be carried across the world to a person he didn't know, and he must convince that person to follow the instructions laid out within. The book had little importance to him personally, yet it meant a great deal to his people. Honestly, how important could a book be if it is written in a language that no one alive can read? He was expected to persuade this person to do what Thaniel commands. What did he know of charisma, of inspiring action in others? The most courageous thing he had done of late was insist that Joppa be brought along, fragile thing that she was.

Something about Joppa compelled Chiave to protect her. He rolled over on his side and looked at the lump of blankets that represented where she slept. Perhaps it was the very fact that no one else seemed to want to keep her alive, herself included. She was a cracked vessel filled with so much memory she overflowed, and it leaked from her at the strangest moments, making everyone around her uncomfortable. Chiave couldn't deny he was included in that discomfort on occasion, but, unlike the rest of them, he had stood that evening behind her in the graveyard as she begged Abihu to wake up. He had seen the heartbreak in her as they walked away from her brother's final resting place. Only someone who had seen that horrible moment, only someone who had watched her at her most vulnerable would understand why she needed to be taken care of.

How could they expect him to send her away? Yes, they were going into danger, but without him, Joppa would plummet back into the darkness he found her in, wandering the landscape without heed to her health or her location. He had no choice but to risk her life by bringing her along. Otherwise, she was sure to die.

It was only after this sort of contemplation that Chiave could rise and face a new day among soldiers who neither welcomed nor understood him. He could feel their derision laying across his shoulders the minute he stepped out of the tent to relieve himself. What did they expect him to do, just drop his commission and retreat back to the loving arms of a family that wasn't really his? He had known his true father for three years, and, in that time, Thaniel had taught him much.

The most important lesson he had taught surrounded a man's honor.

The wintery chill of the morning air around him reminded him strongly of that night sitting before Thaniel's fire in his cottage. Chiave had stoked the fire and Muirinn—he supposed he might as well call her Mylena now, even if only in his head—had brewed them tea from leaves she had dried herself. Thaniel had been discussing the history of the humans of Eidalore, and what had brought them such success in their wars against the Ogres of the North Country.

"A man cannot be judged by his actions as history sees them. History only notes the end results, the successes and the losses. A man may have come of age and never be counted a true man. What is the true ingredient of manhood?"

Chiave thought a moment on this, thwarted by the warmth of the tea and the heat of the flames in the fireplace. "I cannot say, Master. I thought years were the sign that a boy has become a man."

"Honor. It is the honor within a man that truly makes him what he is. Without that honor, he is little more than a beast who walks upright, since a beast is guided by its wants and wishes without regard for others. A man, on the other hand, has filled his days with honorable actions. Most of these history may never notice, and this is alright, for that is the nature of honor. But the man himself will know, and be able to stand tall before his people and before the El and know that he made honorable choices."

Even now, years later and separated from Thaniel by death and so many leagues of land, Chiave nodded at the wisdom of his words. He understood that even though the soldiers did not see the honor of his actions, he knew it was the right thing to do, and would press on for the sake of his manhood. Whenever that might come, he was not sure, but he was positive that if he courted it with brave and decent actions, soon they would be able to distinguish him from the beasts and he could rightly call himself a man.

As he neared the newly stoked fire, he saw that Captain Warrek was talking with his squad, the men and women huddling together. Even his mother Vorynne was among them, and they all seemed completely intent on whatever it was he had to say. Chiave approached the fire and held his icy fingers to the flames to warm them, his curiosity prickling the back of his arms. He wanted very much to know what they were talking about, but, at the same time, he realized the value in allowing the military component of their group to run their organization as they always had. Including a young man in their discussions of strategy might upset those essential routines, and that was no way to be accepted by the soldiers.

It was a pleasant surprise, therefore, when the Captain called him over to their huddle. As Chiave approached, he felt the postures of the soldiers around him change; the energy of the group shifted distinctly toward mistrust. He did his best to ignore it and, instead, focused on what the Captain was saying.

"It seems we have reached the end of the Plains of the Beyond," the Captain began, by way of explanation. "Our scouts have discovered there is some very dangerous terrain ahead and see no way around. This means that you and the girl will have to be protected at all times, and will be in peril from the moment we leave the Plains. Is there any way I can persuade you to—"

"No need to ask, Captain. She comes with us."

Warrek nodded. "Very well then. We will begin our decent as soon as we break camp. Now we have no idea as to how long we will be covering the terrain, and it looks like we will be working off the supplies we bring with us."

"Oh, and did he mention the dragons by any chance?" said a soldier, the one called Gregor.

Chiave's heart skipped a beat, and then another as two opposite emotions warred within him. On the one hand, he was thrilled at the prospect of actually seeing a dragon with his own eyes. However, the bloodlust of dragons was legendary. They were creatures so massive that men seemed but small morsels to them, but that did not stop them from partaking at every opportunity.

While Chiave's insides battled with his mixed emotions, the Captain continued, "Yes, I was getting to that. The land below the cliffs is populated by a horde of extremely vicious dragons. I cannot tell their exact species, but from what I've seen of the carnage down below, this will be some of the most treacherous country I've crossed in my long life. I have met dragons that were civil enough to invite to meet the family. But these appear to be nothing more than ravaging beasts."

"I suggest," began Vorynne, "that we stick in tight formation for the duration of our time in dragon country, and that we move fast. We can expect attacks from above as well as from the ground. Dragons of this small size move much quicker than their larger more docile cousins, so do not be fooled by their size. A dragon of any size can kill with both ends."

"Agreed." Captain Warrek stood up so that the group could see him. "We move assembled and do not break formation for anything. This is not our land. We are trespassing from the moment that we set foot on that valley floor. The dragons will have every right to defend the land they claim is theirs, so we must be on alert at every moment. Understood?" There was a murmur of assent all around. He turned to Chiave. "Understand?" It was Chiave's turn to nod. "Good, then we break camp after eating and get going. No reason to waste daylight when we will have so little of it."

Breaking down the camp went smoother than Chiave would have imagined, considering the threat of dragons on the horizon. He made sure Joppa ate something, and while she giggled into her porridge, he dismantled their tent and litters and packed them away with the others. This would be the last night they would use the tent village, something he would greatly miss once they started into the Dragon Vale as some were beginning to call it. It was nice to have shelter from the elements, even if it were only a thin piece of canvas, and, although his cloak was warm, it was no replacement for a blanket. Still, he could not carry much else with the Greatsword strapped to his back. He continued to insist it was his burden to manage, even though it was sizes too large for him and gave him an ache in his bones by midday.

They left the wagons in a small gully and set free their war horses. Hopefully, the horses would find a home either on the plains or with a farmer, but to bring them into dragon country would be cruel, since they would surely be slaughtered. It meant that from this point on, they not only would have to go without nightly shelter but also have to travel on foot. Chiave steeled himself for lots of sores on his feet and lots of chilly nights.

The soldiers moved surprisingly fast, considering the armor and gear they carried. As they set off across the plains, it was all Chiave could do to walk, what with his father's sword strapped to his back. And Joppa was a constant distraction, always stopping to talk to a flower or dance in the grass. In the end, he decided it best to clamp fast to her hand, which seemed to delight her unceasingly, and she swung their arms as they walked as if they were toddlers. Toddlers going to war. It would be funny if it weren't almost true.

The cliffs appeared on the horizon in a few hours and, with them, the gray-yellow stain across the sky that was the sign of dragons and their sulfurous breathing. The cliffs themselves looked as though gigantic teeth had clamped into the earth, and the valley below was the result of their vicious bite. For a moment, they all stared at the vast smoky expanse below them, each of them seeing the network of caves cut into the rock and the piles of bones lying on the valley floor. If there was ever a moment where Chiave could fool himself into being on a grand adventure where he might encounter dazzling maidens and mythical creatures, he supposed this might be it. But the maiden he had met was broken somewhere within herself, and the mythical creatures were no doubt preparing their teeth for ripping his flesh. If he were to write a story about his life, he figured he might leave this part, the dying part, out of it. Although really, how can you tell a story when you're dead? At this, he laughed at the ludicrous nature of the situation, at the dragons, at the cliff, at the sword and book, and at world that had been so cruel to him. He laughed so hard his sides hurt, laughed so hard those around him looked at him slantwise as if he might have caught a bit of Joppa's illness. Joppa herself saw his laughter and began to cry, great rolling tears splashing onto her leather breastplate, and Chiave stopped laughing if only to keep her from being so sad. What a strange life he was wrapped up in.

Captain Warrek was rounding up the soldiers. "Very well. You know what we are facing. You can see it plainly below. Make no mistake; those bones will be ours if we do not work with vigilance and speed. I anticipate a day or more of travel, and there will be no stopping, no resting, no pause until we reach safety.

"What this means is that you will need to take provisions as you can, relieve yourselves when you must, and never sheath your weapon. We are a strong breed, we of Shadowhaven, and we have faced worse things than a pack of puny dragons. We have looked into the darkness and ripped its throat out. If any of you are afraid, let the fear in. Hold it in your stomach a little while and crap it out again because it can only serve as nourishment, and then it must go.

"When we reach the bottom of the cliffs we will form up immediately. We will take the shape of a multilayered egg, the children and I will form the yolk, then the archers will form the white, and you men of brute strength will be our shell."

Here he stopped to look over the group. There were twenty of them in all, most he had fought with for years, Chiave could tell by the expressions they wore under their scars. The female elven warriors stood willowy and strong amongst their human brethren, but each was a soldier of bravery and honor. Honor. Chiave thought back to his contemplation of honor and then to Thaniel. Suddenly he felt incredibly honored to stand among these men and women, even though he was far from their equal. He felt part of this group, as if it were a new clan that welcomed him, and despite the danger lying below, despite the bellowing of the dragons echoing off the valley walls, he smiled to himself.

"It's a very long way down," Joppa said sensibly at his elbow. She was leaning over the cliff edge to look at the valley below, and Chiave pulled her back just in time before she went toppling over. She had a point, though. Exactly how were they going to get down?

Chiave turned to ask his question to Vorynne, and saw that the soldiers were creating two makeshift harnesses from leather and rope. The Stone Caller in the group, a stoic archer named Clodai bound the ends of the ropes in stone so that the group could repel down the cliff face. Amazed, Chiave watched groups of four disappear over the edge to slide down the rock.

"What are the harnesses for?" Chiave wondered out loud.

"Why, they're for you and Joppa," Vorynne replied, and swooped him up into her arms as if he were still a baby. Perhaps he was still a toddler after all. Indeed, he felt like one as he was tied into a harness bound to Vorynne's chest. He faced her, his legs wrapped around her waist and his arms around her neck, holding on like he had when he was a boy. Vorynne swung herself over the cliff face and, with her Chiave parcel strapped to her chest, began to climb down the rope, exhibiting the hidden strength of her race.

All of a sudden, memories were flooding him of the time before she had been ordered to report to the Queen's Guard. His world was simpler then. He had a mother, a father, and a brother who all loved him. It had been Vorynne who had taught him to use a bow and arrow, and Vorynne who had taken him for his first horseback ride through the forest. He could still smell the mossy musk of the trees around him.

Chiave couldn't take it any longer. He had to know, one way or another. "Did you ever really love me?" He was sniffling, his eyes misty with tears so that Vorynne's face was blurry and he couldn't quite see her expression.

He heard it in her voice, however. At first, there was surprise and then she relaxed as she realized he had found out the truth. "When Fionn was born, I was joyful. To be a mother is a great honor, and though he wasn't a female, I loved him as a daughter and trained him in the ways of our people. But we are elves; we are limited in our emotions, and when you were brought to us, you demanded so very much. You wanted to be held, to be played with. You demanded affection, and this was very hard for me. I am a warrior; I thought myself above such nonsense."

Chiave thought about it a moment. His memories were of a warm, loving childhood. It seemed strange to hear that this wasn't a natural thing for Vorynne.

She continued, not noticing his change in expression. "But it was my duty to care for you. Rentyl insisted that you required two parents' worth of affection, and I relented for the sake of my nation. It was my commission, and I fulfilled it. What I did not expect was how much I enjoyed this duty of mine. Fionn will understand this, as he was there to witness it; you were so foreign to us, yet you loved us completely. Your affection opened us up in ways elves have never opened before. Even as a child, Chiave, you had the power to change others. I do not have experience with other human children, but I wager they cannot claim the same influence that you had over us."

"I was only called away from my commission protecting you when it was clear that Fionn was a strong enough warrior to take my place. He had been trained and had taken quickly to the skills required of a soldier. You see, we were a perfect fit for you, our family. There were two warriors and a clan leader among us, all three capable of providing protection for you and your secret."

"So you knew who I was?" Chiave asked between sniffles.

Vorynne nodded. "We knew the day you were brought to us. You have your mother's eyes, you know. Saebariel would have loved to have known you. Alas, that was not to be. There has been much heartache in that poor girl's life...," she trailed off a moment, then finished, "as in yours. I am sorry, Chiave that you were wrapped in such sadness. Although there is little you can take comfort in, realize that your parents—all your parents—loved you. Your life is a consequence of forces outside of our knowledge or control, and I wish I could tell you that the pain is over. The only thing that is over, it appears, is your childhood." She bent down then, and nuzzled the top of his head gently with her nose. It was a gesture he knew from his childhood, and one, he now realized, that did not come naturally to her.

What happened next Chiave would remember afterwards in a series of flashes. He felt a rush of stiff, hot wind as if the desert in full summer had suddenly descended upon him. He heard screaming to his right, and turned just in time to see someone plucked off the rope. He heard someone call from the top of the cliff "Brooks! They've got Brooks!" He saw a great pair of wings beat a few times, and then they were gone. What remained was a pervasive stillness, as if time itself had stopped. Only the distant beating of wings broke the silence as everyone stopped in shock.

It was too fast and too horrible to register completely what had happened. Chiave's heart pounded in his ears, and a blank numbness flooded his head. The only thing he could think was

It wasn't me, thank the El it wasn't me and then, suddenly, the guilt slammed down upon him as he realized what he was thinking. He finished the journey down the cliff in self-abusing silence, and Vorynne did not attempt to break his brooding mood, instead lowering them to the ground and pulling him from the harness without a word.

Once they were on the ground, the last group of soldiers swung over the cliff face and shimmied down as fast as possible while the archers kept watch for any more airborne assailants. There was a silent agreement amongst them that Brooks would be the first and last to die in the Dragon Vale. When Captain Warrek had arrived at the base of the cliffs, the egg formed around him, and Chiave and Joppa were shoved within two layers of armed protection. After what he had seen on the cliff, Chiave didn't mind a little coddling. Joppa seemed not to notice, and was still jabbering on about salvation to the elven maid who had carried her down the cliff.

They set off as a unit, an oval of soldiers with an interior of teenagers. It was difficult to see in the smoke, and the sulfur began stinging their eyes as soon as they started to move. Each of them had caution wrapped around their hearts, and the mood was tense and expectant. No words or banter passed between the soldiers. In fact, the only voice that could be heard was Joppa's as she muttered words of protection songs under her breath. She seemed to be contemplating something, because she kept looking back toward the soldiers at the rear of the formation and then wringing her hands distractedly. Chiave watched her with a rising sense of panic.

"Shut up girl," Warrek snapped, "you're mutterings will get us all killed." Joppa seemed not to hear him, and continued on in her litany as if she were a priest preparing a sermon.

"The Light will protect us; have no fear. But we must pray. Yes, yes, we must pray. If we do not ask the blessing of the El, how will he find us to keep us from harm?" Suddenly Joppa dropped to her knees, hands raised above her, and she began to pray, her words loud and reverberating off the valley walls. The entire formation stopped, and those nearest Joppa tried to shush her into silence, but to no avail.

"We beseech you, Lord, to look upon your servants and see past our weakness and our pride. Oh, how we have sinned to think we could walk without your Light! Look down upon us, your children, and forgive our sinful arrogance. To think that we, puny mortals, could ever stand against the creatures you have raised from the very soil! Pity us, O great El, and protect your servants. Protect us, though we do not deserve it!" Joppa looked around her, astonished. "Why are you not praying! How can one voice speak for the multitude?"

Chiave could feel the danger wrapping around the group. The smoke was so heavy they couldn't see beyond the formation, and every moment they stopped was a moment that they would be open for attack. He had to assume that because the dragons lived in this smoke always, they could see in it. Wasn't that how they had plucked Brooks off the cliff face? He racked his mind for a solution, something to get them moving, and nothing came to him. Perhaps this was as foolish a mission as Warrek had pointed out all those days ago at the monastery. Well, if they were to go, he might as well die in prayer. He knelt beside Joppa and clasped his hands together, bowing his head. "Amen," he said softly.

Joppa looked at him, cocking her head to the side. "What a strange and foolish person you are! To kneel at a time like this, when there is danger about. Are you mad?" She pulled him to his feet and raised her eyebrows to the captain expectantly. "Well then, shouldn't we get going?"

In silent frustration, Warrek motioned for the formation to continue. A minute later, Alarvel, at the front of the group, motioned for them to stop again.

"Captain, I hear echoes, ahead," she said quietly.

"It makes sense, considering we're in a bloody valley," Gregor barked impatiently.

"No, they are below us."

Warrek grunted loudly, and Chiave could tell his frustration was mounting. "Front three go, investigate, but be quick about it. The longer we wait, the more of a chance we have of attack."

The front three disappeared into the smoke, eerily swallowed by the yellowish fog that surrounded the group. They came back in a few minutes with their report. "A pit, about a hundred leagues wide, uncrossable. The monsters were waiting on the other side for us to fall into their trap. At least ten of them, the beasts all lined up as if at the dinner table."

Captain Warrek nodded. "Well, it looks like that prayer may have protected us after all. We will circle east. Move!"

No sooner had he given the order then Chiave heard them. There was a great bellowing, as if the dragons realized that they would have no easy dinner, and then that same familiar rush of hot wind. Suddenly, the sky filled with black beasts, their scales glinting dully in the smoke-filtered afternoon sunlight, talons and teeth out. They were met immediately with a volley of arrows. At first, it looked like they would all miss their mark, but then Chiave realized the archers weren't aiming for the hearts or heads of the beasts. They were aiming for their wings.

A dragon swooped in close, talons closing in on a footman, and even though the arrows rent holes in his wings, we was still able to fly away with his victim screaming into the smoky afternoon air. A second volley of arrows darkened the sky, and, this time, several dragons howled in pain as their wings were gashed and torn. A fire wielder threw a massive fireball at a nearby dragon, setting the creature on fire. Chiave could hear its skin crackle as it screamed.

Despite all the chaos, the group kept moving, Warrek obviously thinking a moving target would be harder to hit. Chiave considered whether or not the greatsword would be of any help to him, and thought better of it. He had little training in swordplay, and he was positive he wouldn't be of much use with a sword he could barely lift.

Beside him, Joppa was giggling, pointing up at the dragons with her face filled with delight. He wondered at her, slightly envious of her oblivion. It would be lovely to be able to step out of this horror and see things through her eyes. Could it be possible to focus on the beauty of such a terrible thing, the grace of the creature, the power of its movements? Chiave followed her gaze, trying to see what she saw. He saw the dragons, the size of six or more horses, swoop and dart as if they were no larger than gulls. There was an amazing grace in their movements, almost like a song.

Without realizing it, Chiave was raising his hands in front of him, flowing with the rhythm of the dragons, his arms swooping in great arcs. The song rose inside him without bidding, his secret song of Stone Weaving, and he coaxed the rock to form a wall not where the dragon was, but where it would be as it finished its arc. The energy from the song seemed to somehow blend with the magic within the creature, and it was stopped dead, locked in the embrace of a stone caress. Chiave caught himself looking at it with sadness, almost regretting his actions, until he realized that the dragon would have most likely killed the archer it was aiming for had he not acted.

Clodai looked at him in amazement, and then adapted her strategy to mimic his. She began to weave stone around the approaching dragons, and although she missed once or twice, was able to capture three in rock prisons as the formation pushed ever forward.

Where success greeted them there was always a fresh crop of dragons to remind them that danger was their bedfellow. For every five dragons they halted, another ten rose up in their place, and the necessary movement of the formation only added to the challenge. The archers had perfect aim while standing still, but Chiave saw even Vorynne miss more than once because they had to shoot while on the run. There was no chance to stop and rest, and his throat burned from inhaling the sulfurous gases exhaled by the dragons. His eyes watered and his hands ached from the effort of casting, but he did not stop and neither did his comrades.

It was a fight of inches, but inches they won. With every step they took, they made progress, and behind them they left dragons encased in stone or charred to the bone. Chiave thought it a shame that the Air Weavers did not have the chance to cast, because he thought a lightning storm would be an excellent weapon. Air magic required time, and there was little of that as the egg moved across Dragon Vale.

"We're a dragon's egg," Joppa said to him as the light of the afternoon faltered into gloaming. "That's why they're so angry. They want their baby back. They think we're a dragon's egg." Chiave nodded and patted her hand, but he wondered if she were right. Could the formation itself be what was angering the dragons so? There was no time to test the theory, and certainly, it would be suicide to change positions now.

They seemed to be in a space that was more open than before, for the echoes of the dragon calls took longer to get to them. Chiave guessed that they were in the middle of the valley now, and, between casts, he tried to look around for a sign or landmark but saw nothing but the ever present smoke. He considered it a blessing really. He probably didn't want to know exactly how many dragons there were in the valley. It might just break his heart.

Captured by a sudden wave of panic, Chiave turned to the captain and asked, "Do you think we'll survive?" As if to punctuate his fear, a dragon broke through the defense, raking its claws across the lower group of soldiers. They screamed, falling, and the formation closed in, leaving their broken bodies behind.

"Never underestimate the will of man to survive. We have too much at stake here boy. What you bring with you across this godforsaken land is more than just a book and sword. You bring hope with you, and you wear it as your shield. As long as you don't drop your shield, we'll be able to survive. As long as we have you, we'll be fine." He smiled then, despite the madness he stood at the center of, and Chiave believed him. Whether or not he was lying, Chiave couldn't tell, but he wanted so badly to believe him, that it seemed much simpler to acquiesce to his desires than to fight them. What good would it do anyhow?

When the last of the sunlight seeped out of the air, the Fire Caller became a living torch, holding her hand high so that the group could see their opponents diving out of the darkness. The light seemed to irritate their sensitive eyes, and less of the dragons attacked when she began to sing her weaving song. It also could be the fact that so many of their brethren died in a fiery blaze that held them at bay. But whatever it was, the formation was able to move faster once she lit her fist with fire.

Soon after that, the weariness hit Chiave in full force. After so many hours of running, of casting, of fighting for their lives, he could feel the energy drain from him, falling from him with every drop of sweat that poured from his brow. They had been going for so long; the night was inky beyond the insular radiance of the firelight bound by the smoke. He was losing momentum, he wasn't sure if he could cast anymore, if he could walk anymore. With his knees sagging, he stumbled rather than walked, pulling one foot forward at a time. He looked around him and found that he wasn't the only one with weariness in his bones. The entire group looked as if they were losing strength, and that was bad. Just when they thought it couldn't get any worse, they lost their light.

It must have been the bravest of the dragons. Perhaps he was sacrificing himself for the good of his horde, since a meal this rich wasn't likely to wander into the vale often. Or perhaps he was avenging a dead brother or father or sister. Whatever the reason, a dragon, larger than the others descended upon the group and would not be deterred. Its huge black shape blocked the light from Chiave's view. No, it stole the light. The dragon had flown in, somersaulted in midair, and snatched the Fire Caller from the group with surprising dexterity. She wasn't one to give up without a fight, however, and about three beats of the dragon's massive wings later, it burst into flame and tumbled out of sight.

They were left in darkness, without the warmth or protection of the fire. It appeared, at last, that they would succumb to their attackers. There was no one with magic strong enough in the group to repel the dragons, and the archers had run out of arrows long ago. Chiave stopped, literally and figuratively, halting the group as he did so.

"None of us can hold them off alone," he said to Warrek, "But, as you said, we are not alone. We have been fighting them off one by one, and they bring dozens more every time we drop two or three. But we are not alone," he repeated more to himself than to Warrek. Suddenly, he understood his own words. They weren't alone. Why should their magic be cast as such?

"Clodai, can magic be mixed?" Chiave called quickly, reaching out for Clodai's hand as he asked. There wasn't much time, the longer they stood there in the darkness, the more likely the dragons would realize they were vulnerable.

"No," Clodai said firmly, yet clasped Chiave's hand even as she said so. She in turn reached out for the archer's hand next to her, and so on until they connected a chain together, magic users bound by fingers and by blood. "This won't work," Clodai repeated, yet she closed her eyes and raised her hands above her head. Chiave did the same, grasping his mother's hand firmly in his left to complete the chain, and the five of them began to sing.

They were singing their individual Spell Songs, songs taught them by their prospective Masters years ago. Although Chiave had learned his by experimentation, he knew that the words he sung were very different from those Vorynne or

Clodai chanted. They each coaxed the elements to do their bidding, begging the magic of the earth to blend, to mix, to make something new and strong and good. At first, it seemed like Clodai was right, that one Caster's chanting would only interfere with another and no magic would answer their Call, but then it happened. A shield of stone and of lightning and water rose around them, a dome of shimmering watery light. It was all elements and no elements at the same time, and, as Chiave sang, he felt the magic surround them with warmth and love and protection. They did not demand, for who could ask a tree to grow? They asked, and received the blessing of the earth, the blessing of the magic as it heard the call of the magic within their veins.

It wasn't long before the shield they created was put to the test. The dragons came, bellowing as they flew, and pounded against the barrier, only to ricochet off it, howling in pain. The water within the shield had been electrified by the lightning, and the stone that swirled within it gave it strength. No matter how much they threw themselves at it, the dragons could not break through, and were left to howl their rage from the shadows. With each attacker repelled, a cheer rose from the soldiers but also from the magic itself. It was pleased that it could help, and as Chiave chanted, he thanked it. He thanked the elements for sending their representatives to help him. He thanked them for saving him.

And then he realized with amazement that Joppa was right, only she herself didn't even know it. Their chanting was just another form of prayer when it came down to it. While she asked for protection from the El, they had asked it of the earth itself. He wondered if this was what they had meant all along, somewhere within him he made a mental note to research the similarities between the elven spell singing and the human worship of the El. He had a feeling they were one in the same. "Amen," he said, under his breath.

They held the shield for more than three hours, enough time for the sun to rise and for the dragons to realize the futility of their actions. Though the harmony of their voices was rough, it was still elegant in its beauty, even down to the end. Somewhere outside of the song, Chiave heard Captain Warrek announce, "They've gone. The dragons have retreated," and he nodded in his delirium.

"Well that's good at least," Chiave said, and passed out.

In the aftermath of Dragon Vale, Warrek surveyed their losses with a heavy heart. Even before he had a chance to wrap his head around the death toll, however, he sat down on a rock and penned out a map of the area as he remembered it. The fallen would be remembered, and this journey would never again be as deadly for travelers, he vowed it would be so.

After they had realized the dragons were no longer attacking, the group had crossed the last bit of terrain until they reached a gorge that took them up and out of the valley. Had the shield not pulverized their attackers into a forced retreat, that gorge would have meant the slaughter of their entire number; so, even in the face of this horrible event, there were things to be grateful for.

Of the original twenty soldiers under his command during this excursion, ten remained, and, of those, four were badly wounded. Still, the boy had come out intact, as had the book, although one of the guards had fallen early in the battle.

The boy. If that wasn't a surprise, he wasn't sure what was. Not only had he kept a cool head during the chaos of battle, it turned out he was able to fight, and with magic at his disposal at that. He certainly was a mystery, this teenager Thaniel had commissioned to travel halfway across the world. And, as it turned out, he was the right man for the job, since, in the end, it was his quick thinking that saved their hides. Chiave lay in his mother's arms at the moment, having exhausted the last of his considerable strength with that crazy shield of his. Warrek filed that strategy away for later. It could come in handy.

Where they sat and rested was a ledge above the Dragon Vale, and oh was it sweet to breathe air free of smoke or sulfur. The very clothes Warrek wore were saturated with the stench of it. He would gladly welcome a bath and a change of clothes, although where he would find such a thing, El only knew. The trouble was, this was where their journey ended, at least as far as the directions written by Thaniel in the Testament were concerned. They talked of the cliffs of teeth and the valley of smoke, a wall of stone, and a secret door, but then there was some scribbling in the ancient tongue that Warrek could not make heads nor tails of. Here they stood, facing an impenetrable rock wall, and supposedly, he was to find a door somewhere nearby. He considered for a moment waking Chiave, but the boy was so exhausted it didn't seem right to rouse him just to ask him to solve a riddle Warrek himself couldn't figure out.

Sighing, Warrek put the text down and, rising, stretched his weary muscles. Every inch of him ached, and he just wanted to have this day over. Their destination lay beyond the stone barrier, if only he could find a way to reach it. He paced, trying to jog a solution from his tired brain, but nothing came. The more he tried to grasp the thought, the further it flew from his grasp.

While his back was turned, Joppa skittered over to the Testament and greedily flipped through its pages. With a grin splitting her face in two she scanned the words of page after page quickly and with relish. The soldier commissioned with guarding the book was off getting his wounds treated, so it was a few minutes before Warrek noticed the girl had snatched up the book. He tried to pull it from her hands, but she darted away, too fast to catch.

"You cannot keep the Anointed from the Word of the El. How dare you consider such a thing!" she chastised him, making quite a spectacle in front of the soldiers. Warrek set his jaw and attempted a second time to retrieve the book. It was not a plaything. Again, Joppa pulled away from him, this time opening the book to the page marked with Thaniel's scrap of cloth. She turned the enormous book this way and that, studying the notes in the margins, and finally dropped it unceremoniously in the dust at her feet and turned to face the stone wall behind her.

Joppa ran her hands across the rough surface of the stone, tracing cracks with her fingers and stretching her arms to their fullest extent so that she could embrace the rock in her own fashion. "We have work to do, you and I," she said to the stone, and kissed the rock as if she were saying hello to a playmate. Then she lifted her hands above her head and throwing her head back so that her chin lifted toward the sky she called out:

Zuapiur Piur, noa zuapliuoavr toa ae eakoateavr ae noa voax,
 Noa kiu paorleavr lea laonguoa dea lea Faokiuoaniueaz,
 Lea Aonkiueanz Uonz kiu zea niuxeaz daen toavr zean,
 Tiureavr reatoaouv lea Tuoteaz ea laoiuz noa paozoavr.

Zuapiur Tuoteaz doun zeakreatz prouteagh lea vouleauorz dea lea luomiuear,
 Noa ki deamaondoavr ae eatreaz moantrea lea xeamiun,
 Paorv toavr koaeauor ea ean lea zaenktuoaer priuveat,
 Tiureavr reatoauov lea Piur ea laoiuz noa pauzoavr.

She stood back then, smiling a small, knowing smile. As she did so, a rumbling began deep within the rock, and a massive fissure started along the base of the wall. The great crack split the rock wall from the cliff they stood on, then traveled up the stone face right in front of where Joppa stood. The crack opened wider, and wider, until it was wide enough for three men to walk through, shoulder to shoulder, and then the shaking stopped. "Thank you," Joppa said to the rock, and then sat down on the ground where she had left the Testament, and began to read.

Warrek was beyond amazement by this point. He had seen so many outlandish things, he couldn't fit anymore astonishment into his being. So he shrugged, and went to wake the boy, who had somehow slept through the earthquake. "Must you?" Vorynne asked, protectively holding the young man against her shoulder.

"You know, Vorynne, that he is no longer your child," Warrek was not about to mince words after they had come this far. "After everything we saw last night, it should be clear to you that his childhood died long ago. He is the reason that we came here, and, although I am sure he could use more rest, now is not the time for sloth. Now is the time for action."

Nodding, Vorynne shook Chiave gently, and he roused slowly, looking around him, unsure of his location. When he saw Warrek looking down at him, however, he sat right up, instantly awake. "Did we live?" was all he said.

"Yes, we lived," Warrek said with amusement, "and now is your time to get to work. We are here."

Chiave stood on shaky legs and, together, he and Warrek faced the crack in the rock wall. With only a moment's hesitation, Chiave walked up to the crack, and then stepped through. Warrek was only a step behind him, unsheathing his sword as he went.

What he found and what he expected to find were two completely different things. Rather than a cave, Warrek stepped into a bower, a flower-scented grove of trees that looked as if they were grown from magic themselves. He blinked twice to clear the fantasy from his eyes, but when he opened them again, nothing had changed. Behind him, he heard the astonishment of his squad, and he didn't blame them really. To traverse the hell of the Dragon Vale only then to step into a paradise was truly difficult to believe.

As they walked through the trees with Chiave in the lead, little bells chimed everywhere, and the air filled with the scent of the sweet perfume of flowers and something else even sweeter that Warrek could not put a finger on. Between the trees darted woodland animals that seemed neither afraid nor surprised by the soldiers. The air was filled with color, and then Warrek realized that he was wrong. The air was filled with something, or someone who radiated colored light, and, out of the corner of his eye, he caught sight of what it was and finally, after everything, felt astonishment once more. They were in a grove of pixies.

"The legends are true," he heard Alarvel whisper reverently. "I only thought they were stories told to children to remind them of their magical heritage. To think, all this time, that they actually existed, and all the way out here, in such a barren place."

Chiave had separated himself from them by a few feet, and, as Warrek approached him, he saw that Chiave had reached a clearing. The clearing had at its center a glassy pool, swirling with magical power. Warrek wondered if it were part of the Well of Zyn, or at least related to it somehow, but dared not speak. What stayed his tongue was the arrival of a person who demanded silence.

At first, she was just another pixie, perhaps a little brighter than the rest. But then she changed, shifting into an elven form so glorious it nearly broke Warrek's heart to look at her. Her golden-white hair flowed about her shoulders like wisps of smoke, and her eyes glowed bright with a keen understanding of all things. She stood regal before them, her head held high, and, as her eyes alighted upon him, Warrek felt a warm calm spread through his chest.

When she spoke, it was with a voice filled with music, music like the Spell Songs, but deeper, richer, and ringing true like the bells they heard in the grove. The contrast between her words and her voice was, therefore, all the more striking. "Greetings, Warrek of Shadowhaven. Have you come to beg forgiveness for the death of my daughter? Well, you will not find forgiveness here. A pixie lives forever, unless cut down by violent hands, and you, sir, are responsible for that cutting. I doubt very much there is anything you can say that will keep me from killing you right here where you stand."

## CHAPTER NINE

Mylena was once again wandering the dream castle of her childhood. She lingered in the foyer this time, smelling the mustiness of the tapestries depicting the magic singing of the elves. She wondered absently why, after so many years, the country still divided itself along racial lines. Were they not all citizens of the same realm, ruled by the same queen?

The thought of the queen brought Mylena back to her original purpose, so she climbed the hulking staircase and took the left fork where it split open at the top like a ripe fruit. At the end of the corridor, the Golden Owl doorknob leading to her father's room scowled down at her in derision. It judged her for her weakness, for her lack of warrior blood. The bird turned its great golden eye to watch her unblinkingly. It seemed to dare her to try to enter her father's domain. You are not welcome here; you are nothing but a peasant girl.

Shaking her head as if to clear the voice of the bird from her mind, Mylena turned left into the hallway leading to her own apartments. She slipped into the anteroom, letting the soft white gauze curtains brush along her face and hair. The scent of potted flowers filled her head with their powerful fragrance, flowers put there by her mother. Her mother had always filled their living space with other living things, things that reminded her of her home so very far away. She didn't talk much about her life in the Pixie Grove, mostly because of the estrangement between her mother and herself. Mylena knew that the disconnection hurt her mother greatly, but there were never words to speak about such a delicate subject. There was never room in their relationship for that much honesty. They were three generations of women who couldn't talk openly about the most important things. Mylena wondered where it would end.

Everything was there as she remembered it: the nightgown dancing on its peg by the bed, infused with life by the cool ocean breezes; the dressing table with its brushes and combs laid out by the serving girls. The pillows on the bed were plumped and ready for an afternoon nap, begging her to lay down for only a moment. The heady fragrance of flowers, the tinge of salt on the air, everything about this room spoke of relaxation and calm. She had never noticed it before, but her bedroom had been more of a sanctuary to her than any chapel she had knelt in. Here, she felt safe to be herself; here, she could spend her days staring out at the sea. Reflexively, her eyes drifted to the doors that opened onto her balcony. There stood the figure, tall, imposing, eyes looking out at the ocean with a sad, lost expression.

Mylena approached, her stomach knotted with fear. Whoever this person was, she stood to judge her, to condemn her for her weakness and pride. She knew it to be so; thus, this time, she determined that there was no avoiding such derision. Stepping lightly as she crossed the room, she inhaled the aroma of the potted flowers to bolster her confidence, and reached out a diffident hand to touch the shoulder of the visitor. She turned, and Mylena came face-to-face with the last person she ever expected to see again.

The Warrior Queen Saebariel stood before her, tall, and regal. She was so tall that she always looked down on Mylena, and, in her heart of hearts, Mylena suspected this was not only a physical action, but also an emotional one. How could a queen of such power and beauty help but be disappointed by a daughter whose greatest asset was her hair? Mylena looked up into the deep wells of her mother's blue eyes, and imagined she could see the pain within them.

Her mother began to speak, words tumbling out urgently. She reached a hand out and put it on Mylena's shoulder, but the weight was too much for her and she had to step out of the embrace. The waves of the ocean, even though they were several miles below, drowned out whatever her mother was saying. No matter how hard she tried to communicate, all Mylena heard was roaring. The sound of the sea ate up ever sound, loud enough that she could hear it when she woke. All that was left was the sadness in her mother's eyes, and the ever-present smell of flowers.

He was so exhausted, Chiave thought that he might be seeing things. So much had happened in the last two days, he considered the pixie queen might be a figment of his overstretched consciousness. So, as she railed against Captain

Warrek for the death of her daughter, he wobbled on his feet and grabbed Joppa's arm for support. She stared at him, shocked, and awkwardly, he felt as if he were grabbing the arm of a stranger. Quickly, he pulled his hand away and stepped forward into the clearing to stand beside Warrek.

Chiave could see the pain and surprise on the captain's face as the regal woman condemned him for something he didn't do. From what he could understand of the situation, Captain Warrek wasn't even in the country at the time of the invasion. Hadn't they spent three years abroad sent on a mission by Counselor Arndorn? How could he possibly be responsible for Queen Saebariel's death?

It irritated him how judgmental this pixie queen was being. The irritation boiled within him and mixed with the aching in his bones, with the sheer exhaustion he felt, and with the small light of pride growing in him, knowing they survived certain death in the valley below. And after all that, after all the death and carnage and sacrifice, after all the distance they had come, this was their welcome? Without thinking, Chiave wrenched the Testament from Joppa's iron grasp and took a defensive position in front of Captain Warrek.

"Queen of the pixies," he began before Warrek could react. He could fairly feel the shock of the man behind him, but did not turn to verify it. "We have come far and suffered much to speak with you. Captain Warrek had no way of preventing the siege on Shadowhaven. Although sworn to protect the royal family, he was sent on important business and could not be at the capital to protect your daughter."

The faery woman before him drew herself up, and Chiave could have sworn he saw her grow taller. Her eyes widened a bit in surprise, and then she tossed her head dismissively. "Inventing events will not cloud the fact that my daughter was murdered. Why should I believe the words of a boy barely stepping out of his childhood?"

"Inventing events? My Lady, there is no invention here. Any person living in Shadowhaven can tell you of the realm's takeover by an insidious villain. It is that villain who killed your daughter, burned our capital, and destroyed our kingdom."

Her eyes lit with triumph. "You say the kingdom is destroyed. I say you are lying. You say the world is thrown into chaos. I say look around you. Is this chaos, little man? Is this destruction? The world is perfectly peaceful, everything in order. It is you who are throwing it out of balance. It is you who are toying with the fabric of existence. You come here, you stand before me with your army, their weapons drenched in blood, and you tell me the world is in peril. Little man, I do not believe you."

Chiave took a step forward and threw the Testament at her feet. The book bounced once, and then came to stop, opening to the page marked with Thaniel's piece of cloth. As he did so, his lessons with Thaniel back in Kir'Unwin boiled forth from his recollection. There was something here, about that pool, about the pixies. "We were sent by Thaniel, a man I was told you respected. The siege is fact, not some fantasy dreamt up in the mind of some fevered teenager. If it were a fiction, I would be the first to welcome it. It would mean that countless people whom I have loved would still be here, your daughter among them.

"You don't believe me. You don't have to, but you will believe your own eyes. You, oh great queen, have the power to see these events for yourself. If I am wrong, then we will leave here without your aid. If I am not, then come with us to Haven City, defeat this monster, and rid Shadowhaven of this evil once and for all."

The pixie queen considered him for a moment, looking down at him along her nose. "You presume to know much about me boy," was all she said. She appeared to be considering.

"With all your vast amounts of power, surely you owe it to your daughter to see the truth of her end." Chiave did his best to keep the pleading out of his voice. "Saebariel loved Shadowhaven, built the kingdom with her own two hands. I ask you now, oh great queen, to step into the past. See the events I speak of. Hear the wailing of the wounded and smell the smoke of the fires in the capital."

The air in the grove seemed to congeal, and for a moment, nothing moved save the pixies flitting in the air around them. Truly, had it not been for the little beings of light, Chiave might have thought that time itself had stopped. The pixie queen looked from him down to the book, and with a flick of her wrist, a dozen pixies flitted down to the tome. They pulled it from the ground and held it so she could read Thaniel's notes in the margins. Little clouds of dust rose around the book, churned up from the small puffs of air sent by the flapping of their wings. The pause lengthened, and Chiave resisted the urge to shift on his feet, sore as they were from the Dragon Vale gauntlet.

Finally, the spell was broken, and the pixie queen addressed him. The words used surprised them all. "Very well, little man, I will travel the roads of time and see for myself atrocities that you say occurred. Shying away from the truth is never the pixie's way. Let it not be said that Ysle is a queen without a heart." Without another word, she turned her back to them, and began to sing a soft Spell Song Chiave didn't recognize. It was as if she wove a completely new type of magic, one separate from those of the Elves. His curiosity piqued, he made a mental note to research the magic of the pixies when the world was once again in order.

The water of the Reflection Pool rippled and then glowed with a bright white light. It was this light that was apparently the goal sought by the queen's spell weaving, for, without a glance back, she stepped into the light and was gone.

Ysle, queen of the pixies, had stepped into the Light of the Reflection Pool only three times before. Since The Retreat, when she moved her nation to the most remote location imaginable, she had lived with the seclusion only through the knowledge that she could reach out to the outside world whenever she wished. Still, that ability had rarely been used, and her travel outside the Pixie Grove had even been rarer still. The seduction of their ultimate seclusion had claimed not only her people, but her own heart. She began to believe that the paradise built by their magic represented the world at large, and little evidence was presented her to disprove this fact. It wasn't until she felt the spark of Saebariel's light snuff out that she remembered there was even pain in the world at all.

The feeling always surprised her, the intense cold being the most shocking part of it. All her life, she had associated light with warmth, the brightness of a companion's spark, the heat of flame and fire. But within the magic stream, the cold hands of time ripped all warmth from the light, and she was left feeling the icy chill of the past. Focusing on the moments the boy had described, Ysle turned her heart toward the edge of her mind, stepped through a moment, and immediately felt the chill leave her bones.

It took her several minutes to acclimate to breathing air again, to feeling blood pump through her veins. When she had forced herself to relax once again, Ysle looked around her. She stood at the mouth to a mountain pass, the evening sun having already sunk below the horizon. In the cool autumn air, she could make out a series of crude human-made buildings to her left a little ways down the path.

At her feet stood a small altar, an elegant piling of stones where old sticks of incense and wilted flowers stood in small crevices. The altar spoke to her, reminded her of all of the human endeavors in these lands, things she had heard through her daughter and through her travels along the roads of time through the Reflection Pool. There was deep meaning in the workings of man, but they created using the most rudimentary of tools. Their fear of magic had limited their potential as a race, so they were left with an even more limited understanding of how the world really worked. She considered fortifying the altar with magic of her own, but was interrupted in her musings.

Out of the pass trooped a contingent of elven soldiers, peppered with human men and elven women bearing shields and swords. At the front of the squad was a man she recognized and abhorred, Captain Warrek himself. She bit her lip at the sight of him, and stepped back into the shadows lest she be tempted to rail upon him. The little army seemed to be celebrating their arrival, whooping and slapping each other on the back, heedless to the danger that pulsed in the very air around them.

Behind the soldiers, a pair of men were leaving the largest of the buildings, one leaning on the arm of another. The taller of the two seemed a slim young man, his robes hanging off him as if they were made for a man twice his age. His dark eyes darted nervously around him, looking for danger in the shadows. Yet he continued to lead his companion to the altar, walking slowly through the squad of soldiers, taking care that the old man could shuffle along at his side without disturbance. And old he was, bent with age and white-haired, his sightless eyes as white as his hair.

When the monks reached the altar, they knelt before the small pile of stones. The youngest of the two seemed not to see Ysle, despite having the use of his eyes. A chanting began, not the Spell Singing she was used to, but a rhythmic, prayerful undertone that wasn't filled with music yet was still musical. The elder of the two raised his wrinkled hands to the sky, his blank eyes scanning the darkening sky.

Suddenly Ysle felt a sadness press on her heart, a sadness she recognized all too well. The smell of death wafted on the breeze, and a second chill spread upward through her feet and into her core. The shadows around the holy men seemed to solidify, and they slithered on the ground as if having a life of their own. And then they were suddenly alive, attacking the men as they prayed. The soldiers ran for the safety of the building, shutting themselves selfishly behind the protection of thick oaken doors. Ysle held back, understanding deeply that the past could not be altered. If she could be more than an observer, why wouldn't she step back and save her own daughter? No, she knew all too well that to change the past would be to threaten the present, and that she could not risk.

The screams of the monks were almost too much to bear, their voices echoing off the walls of the mountain pass. The shadow creatures tore with claw and teeth, darkness seeping from their very skin. It was horrible to watch, yet Ysle knew that if she didn't stand as witness, no one else would. She forced herself to watch the carnage, etching the dying screams on her mind.

When, at last, the life had seeped from the monks, when the shadow monsters had slinked off into the night, Ysle stood there for a while, chewing over the meaning. Perhaps the boy had been right, that there was true cruelty at work here. Perhaps she was correct, and this was simply an isolated incident. The silence of the evening swept around her, seeping into her bones, and with it, came a resolution. She would reach out again and seek another moment, the moment she had been most avoiding contact with. It was the only way to make sure, to be convinced that the world was as the boy said it was.

She reached out a hand into the dying autumn light and then pulled back in obvious hesitation. It wasn't something she wanted to see; in fact, she had constructed a perfect wall around herself in order to keep out the truth of this moment. With a sigh, she shook herself lightly and reached out again a second time to pull the light from the air. With a soft song, she created a door of light, and focusing her mind on the one moment she hoped never to experience, she stepped through.

The familiar cold enveloped her, and Ysle thought of the nature of light. So many associated light with warmth. Well, sunlight was warm, but the true light, its heart, was cold and hard and more unforgiving a taskmaster than any might suspect. Light did not recognize the wielder as other elements might. You could not command light to do your bidding, nor could you ask it a favor. While the other elements in the world felt compelled by the songs of the elves, not so with light. Light felt itself separate from the living creatures of the world. Unconcerned with their daily troubles and battles, light simply shone, and it was impossible to talk it out of or into anything.

Perhaps because of their stature, or their speed, the pixies saw light in a very different way. Ysle wasn't sure if it was always the case, but the pixies of Shadowhaven seemed to hear the singing of these tiny travelers that rode upon the light. The light itself was immovable, eternally unconcerned, but there were little invisible particles that flowed along within the Light, and those travelers loved all creatures, and were keenly interested in anyone who would talk with them. This was why Light Wielding was so very difficult; you had to be very small to hear the singing of the particles.

It was those little songs that swirled all around Ysle now, and she responded in short bursts of song, explaining where she had to go and, more importantly, when she had to go. The curious, eager little light particles paved the way for her, carving a space through the frigid roadways of time, their chittery little songs echoing in her ears.

When the portal opened at last on the other side of time, Ysle stepped from painful brightness into darkness. She heard the particles express concern for her, standing there without any light at all, but she pointed them to a light source across the way from her, one so familiar they fairly trilled in glee. It was a pool, a sister pool to the Reflection Pool that Ysle lived by in the Pixie Grove.

This pool was the source, it was true, older than time, the waters churned with vibrant blue waves as if someone had just skipped a stone across the surface. No one had disturbed these magical waters, not since Thaniel had bound the Well of Zyn behind a shield tied to his family's blood. Squinting, Ysle looked at the magic work. It was crude, no doubt, since he was human and could claim no magic of his own. But he had studied the elves and understood the secrets of his wife's ancestry, and he understood the power within the Well as no elf had before. He had created a ward that no man or elf could break. Well, it could be broken, as they well knew, as anything tied to blood could be destroyed.

It was the thought of the shield charm that brought her back to her surroundings. As much as it thrilled her to be within range of the Well of Zyn once more, Ysle was wrenched back to the reality of the moment she stood in. The cavern was dark, vacant, but above her, the sounds of voices echoed at the top of the cavern. With a naturally domed interior, sounds bounced strangely in this place. Voices so very high above should not normally be heard on the cavern floor, but the walls made it so.

Ysle stepped back into the shadows, resisting the urge to approach the Well, and waited for the owners of the voices to approach. She spread her hands along the walls behind her, feeling the unnaturally smooth stone surface, here and there marked with cracks from the weight of the mountain pressing in upon it. She had to wait a long time, but age had given her patience. Was she not the woman who had saved her own people from extinction and prepared a new grove for them to survive in? Was she not the woman who had waited 100 years for a husband to return who never would? She could be patient. She was patience.

When the light from their torches finally illuminated the darkness of the cavern floor, Ysle watched through slit eyes the scene unfold before her. There were men here, strange men she did not recognize—humans from a distant land. The soldiers who spread throughout the cavern wore mismatched armor that looked as if it were scavenged off the dead, and probably was. Their leader was a man of moderate height for a human, his great girth a stark contrast to the male humans of Ysle's acquaintance. He wore flamboyant robes in colors just a little too bright for his dark complexion, and his black eyes, focused completely on the Well of Zyn, were filled with a lust she had not seen in many a year.

Words were exchanged, but Ysle paid little mind until they brought her daughter into view, broken and bloodied from torture, yet still strong despite the obvious pain. Nowhere could be seen Thaniel's soldiers; in fact, the only person she recognized was a toady from the royal court, although his name escaped her. He was speaking now, with the smug authority that could only come of betrayal. Ysle was having a hard time understanding why her daughter would be brought to this place. If the lustful madman had already taken the city and the castle above, what more did he need? Then, with a wrenching in her heart, she understood. None of it mattered, nothing above their heads. The kingdom was but a stepping-stone. It was the Well he wanted. With a wrenching in her heart, her nails scraped the stones and she forced herself to keep from stepping forward to save her daughter. Already nauseated, Ysle nonetheless forced herself to bear witness.

The odious, power-hungry fat man came and said something directly to Saebariel, touched her cheek as a lover might, and then, without ceremony, indeed, with a smile, plunged a dagger into her heart and then her stomach. He then turned, and while one of his henchmen collected the queen's blood, he grinned. Through her disgust and rage, Ysle saw him paint her daughter's blood on the shield and saw the shield rebel. It was but a small comfort.

She waited until they had all left, taking their torches and their treachery with them, and then Ysle knelt down before the body of her daughter. Saebariel had always been a little too beautiful, and now though broken and bloody and no longer alive, that beauty lay with her still. Though her voice was hoarse with grief, Ysle bid the light particles living around the Well of Zyn to aid her, and they left off their duties for a while and came to lift the body from the floor. Wrapped in the arms of light, Saebariel looked nearly alive, but not nearly enough. Ysle turned her back to the fount of her magic abilities, and formed a doorway, and together mother and daughter took one last journey.

She stepped out onto a mountainside alongside Illuminata Castle. The night was dark and silent except for the distant pounding of ocean against shore. The light particles laid Saebariel gently on the ground, and awaited their next order. No Stone Weaver was she, but still she asked the particles to help her dig a grave, and they did so, gratefully. Ysle buried her daughter on that mountainside, overlooking the sea and the land she had loved. She marked the grave with starlight, so that, even in the darkest of days, Saebariel would never completely be in shadow. Ysle said her last goodbye to her only daughter, and then stepped into another portal, this time, with no fixed image in her mind of a time, only an opportunity.

Stepping out of the light, she found herself again in the cavern housing the Well of Zyn, but at a moment different from the last. This time, she did not worry herself about detection, and stepped onto the stone with a firm determination, her shoulders squared and her head held high.

The fat man was there before the Well, sweating profusely, the stench of frustration seeping from every pore. It was hard to imagine how nature allowed such a creature to exist, let alone attain magical power. She understood his magic as the antithesis of her own; he called upon the shadows while she sang to the light.

At first, he didn't notice her, and when he did, there was morbid fear and shock in his eyes that surprised even her. She knew herself to be imposing in her humanoid form, but did not expect to instill such fear.

"Saebariel…" he breathed, and then she understood. Familial resemblance was at play here, and working to her advantage. Ysle stood for a moment, allowing the fear to work through him, and when he finally spoke again, it was in a voice shaky with uncertainty and forced bravado.

He made as if to turn and call his guards.

"Don't bother," she said haughtily. "Only you can hear me. Only you can see me."

"Who do you think you are," Sargon asked angrily, "coming into my palace without invitation? Do you have any idea who I am?" He stood up to his full height to look as imposing as possible and failed miserably.

Knowing he had no true idea of who she really was, Ysle decided she was allowed a certain amount of embellishment.

"Your palace, little man?" she intoned, stepping forward to loom over him. "Whoever said it was yours? My people built this cavern and the castle atop it. There is nothing here that is yours. As for who you are, I care not. There is nothing about you that could impress me. You are merely a gnat landing on a diamond, waiting for the true owner to arrive and squash you out of existence."

The insult served to bolster him, and it appeared that he felt compelled to proclaim his prowess as all true cowards must. "I am Sargon the Terrible, Master of the Ombrid and destructor of worlds. There is no one who can defeat me. I wield the very darkness as my weapon, and the shadows of the night jump at my very command."

Ysle actually felt laughter rise within her, but decided against it. Instead, she took a different tack, "How nice for you. Tell me, how often do you have to repeat that to yourself at night to help you sleep?"

It seemed to have the right affect, because the little man sweated and fumed, reddened and swelled. "I demand you tell me who you are. Who is it I am sending my minions out to destroy?"

At this, she did allow herself to laugh, a high, ringing laugh that echoed off the stones and bounced off the shield enveloping the Well of Zyn, which pulsed in response to the music in her laugh. "The gnat demands my name? By what authority do you claim to require such information? I answer only to the queen of this place."

A cruel glint shone in his black eyes as he replied. He obviously felt he had backed her into a corner. "I demand as the one who killed 'the queen of this place.' It is by my own authority that I speak, and no other."

A stabbing pain in her heart throbbed at the mention of such a cruel act. It was the only blow he could deal her, and, by luck, he had struck deep. "Then I am Ysle, queen of the pixies," she spat out, her eyes narrowing, "and I think it best that you remember that name. It will come in handy when I arrive to kill you."

"Hah! What can you do against me and my horde of shadow demons? So come, I dare you. The Ombrid grow restless. The magic I cast is built of darkness itself, and I will watch as you and your little winged friends melt in the shadow of your own destruction. Please hurry; I hunger for your blood."

Admittedly, Ysle was no longer paying much attention to this Sargon. She was thinking instead of the boy Chiave, waiting for her in the future, waiting for her answer, waiting for acknowledgement that what he said was true. It was a moment, therefore, before she realized that she was required to speak, and, no doubt, fearfully. "You hunger for your own death, little gnat. I welcome these minions of yours; what did you call them, the Ombrid?" Any information would prove useful, particularly information about the enemy.

"They will eat your eyes from your sockets and then you will rule over only the maggots in your skull," Sargon replied, smiling.

Ysle was positively bored and said so. "I tire of this little game, gnat. Had you been a more dynamic conversationalist, I might have stayed around to chat. But, as it is, you bore me. I thank you for the information, but I really must be getting back to matters of real importance."

She had overcome being a thousand times more powerful that this little dabbler in shadow magic. True, the creatures he commanded were a real threat, and would have to be dealt with, but it could only be through luck that this worm happened to stumble upon the means to control them. She would have been more curious if he weren't so very pathetic. The stench rolling off him was simply too much to bear, so she turned and stepped into the last portal, and asked her friends the particles to take her back home. Behind her, she could hear the little wizard roaring in anger, but she didn't care enough to pay attention to what he said.

It was several hours' wait before the pixie queen returned, and Warrek's soldiers spent that time resting. Chiave wanted to sleep, badly so, but knew it best that he keep awake and alert for when he received his answer. Instead, he watched Joppa, who was spending her time communicating with the pixies.

Joppa first would hold out her hand to a pixie and when one alighted on her palm, she would curtsy awkwardly. More times than not, the jarring movement would send the pixie rolling off her hand in a fit of giggles. They found her fascinating, this odd little girl with the wide, dark eyes that never seemed to rest.

"She's a strange one," came a voice from behind him, and Chiave looked up to see Aebrin settling down beside him.

Immediately he stiffened. He had had little contact with Joppa's brothers, and, indeed, neither had she. He recalled the first reunion the family had in the monastery, her refusal to acknowledge their existence, as if all her brothers had died with Abihu. He sighed to think of it, but he seemed to be the only person she would connect with.

"I don't hold nothin' 'gainst you, lad," Aebrin said, as if reading his thoughts. Chiave idly wondered if the trait was passed down from their parents. "Joppa has been broken for a long while. I did me best to help her, but she would have none of it. You saw what happened back at the monk house. The twins were always a set of their own, separate from the rest of us. We never understood them, see? Abihu with his knowledge and Joppa with, well, being a girl."

Aebrin picked up a stone and tossed it in front of him. "We've seen so much; it's hard to believe there are still wonders in this world. She a wonder, Joppa; always has been, sensitive-like. I thank the El she found you, that she trusts you, and, goodness knows, you've proven yourself to be worthy o' that trust."

Chiave looked up at Aebrin, who was watching his sister with a strange look in his eye. "You don't mind me looking after her?" Chiave asked. There seemed more weight behind the question than he realized. He found himself holding his breath, and it dawned on him that it would hurt very much not to have Joppa around. She was so very separate from this world, like Aebrin had said. She seemed to be the only thing keeping Chiave from getting swallowed by the shadows of evil that surrounded him.

"Nah, my brother Zolokai is head o' us Joramsons out here, separated as we are from our Pa, but he seems to think she's better with you. And she is; I know. I can tell. There's more Joppa in her when she's around you. Just look," he said, pointed to the girl, who was twirling in a circle and giggling, surrounded by a cloud of pixies. "There's a girl full o' Joppa if I ever seen one."

Chiave nodded and was about to respond when a great light filled the clearing, nearly blinding him. A bright light flashed over the Reflection Pool, followed by a swirling fog that seemed to pour out of the center of the light. From this opening in space, the pixie queen stepped out of thin air and into the clearing. Hastily, Chiave stood, brushing off his pants. She approached him, her eyes unreadable. For a moment, she just stared at him, her expression solemn, and the entire clearing seemed to lose sound. Knowing that this was not the time for impatience, he waited, not daring to move. When she finally spoke, it wasn't what he had expected.

"Look around you, boy," she began, waving her hand to indicate the clearing. "These are the only pixies left in existence. Once, we roamed the earth and numbered like the stars. We lived alongside the races of men, until their slaughter and bloodshed took our lives as well as their own. They have lost so much, by virtue of being so very small. For the sake of my people, I cannot do what you ask. I cannot help you."

## CHAPTER TEN

Was it always this complicated ruling a nation? Sargon was beginning to regret his ever having heard the words "Well of Zyn." He sat on his throne—carved from stone, though surprisingly comfortable—and did his best to ignore the whining of his minions as they brought him news from around the kingdom.

The throne room had changed quite a bit since Sargon had taken up residence in Illuminata Castle. At first, he had considered ripping the trees from the unnaturally healthy soil that served at the throne room floor, but, in recent years, they had served a much better purpose. A dozen bodies hung from the branches of the stately trees, each oozing their body fluids into the roots of the mighty plants that held them. It gave him no end of pleasure to know that Saebariel's trees were now feeding on elven blood. Since he had begun this practice, the trees had all but withered. He was beginning to think he had a bit of a black thumb when it came to plants. No matter. They served their purpose, and that was all that was required.

A buzzing rose in Sargon's ears, and he swatted and rubbed at his ears to try to alleviate the annoyance. Only after several unsuccessful attempts did he realize that it was someone speaking that served as the source of the irritation.

"My most dread Lord," the peon was saying, a sniveling elf who had served in Arndorn's stead since that unfortunate evening when he ended up with the wind wrung out of him. Such horrid way to die. Sargon smiled just thinking about it. This one had little ambition and even less backbone, which made him perfect for his job. "The people of Haven City are dying of thirst. The waters of the canal can no longer serve as a fresh water source now that so many have given their lives to serve your cause. With their remains clogging up the water system underneath the city, some fear a pestilence will ensue."

"Really? A plague in the city?" Finally, Sargon's attention was held. "Do you really think so?"

The Chancellor blinked awkwardly at the floor, clearly confused. Not only did he not have any backbone, he apparently had no wit to speak of.

"If there is to be pestilence, then I best get my good robes pressed. It's not often such a splendid event happens upon our doorstep."

"Sire, if you but let the people leave the city, they would no longer be a burden to you." The Chancellor shifted on his feet, seemingly surprising himself with his uncharacteristic show of assertiveness. He almost looked up at Sargon, but caught himself in the nick of time and dragged his gaze back to the moss-covered floor.

Sargon tented his fingers piously. "But they are no burden! Far from it, I love the people of Haven City, and cannot stomach the idea of even one of my precious populace leaving the city." He smiled. "Now, seeing as how pestilence is coming, don't you think we should show it a proper welcome? I should think fifteen bodies hanging from the canal entrances should do it, don't you? And Chancellor, as a reward for all your service, you may select who shall be sacrificed."

The elf paled, which was quite a thing to see, considering how sickly white they all were to begin with, and backed out of the throne room to carry out Sargon's wishes. Sargon was finally able to sit in peace, with only the dripping bodies and the sanguine trees as company. Somehow, the day wasn't turning out too badly.

Even in the most dire of circumstances, routines arise. After everything that had happened, Mylena found herself slipping back into what she knew much faster than she cared to admit, even to herself. Kir'Unwin relocated to its new location in the middle of the Eye of the World, and, within a few short weeks, buildings were woven, streets laid out, and the oasis was a village eerily similar to the one she had known and lived in for three years.

Rentyl had seen to it that she had a place of her own, and, at her request, raised an apothecary's shop on the edge of the village. Every morning, she would rise, as she had in her old life, stoke the fire, and prepare the shop, whose limited supplies still managed to provide curing for most ailments.

The difference, of course, was that she lived alone and that people were coming to her for healing rather than to her father. Mylena simply wasn't able to work the wonders her father did with herbs, but she did help when she could. Taming the wilderness of their new home was dangerous work, and there were more injuries and illnesses every day as the Unwin Clan acclimated themselves to the valley.

This morning, Mylena rose and began her routine earlier than usual. Dressing, she then coaxed the coals in the fireplace back to life, adding new pieces of wood to fuel the flames. She brewed some tea over the fire, and poured herself a steaming mug, which she took with her to the front shop area of the cottage. In this version there was no thick red curtain, no shelves lined with gleaming bottles. The bottles were there, but they were few in number and mostly newly blown, as most of the old apothecary's kit was left behind. The herbs themselves, in this part of the realm, were strange to her and required much experimentation.

Finishing her tea as she tidied up her little shop area, Mylena made note of the items she was running low on. The rhythm of the day was soothing, the routine pleasant, and the crisp winter air that greeted her as she stepped outside was a welcome contrast to the warmth near the fire. Bundling in her shawl against the cold, Mylena set out for the eastern edge of the Eye, basket in hand.

It helped to get out of the cottage whenever possible these days. Everything about this place was tainted by his absence. All of the people looked at her differently, and it wasn't simply because of her hair. In their eyes, she was a symbol for everything that had gone wrong in their lives, and she was sure they were expecting the evil to find them here in the north despite the protective properties of the Eye. The monsters she had faced in the forest would come; she was sure of it. So were they. It was only a matter of time.

The accusing glances of the villagers, whether real or imagined, made her gathering trips nearly the only time that she felt at all happy these days. Out among nature, walking in the ankle-deep snow with her basket at her side, she nearly burst into song—until she remembered the golden butterflies in autumn and the strange rainstorm that had simply appeared out of nowhere. Strange things happened around Mylena, and she couldn't quite convince herself she wasn't the cause.

An hour or so away from the oasis, a small stand of willow trees sheltered the only known patch of sourgrass Mylena had found in the valley. While bitter to the tongue, it was the only cure she had come across for the truly upset stomach. Carefully, she pruned away a moderate supply, mindful not to overcultivate and, thus, destroy the precious resource.

An unexpected wave of grief washed over her, and Mylena collapsed to her knees, pruning knife in her hand. The pounding fist of sadness railed upon her, and she watered the grasses with her tears. It normally came like this, unexpectedly and swiftly, catching her at the worst possible moments. Above all else, beyond the guilt and worry and anger and frustration, she simply missed her father.

She let the grief in, giving it full reign of her being, sobbing at the sheer unfairness of it all. It seemed like an eternity until she had herself under control, but when she did, Mylena stood, wiped her eyes, picked up her basket, and returned home without another tear. Looking back on it later, she would realize that above and beyond leaving her tears on the mountainside, she had left her childhood there as well. That was the day Mylena turned twenty years old.

"A toast to your incredible accomplishment," announced the King of Eidalore, raising his bejeweled goblet high so that all in the banquet hall could see the gesture, "surviving against the greatest of dangers. To survival!"

"To survival!" came the obligatory echo from a hundred voices.

"Brave Captain Harridan has returned to us from the wilds of Shadowhaven to report on the troubles our kin are having creating their little society," King Odar continued after draining his cup of its contents. "Would we all be so selfless in the cause of our people. We applaud your daring, young man, and bid you sit at our side and tell us of your exploits." With that little speech delivered, the king indicated an empty chair to his right, and settled into a richly carved wooden chair of excellent craftsmanship.

King Odar was the eighth in his line to sit on the throne of Eidalore, the most powerful of the human realms. As one of lineage, he had grown overly fond of the decadence of his position, and availed himself of both wine and women as often as the desire struck him. Odar was in his middle years, graying at the temples from the excess of his lifestyle, and quickly forming a paunch around his watery green eyes. He had never really expected to be king, having much preferred being a lascivious prince of the realm, so was almost as surprised as the king his father the day his father choked on a chicken bone at dinner and collapsed, dead.

Where his father had been keen on expanding his territories and power, Odar was keen on expanding his stomach. So when reedy Captain Harridan arrived with his battle-scarred group of warriors, Odar, at first, only thought of throwing a feast. Revelry was his natural reaction to most situations, whether appropriate or not. The more time he spent around Harridan, the more he came to admire qualities he had never found in himself: honesty, loyalty, a keen sense of honor. Odar recognized that a king ought to have these qualities, and as he gnawed on his fifth leg of turkey that evening, his wine-soaked brain formulated a plan.

"What do you think of Eidalore, young captain," King Odar asked conversationally.

Captain Harridan put down his meat and cleaned his mouth with his napkin before he replied. "All the tales of Eidalore's power and majesty pale in comparison to its reality. That is exactly why I have come to beg you, oh great king, to bind your assistance to our desperate cause. The troops you send can ensure the survival of Shadowhaven, and the perpetuation of our way of life."

"Yes, yes, I know all that," Odar waved a hand in front of his face, as if shooing a fly. "I am more interested in how you like it here. Eidalore is old, immeasurably so, and has amassed a great deal of wealth. I could easily send you back with the army you ask for, I could send three armies and still see no dent in our military force. How many do you command back in your little country? Ten? Twenty men?"

Harridan was obviously confused and thrown off balance. He didn't know exactly where King Odar was taking him, which was exactly how Odar wanted him to feel. He let the confusion fester a bit in the young man as a darling little blonde serving wench pour him two more goblets of wine, which he drained in quick succession. He made a mental note to inquire after her health once the feast concluded. Then he sat back in his chair and eyed the banquet hall spread before him.

"Sire," Harridan began slowly, "I command as many soldiers as Captain Warrek assigns me." It seemed as if he were going to say more, but he stopped there and took a small sip of his own wine.

"That is exactly my point, son," Odar said, still keeping his eyes on the crowd. "You're not appreciated down there in Shadowhaven; that much is obvious. It's a lost cause, anyhow, from what I hear. That Sargon fellow is sure to wipe the floor with Warrek, no matter how many soldiers you throw at him. He commands demons, I'm led to believe, and demons are damned hard to fight.

"No, I'll put it another way. You can go back down to Shadow Hovel and fight a war you are sure to lose commanding fifty men, or you can stay here and command my entire army." From his right, Odar could hear the current Captain of the Guard choking on his dinner in disbelief. Well good. The man had little respect for the king, anyway. Regardless of how Harridan replied, at least this would teach that pompous knight not to get too comfortable in his position.

"My lord," Harridan protested, "I am but a militia soldier, untrained and untested in commanding any large group of soldiers.

"Yet here you are, having successful led a group of battle-hardened soldiers through very dangerous territory to ask a king for help. I would hardly call that untested. You are brave and loyal, yet you are an unsung hero. They don't see your potential, but I do. Stay here in Eidalore, Harridan, and receive the tribute worthy of a hero." Odar clapped the boy on the shoulder with a wide, beefy hand, in a gesture he hoped came off as genial. He was never quite sure how "nice" went. He considered saying something more, but instead turned back to the blonde serving wench, and beckoned her over. This evening wouldn't be a total loss.

Fionn found her washing clothes in the creek, and though he told himself to give her space, the weeks had spread between them and made him miss her to the point of distraction. Mylena did not look up as he approached, and the puffs of cool breath issuing from her in the cold winter air did not even change direction.

"The winter snows here bite our breath and paint our toes blue," he began, a little awkwardly. All the grace of his people seemed to fail him when he was around her. Kanefionn, archer extraordinaire, actually felt clumsy around this slight woman bowed with grief. Her internal pain made her all the more beautiful, changed her from a girl to a woman, and Fionn felt guilt sour in his belly to think of it that way. The guilt did not stay his hand, however, as it began to trail its fingers in her vibrant red curls. Like dipping your hand into liquid fire it was, he thought idly, distracted once again by her beauty. This close to her now, all he wanted to do was grab her up into his arms, but he knew the wisdom of restraint.

"I miss you too, Fionn," Mylena said, still not rising or looking at him. She looked completely frozen over by the cold, stuck in time eternally washing clothes in a frigid creek. Only he never stopped touching her hair, so he knew that she froze herself and was not affected by the temperature.

"Can't we go back, back to an empty oasis, just the two of us and the stars?" Fionn seemed to be begging her to pull some magical miracle out of her pocket, but he couldn't help it. It was his dearest wish, and should nothing else come of it, he felt it should be spoken aloud. "I would give every ounce of magic in my blood if it meant a chance to go back to those days with you."

"But we can't go back," she protested, looking up at him, and he could see she was crying. Perhaps she had been for a while; he could not tell. "The village came, my father died, and the evil approaches. No matter what we want, the world continues on. It plods on, trampling everything in its path."

He knelt beside her then, taking her face in his two hands. Mylena looked up at him, tears streaming down her face without let up. "Why is it that everything I love leaves me?"

"I will never leave you," Fionn vowed, then leaned down and kissed the tears from her face. "I will always be here for you, with you, because of you." He kissed her lips then, lightly, and then more hungrily, a kiss born of weeks of anticipation. Even more surprising was when she returned the kiss with all the passion he felt and hoped she did as well.

"And I will never stop loving you," Mylena whispered, nestling against his chest. Fionn held his breath lest he break contact even for an instant. They stayed there in that moment for what seemed like hours; somehow, it felt as if they had indeed managed to find a way back in time to their secluded days when the Eye of the World looked down on only them.

They stayed in that moment until Vorynne appeared across the creek, her expression unreadable. She said nothing for a moment then turned her back and said over her shoulder, "It is good to see you again, son. Your brother would have a word with you." Then she walked into the trees.

Chiave arrived at the Eye of the World exhausted and defeated. He had talked over the events of the past weeks with Captain Warrek, and the captain had agreed that going on with their plans was the only wise course of action. The tricky part came in that not only did they have to convince the princess to return with them and lead an army to conquer a captured city, he couldn't let her know that, without Queen Ysle, they would, no doubt, fail in their attempts to perform the task Thaniel had set before them.

The task. It made Chiave sigh just to think of it. He didn't understand half of what he had read in the book, and he certainly didn't understand the words Joppa knew. But he knew the three of them—he, Mylena, and the Queen Ysle—were meant to perform a ritual in the bowels of the castle, a ritual that would save their people. The instructions were so cryptic, Chiave barely understood them, but he did know he needed the princess, if not to make the ritual successful, then at least to get the people of Shadowhaven rallied enough to fight their oppressor.

They hadn't left the Pixie Grove completely empty handed. As the squad had exited the magical forest and deposited themselves out above the Dragon Vale, a small messenger named Gace appeared. She was precocious and refused to assume a humanoid form, which made communication difficult. In fact, she would only speak to Joppa, whose dancing had entranced her. Through Joppa—and, therefore, through Chiave, since he was the only one she would speak to—Gace told them that she could lead them to the princess. Without any other clear way of finding the girl otherwise, Warrek accepted the offer and, indeed, she proved to be an excellent guide.

Gace not only knew where to find the princess, she also knew the safest and fastest routes through the craggy expanse of the mountains she called the Jagged Teeth, a giant maw that opened around the volcano housing the Eye of the World. Indeed, they looked like massive fangs bared at the wintery sky. It took a week of careful travel to cross the Teeth, and, the entire time, Gace refused to communicate with anyone but Joppa. It made conversations with the pixie incredibly difficult, but Joppa found it endlessly amusing to suddenly be playing translator.

On the morning of the eighth day, the smooth bowl of the Eye of the World came into view, and, by mid-afternoon, they were sitting, drinking tea with Rentyl, who seemed very surprised at the changes in Chiave. He supposed it was true; he had gone through so much since he had left Kir'Unwin lugging a book, a sword, and an entire new history to assimilate into his life. He had spent a lot of time thinking about Rentyl and Vorynne, and had come to the conclusion that they may not have begotten him, but they raised him, so they were as much his parents as those he was connected to by blood. He was happy to see Rentyl, therefore, and embraced him warmly.

Shortly after their arrival, Vorynne had gone to retrieve Fionn. He arrived soon after with the princess Mylena, who looked tired, confused, and ultimately sad. Well, she had great reason to be sad, Chiave thought, more than even he had.

Captain Warrek rose and knelt before her the moment he saw her. "My Lady, it is great to see you alive. As I pledged my life to your mother, I again vow to you to protect you with everything that I am."

Mylena looked down at him, a look of irritation and confusion clouding her face. "I ask for no protection. I have my clan, the village. That is all I need. You are free from any vow, Captain, as my parents no longer breathe. As my mother is dead, I see no reason you should waste your time following me around as I gather herbs."

Captain Warrek was taken aback, and several of the elves gasped openly. It appeared that he was genuinely at a loss for words, and Chiave understood why. Warrek saw her as he remembered her, a member of the royal family, heir to the throne, but she did not see herself in the same way. Mylena had lived for years in hiding, had come, it seemed, to prefer the work of an alchemist, and didn't seem to understand why they had come. Chiave had spent those years with her, so before he could talk himself out of it, stood up.

"Muirinn?" he began, intentionally using her guise of a name, "you know me, don't you?"

She turned to look at him, surprised to see him standing there amongst the soldiers it seemed, dressed in his armor, a massive sword strapped to his back. She smirked after a moment, crossing her arms. "Why, Chiave Stoneweaver, what have you gone and done? I recall expressly forbidding you from growing up, and now look at you, a soldier and so much more confident than when we last met. Don't tell me that you have come to swear allegiance to me as well?" There was a pleading in her eyes behind her smile that told him there was less jocularity in her question than one might think.

Chiave shook his head. "My allegiance has been sworn to Shadowhaven. I promised your father that I would do everything I could to save her people from the dire circumstances that have befallen her. It is why I have come here, to speak to you, to ask of you what I have been asked. To ask on your father's behalf." He turned to the elf most recently entrusted with the Testament and gestured for her to bring the book forth. To his surprise, she followed the silent command, opening the book so that Mylena could see her father's writing along the margins of the marked page.

"He asked me to bring the book to you, to show you that it is time. The time for hiding is over. The time for leading your people home is here."

"Lead?" She looked from Chiave to Warrek to Fionn, clearly disbelieving what she heard. "Who would follow me? And why should I want to lead them? Hasn't there been enough death and suffering already? Haven't enough people fallen? But no, you want me to ask others to die just so we can take back the city. Who's to say Sargon isn't doing a fine job as a ruler?" Even as she said the words, he could tell she didn't mean them. But even so, he decided she needed to hear the truth.

"Word reached us from spies in Haven City. Sargon has closed off the city and will not allow food or supplies in nor citizens out. He slaughters them by the dozens for his horrid spell weaving. The heart of the nation is rotting from the inside, and the people have no hope. They believe all lost. But all is not lost. You are alive. You have survived. You exist, and you will be their hope. You will be the one reason they have to strive to keep going, to continue fighting for air despite being drowned in Sargon's hate. You are our hope," he finished simply, "and we would all follow you," and knelt before her, his head bowed. Around him every man and woman, human and elf, knelt beside him, a powerful statement that she could not ignore. Looking off to his left, Chiave saw that Fionn, too, knelt at Mylena's feet.

She said nothing for a long while, and then Chiave felt a hand on his shoulder, and looked up to see Mylena gazing sadly down at him. "I cannot deny our people hope, Chiave. But know that where I travel death follows, and in my wake, only the dead remain. I cannot promise success, but yes, I will come."

"Plans must be made," Captain Warrek was saying the next day over a hot mug of mead, sitting in front of Rentyl's fire.

The elf nodded, and began to pace. "The clans must meet. It is the only way to get a consensus on how many we can expect to join with us. Kir'Tazul, or what is left of it, cannot help us, as those are the citizens of Haven City. They have enough to deal with, trying to keep alive."

Warrek bit his lip in anger. How could a person be so very evil? he thought. How could he do that to innocents? Did he not wish to rule over them? Why slaughter them by the hundreds? "What about the other three?"

"The mountain-dwellers of Clan Kashel are a solitary folk," Rentyl mused, "Living so far west has protected them from much of the torment us lowlanders have had to deal with, but I do think they will send assistance, even if in small numbers. Midras the seafarers are a clan rich in wealth, so have much to lose from Sargon's occupation. I expect we can rely upon a large supporting force from them. Midras is nearly five times the size of Unwin. As for Lothyn, they are led by a bitter old Water Singer."

Warrek scoffed. "Bitter? I thought all elves were calm, wise folk."

Rentyl shook his head, "I know Morge. He is as bitter as the poisons he brews. There is only one way to convince him, and that is in person, appealing to his instincts for self-preservation. I therefore recommend a meeting in the Wasting Sands. If we show up in his desert, Morge cannot ignore us."

"I expect my troops within the city to rally once they realize we are outside the gates," Warrek stated as he emptied his tankard. "And once the princess makes her appearance, the people will flock to our cause, and our numbers will grow. Will she really come, do you think?" he asked, suddenly changing the conversation.

"I wish I could say I know the girl better than you. I have only spent a few years with her in the clan, and I can see she is strong of spirit. Even without her father, she has continued to serve the community, healing the sick. I would not wish to trade positions with her for every drop of water in the Well of Zyn. But yes, to answer your question, she will come, she will lead, and if the need arise, she will die."

## CHAPTER ELEVEN

Conceived in wisdom, the plan was set in motion the very next day. Warrek sent elven emissaries to the Kir'Kashel and Kir'Midras, requesting representation at the meeting in the Wasting Sands. The warriors of Clan Unwin girded themselves for war, Fionn included. It was the first time that he would be allowed to fight alongside his mother and the rest of the army, and he felt proud to be included, even in such dire circumstances.

Fionn joined a handful of others of the Unwin Clan who decided to march under Warrek's banner. At about midmorning, the squad was packed up, armor strapped tight to their weary bodies, their newly chosen packhorses laden with food and ammunition and whatever else the village could provide. There was an eerie quiet settling over the village as the group formed up. It was as if the war had already begun, here in their hearts, in the hearts of the children, women, and elders left behind, as if it had begun in Kir'Unwin.

Indeed, it had. As he slung his bow across his back, Fionn recalled the terror of a few weeks ago, of the monk and the book, of the brave soldiers, his father included, who stayed and fought so that the village could survive. So much pain had already come to these people. His clan had adapted first when the country fell to Sargon and now as his hounds were unleashed on his populace. Part of him wanted to blame Vidius—Thaniel as it turned out, all along hiding among them—for bringing the violence to the innocent folk of Kir'Unwin, but he realized how childish an impulse that was. It wasn't Thaniel's choice to unleash the demon Ombrid. Sargon the Mad had done that, had taken everything good about Shadowhaven and corrupted it. It was Sargon who needed to pay. Thaniel had already left this world and all the debt he had accumulated here.

Kir'Unwin had few horses to offer the warriors, about six in all remained after the trials of the last few years, but they gave them up gladly in support of the effort. Four of the steeds, tall elegant palominos the lot of them, were used to transport goods. The widest and strongest of them Warrek requisitioned as a replacement for his own beloved war horse, a beautiful and proud beast who, no doubt, was ruling as king over their war steeds on the Plains of Beyond. The last horse they reserved for Mylena, since she was not trained to travel these distances on foot.

It made sense, Fionn thought. It was time that she began to reclaim her royal station, and walking amongst the soldiers was no way to do that. She was a princess, whether or not she wished to be, and that both filled him with pride and daunted him. On the one hand, they had been drawn together by circumstance, two young people thrown into danger without context. However, things had changed when Chiave had brought the King's Guard into the Eye of the World. No, things had changed before then, when her ruse had collapsed, leaving only the truth and her grief. Even with the world in chaos and uncertainty unraveling the future, their hearts were still bound together, and Fionn felt his heart swell as he saw her mount up on the last palomino in preparation for leaving the valley.

Fionn watched from a distance as Mylena settled on her steed and turned to talk to what looked like the very air beside her. On closer inspection, Fionn saw the pixie Gace flitting beside the princess. He remembered the little creature taking an instant liking to the princess the moment the troops had arrived in the valley. He didn't understand the nature of the attraction, but as he was so enamored of Mylena he couldn't begrudge anyone else feeling the same way.

Once Mylena was mounted and positioned alongside Captain Warrek, the second-in-command, a gruff and lanky soldier named Gregor, gave the word to move out. As Fionn turned his back on the town and began to wind his way up out of the bowl of the valley, he felt a chill seize his heart, as if an icy hand had gripped it and, for a moment, squeezed. At the same time, he felt a pull behind him, a warmth tugging him back toward the oasis at the center of the valley. It was as if the lake were begging him to stay. The foreboding lasted but a moment, and Fionn attributed it to the wintery temperature. By the time he had left the Eye of the World completely, the incident was forgotten.

By the time they had descended the volcano and crossed the foothills into the Plains of Beyond, Fionn had forgotten about the foreboding and was in high spirits. "The Well shines within you this day," came a voice from behind him. He turned to see his mother Vorynne approaching from behind him. She looked as young as she did the day she left for Haven City six years ago. Vorynne was the picture of health, the picture of a strong, proud elven warrior, and, though he never met her, in his mind's eye, Fionn imagined the Warrior Queen herself could not have been as beautiful.

"I carry the blood of the world within," he responded in the traditional manner. When had speaking to his mother become so formal?

Vorynne smiled at him, and looked at him from the corner of her eye keeping her head and shoulders facing the road ahead. "You've grown tall, Fionn, even taller than I." It was a compliment, and he took it as such. In their culture, height was a sign of strength, and all the greatest elven warriors in Shadowhaven had stood above six feet. The thought, as did so many others, brought his mind back to Mylena, who came barely to his shoulder. He had seen evidence of her power, though, and he supposed magic and strength were two different but equally important things. Perhaps her short stature was a byproduct of human blood, Fionn mused, although her father had been as tall as he was. He thought it best that such a little mystery of little consequence be put off until peace once again reigned. Then there would be time enough to ask Mylena everything he ever wished to know.

"I am glad you have made it back to us," Fionn said a bit awkwardly. "With all the war Shadowhaven has seen, it appears you have been fortunate enough to have lived." Somehow, the words came out more accusatory than intended.

Vorynne looked at him a moment and then said in her usual reserved way, "I live as long as I am needed. There are still wars to fight yet, and they will need all the capable archers they can find. I am simply grateful for the opportunity to fight for the realm I believe in."

"It appears I shall have the opportunity as well, despite what I thought." Fionn couldn't keep the bitterness out of his voice.

"Fionn," Vorynne said, her voice full of feeling, although her manner did not belie such emotion, "you have always been like a daughter to me. I trained you myself, and it was with pride that I left you to protect our family. There is no joy in my heart today, knowing that your training will now be put to the test. The elements have spoken, however, and events draw us to conflict. I am glad to have you by my side, Fionn."

The word rang in the air a bit after she said it. Fionn couldn't recall a time when she had called him by his name, even as an infant. Such a familiar term made him suddenly uneasy, as if this overflow of affection meant that something was about to change, and his mother felt it wasn't going to be good. He wasn't sure how to respond, so they walked along in silence for several hours, a companionable quiet wrapping them in mutual solitude as they crossed the Plains of the Beyond. Fionn reached out his hands and let the gray-green grasses tickle the palms of his hands.

This was it; he was marching off to war. Well, he was marching off to a war council, but then to battle. Finally, after all this time, he was going to be numbered among the warriors of his people, the brave women and soldiers who had kept his clan safe. He had waited his whole life to walk into battle next to his mother, and now it was happening. He couldn't help but smile.

It took two days to cross the Plains of Beyond, and there was little incident beyond a horse slipping on the wet grass and tossing Captain Warrek for a spell. His original troops seemed to find it amusing, but Warrek was not at all pleased with ending up on his rear in front of the new recruits. On the beginning of the third day, the Plains emptied onto the desert expanse of the Wasting Sands. The region resembled an ocean made of sand instead of water, with rolling white dunes stretching as far as the eye could see. Chiave asked Rentyl how people could live in such a desolate place.

"The world has many people in it, Chiave," he replied sagely, "and as many places. Some people and places fit together perfectly and others do not. Lothyn'Kir is a place where those who prefer solitude live. The desert suits them, just as the forest suited us."

"Not anymore, though," Chiave said quietly.

"True," Rentyl replied, "not anymore."

The uneventful nature of their travel continued as they entered the desert. Joppa spent most of her time milling about the princess's horse, talking to the pixie and the horse itself alternately. Chiave made sure she was out of the way during more important occasions, such as the assembling of the troops and mealtimes, but, otherwise, the wide expanse seemed to suit her. He thought about what Rentyl said, and considered what Joppa would select if she were given the choice of locations to live in.

"Where would you live if you could?" Chiave asked her as they ate a sparse midday meal on the dunes. "Would you live here, for instance, on the desert? Or perhaps by the sea?"

Joppa considered her plate of stew a moment, then her fingers, then looked up, her face filled with a rare lucidity. "I would live on the grave of my brother," she said, and he could see she meant it. The grief was still just as fresh for her as it had been those months ago when she lost her twin. The delicate nature of her mental state would most likely keep the pain acute throughout her life. Indeed, there were times when she mixed up events, where she would believe herself to be standing in a moment in the past. There were even times when it appeared that she wasn't even herself, when she talked strangely as if she were a completely different person. He believed her when she said she would live at the monastery. Perhaps that would be the best place for her once all this ugliness was settled.

The ugliness. He couldn't quite come to terms with what he was wrapped up in. To Chiave, the world had taken on a surreal quality, where children were given positions of power and adults bowed to their influence. Only in a dream world would he be put in such a place, traveling across the world, carrying a book and a sword and only half a notion of what he was doing. Only in a dream world could any of this be possible. Yet here he was, armor-clad with a greatsword strapped to his back, marching along with battle-hardened men and women, elves and humans. And the most surreal part of it was, he could technically call himself battle-hardened as well. Had he not survive the onslaught in the Dragon Vale where others had not? This world was a strange, dream-like place, but it appeared that he belonged there.

Three full days were spent in the Wasting Sands, and it wasn't until the night of the fourth that Rentyl stopped the company and spoke with Captain Warrek. "From here, I am to go alone. Nothing will spook Morge more than an entire phalanx of soldiers mucking up his terrain."

"I'm fine with that," responded the captain in a tone that screamed he was nothing of the sort. "I only ask that you bring along your boy there. He's shown a quick wit in strange situations, and may prove useful."

Chiave understood more about Warrek's request than anyone could tell. As a member of the company for several months, Warrek would rely on Chiave to keep his ears open and report any strange happenings. If his life had been different, if it had been less surreal, he would have refused to spy on his own father. But events had taken the exact course that led them to this moment, and he realized that Rentyl might not be as forthcoming as Warrek might need him to be with information vital to the success of the campaign. And more than that, Chiave agreed with him.

Rentyl nodded. "When we have made contact and prepared Morge for what is to happen here, I will send word."

"The clan leaders should be arriving here shortly," Warrek said meaningfully. "If you can't convince Morge to open his sympathies to us, then we will have to proceed without him. My question is this: will he actively resist us being on his land should he decline participation in the campaign? Am I going to have to fight him and his clan before going on to fight Sargon himself?"

"Let us hope it does not come to that," Rentyl said with a cagey smile.

If Chiave had not been convinced of his father's unique motivations before, he certainly was now. He met Warrek's eyes and nodded once to show he understood the situation. Then he followed his father off into the night.

The moonlight gave the sand dunes an eerie glow, as if the El had come along and painted the world with a blue brush. Because of the reflective nature of their surroundings, no torch was needed to light their way. Rentyl plunged into the heart of the desert without pause and without explanation. He too expected obedience from Chiave, obedience without explanation. Again, Chiave was not surprised, not even irritated. Respect for his parent's wishes had been instilled in him early on, and the expectation of that respect had been a large part of his life. Instead of resenting his father for not understand how much Chiave had changed, he followed Rentyl silently into the desert, concentrating on the route they were taking.

After several hours of walking in a seemingly random direction without landmarks or indications of where they were, Rentyl threw up a hand to stop Chiave's progress. Chiave looked around the spot where they stood, but saw nothing but more rolling sand dunes sparkling in the moonlight. Rentyl was standing stock still looking up at the dune in front of them, and then, strangely, he smiled.

"I am tired of walking around in circles," he called out to the night. "Aren't you the least bit curious what this is about, you crotchety old man?"

"I don't have the energy for curiosity," came the reply from over the dune. Soon a figure followed the voice over the rise, an elf leaning heavily on a gnarled stave. In the darkness, he looked more like a wraith than a man, his features were cast in shadow, and his pale hair, glowing in the moonlight, was braided with beads and strips of leather.

Everything about the elf looked worn, from his leather armor, cracked with age, to the chipped and rusted axe hanging from his hip that could clearly do with some attention. Chiave had never seen an elf like him, and, for a moment, doubted this was the person Rentyl had spoken of. But then he crouched down and lay his hand on the sand, singing in a rumbling baritone, and water seeped up from the sand into his hands. He drank then, acting as if they weren't even there. It was his attitude more than anything that proved his identity.

"You had energy enough to track us these four long days. Did you expect us to steal your sand?" Rentyl was still smiling, the light of mischief glinting in his gray eyes. He squatted down so that his robes pooled around him on the dune and waited for a reply. The reply didn't come for quite some time, yet he still sat there, looking as if he were sitting back home in his study pouring over a manuscript. Chiave wondered at how at ease his father appeared, here in the middle of the desert.

"What damned reason do you have for coming, Stoneweaver?" The question came after what seemed an eternity. "Tell me quickly before I crap myself from boredom." Morge scratched himself indelicately as if to prove his point.

"War is coming, Morge. You cannot deny the torment Shadowhaven is under—"

"I can deny anything I please. I deny Shadowhaven even exists," Morge cut in mercilessly. Chiave sensed that he was finally getting to the meat of the secret his father was keeping from Captain Warrek. In order to convince the Lothyn'Kir clan leader that he must aid in the battle, Rentyl would first have to convince him that the realm was valuable enough to be saved. How exactly did Saebariel rule people who refused to acknowledge her leadership, he wondered.

Rentyl continued undaunted. It appeared that conversations with Morge often took on this sort of tone. "Uniting the peoples of this land under one banner is a fact, Morge, whether you accept it or not. Also, a fact is the rape and pillage of this land and its people by a mad tyrant bent on seizing the Well of Zyn for his own personal use. The seeds of Sargon's corruption are traveling the winds, Morge, and the winds will reach even your precious Wasting Sands. You may have hid from Saebariel and Thaniel, but you cannot hide from the demons Sargon commands. The taint of their kind will reach here as they reached Kir'Unwin. I stand before you today as living proof of the evil Sargon has unleashed on this world." Rentyl turned his head lifting back his long pale hair, and, for the first time, Chiave saw the price his father had paid for fighting the Ombrid; his left ear was missing, and, in its place, long scars ran from his hairline down his neck and out of sight.

"That's a lovely little trophy they left you, Stoneweaver; pity I wasn't there. Sounds like it was quite a fight. So you lost a piece of flesh and some soldiers, but what is that to me?"

"Never belittle the death of my clansmen," Rentyl growled, standing. "Perhaps I was wrong about you, Morge. Years ago, you would have joined a fight simply for the joy of battle. Have you become so rusted in your limbs and blind in your eyesight that you cannot fight or see the world crumbling around you? I have little time, yet I see I am wasting it talking to a desert-mad fool like you. The poison you wet your arrows with has obviously poisoned your heart as well. Enjoy your sand while it is still free, Morge Watersinger, and may you choke on it."

Rentyl turned on his heel and walked back up the dune without another word. He neither paused to wait for an answer nor turned to see if Chiave was following. Chiave looked at the weathered man crouched on the sand for a moment then ran to catch up with his father.

"What...?" Chiave began when he was walking next to his father, but stopped when Rentyl shot him a look. They finished the trip back to the camp in silence, which, as it turned out, was not all that long. Rentyl really had been wandering in circles all that time. When they reached the camp, most of the company was already bunked for the night, and, with a nod, Rentyl indicated that Chiave should follow suit. As he laid out a blanket and settled himself beside the sleeping form of Joppa, he watched Rentyl sit down to stare at the smoldering flames. He would still be there when they awoke in the morning.

There was much that Mylena did not understand about her circumstances. If one were to ask her why she was standing in the early morning cold in the middle of the desert wrapped in her traveling cloak, she wouldn't have been able to give an answer. An answer was there, although she wouldn't have admitted it aloud. She was there to perform penance.

Not that she didn't trust the judgment of Captain Warrek and the others. She was certain they knew more about the people of Shadowhaven than she ever would. Perhaps that was the point of it, too. She didn't feel like a queen. Her entire life, she had been waiting for that moment when she would suddenly awaken some inner power within her that would signal that yes, she was worthy of being the daughter of Saebariel. But that awakening never came. Instead, Sargon overthrew the realm, and she fled with her father into hiding.

Mylena sat down and began absently trailing her fingers in the sand. It was surprisingly cold in the lower layers. She remembered the cold mornings in Kir'Unwin when the world seemed simple and straightforward. Once they were in hiding, Mylena seemed to have a purpose for the first time in her life. It wasn't some grand illusion, some ultimate expectation of greatness. No, she was able to set bones, heal wounds, cure headaches, and that work was, to her, a more fulfilling purpose than anything she had been raised to do.

But you can't run from the past, it seems, and here she was, sitting on a sand dune on her way to lead an army to battle, all for the parents she failed. She wondered if she had been more of a princess back then, could she have prevented it? Her head filled with the memories of the thugs pouring into their rooms, of her father pulling her through a door she never knew existed, of her mother screaming in outrage.

"Breakfast time, m'Lady," twittered a voice near her ear. Mylena turned to see Gace fluttering beside her, the pixie's bright light and broad smile a great bolster to Mylena's mood. She knew why the pixie had taken a shine to her, as it were, but she wasn't sure she deserved the attention. Simply having pixie blood didn't make her special. If that were the case, then they would be putting Gace on a horse and forcing her to lead armies. Still, as she had been taught throughout her life, she kept her pixie origins a secret, and feigned surprise at the little creature's affections.

"I will come in a minute." Mylena shooed Gace off and stood up. She wasn't about to be hurried, now that she was a princess again. Didn't she have the right by blood to be a bit difficult and late? Biting her lip, Mylena attempted to shake the sand out of her skirts, and turning came face-to-face with the strangest elf she had ever seen. He looked more like a beast than an elf, all hunched over and leathery.

"You're the daughter, aren't you?" he asked, standing too close for comfort. "Tell me, princess," he nearly spat out the word as if it tasted rotten in his mouth, "why do you go to war so easily? Are you not a lover of peace, as all humans are?"

Mylena blinked a moment considering whether or not to answer the stranger. He looked dangerous, wild even, but something in his bright blue eyes spoke to her. "Even the elves prefer peace to war," she recited from lessons taught her by her mother. "We fight only when necessary, to preserve the delicate balance of what we have created." There was more, about how Shadowhaven was a land free from racial hatreds, a place where races could coexist despite their differences, but she thought that might be too much for this beast-elf, so left it at that.

He cocked his head to one side and sniffed at her like a dog. She could tell he was trying to unnerve her, and she almost smiled. To think that anyone could unnerve the daughter of Saebariel; it was enough to make her laugh. She allowed herself a small, haughty toss of her head to rearrange her curls.

"You didn't answer my question," he baited, still sniffing.

"You don't want an answer; you want an excuse," she replied, her tone beginning to match her posture. "You've come to ogle at the reason we're here, and since you've already made your decision on the matter, I can only think you are looking for an excuse to back up your assumptions. I will give you none. My reasons are my own."

"Fire in the heart to match the fire in the hair, you are your mother's spawn, aren't you, you little wretch?" She had struck a nerve, enough that he felt he had to lash out. Her wild shot in the dark had rung true. She smiled.

"Are we done here? You bore me." Mylena made to go back to camp, but he grabbed her arm and held her there.

"You'll require my services should you wish to succeed," he said in an oddly deferential tone, "I was a great help to your mother once upon a time."

Mylena looked down at his hand on her arm, pointedly indicating he should release his grip. He did so, even going so far as to step back to allow her a bit of space. "You knew my mother then." It was not a question. "What assistance can you provide that I cannot get elsewhere? There are other clans besides Lothyn, my friend, and I do not need yours."

He smiled a bit and said in a low tone, "You'll need my numbers."

"Oh? Am I to assume I have it then, this assistance you offer? How many swords bring you to the fray? Speak quickly; I have things to attend to." It was a lie, a great foolish lie. Mylena had only sitting around to do. It wasn't as if she were included in the campaign planning. Most days, she felt more like window dressing than anything else. Still, she put all her conviction behind the lie, and let it stand on its own two feet under his scrutiny. And then she waited.

Morge eyed her for a moment and then said, "Ten thousand." From what Mylena had overheard of the discussions of the clans, this was four times the estimated population of Lothyn'Kir. Exactly where were they keeping these people?

"Then come, Morge of Lothyn," she said as she turned without looking at him and began to make her way back to camp, "it appears we have something to discuss after all."

Through the steam of his morning porridge, Chiave saw Princess Mylena approach, accompanied by Morge, looking as irritated as ever. They were the most unlikely of pairs, and stranger still it appeared as if she were leading him around by the nose. They stopped to speak to Captain Warrek, who nodded and said little, but apparently, it was enough. Chiave soon became distracted with trying to keep Joppa from giving Gace a porridge bath, so when we looked up again, he was surprised to find that the company was already on the move.

"Where are we going?" he asked Rentyl, who was standing around looking smug.

"Why, to Lothyn'Kir of course. You didn't expect us to spend our time here in the desert huddled in tents, did you?"

"But I thought this was Lothyn'Kir," Chiave protested, feeling suddenly foolish.

"Come along, boy; it's time to readjust your thinking," Rentyl said knowingly.

With the camp packed up and the company assembled, Morge set off in the most unlikely of directions; he began to travel back the way they came.

"The ugly elf is confused," Joppa said, a little too loudly.

"The crazy girl is blathering," replied Morge from the front of the column. It appeared that his hearing was sharper than one would expect of someone who had lived all those years in solitude. Perhaps it was that he was not used to the human voice, so was more sensitive to it. "You assume I am confused, but you are wrong."

"You assume I am just a girl, but you are wrong," Joppa replied, nonplussed. Morge barked a harsh guffaw in response, but said nothing.

Morge led the company to a copse of trees they had passed in traveling to the Wasting Sands, and then turned south without a word. Chiave watched Rentyl for signs of unease, but saw none. Either his father had been here before or trusted Morge enough not to lead them into a pit to be fed to dragons. Chiave shuddered at the thought, the memories still a little too fresh to jest about.

When they had walked seemingly forever and Chiave's feet had begun to protest, Morge stopped the company with a wave of his hand. They stood in a large valley walled in with dunes. It looked like all the other parts of the desert Chiave had seen, except perhaps a bit bigger. They all looked around them in curiosity, exchanging skeptical glances, and then Morge let out an ear-piercing whistle. In response, two figures stood, rising from out of the sand itself it seemed, and began a low song that echoed off the dunes. Chiave recognized the phrases used, and turned to see a break opening in the dune to their right. It was a massive door, several men high, and beyond lay only darkness.

"Welcome travelers to Lothyn'Kir," Morge said ceremoniously, and then set off into the passageway.

It took several moments for Chiave's eyes to adjust, and when they did, he still didn't believe them. He was standing in the midst of a sandstorm frozen in time. At least that was how it looked at first glance. Great walls of sand rose above them, ending in darkness above their heads. They seemed to undulate and move as sand moves in the wind, but when Chiave reached out with his hand to confirm what his eyes were seeing, he found the walls were solid to the touch.

"Don't dawdle boy," Warrek called to him, and Chiave realized he had separated from the column. Not a good idea in such a strange and unfamiliar place. Quickly, he ran to catch up and reached his original position just as they were leaving the sand corridor.

The corridor itself opened onto a great cavern so large its extremities were lost from sight. To their right, a river of sand coursed along with the speed of a normal water river, wide enough to require bridges built across it. Beyond the bridges appeared to be an island formed of sand and, on the island, a cluster of buildings. Now that he recognized what they were, Chiave saw that buildings were rising along the walls of the cavern all around them, their doors looking like dark eyes as they rose up and out of sight. Still, they saw no people, which was the strangest thing of all. This magnificent city, created from the desert itself, seemed to be completely empty of life.

As the company made its way across the fourth bridge they came to, Chiave dropped back to walk alongside Clodai. She still bore the scars left her from the Dragon Vale, but she walked with her head held high as any soldier of Shadowhaven might.

"This city," he began in hushed tones. Somehow he feared his voice would echo into the cavernous space they traversed. "How is it possible? I see no stone here. What exactly are they weaving?"

Clodai smiled lightly, a smile that never reached her eerie white eyes. "No stone?" She bent down and trailed her hand in the sand river. When she pulled it out again, she cupped the warm sand in her palm. "What is sand, Chiave? Look beyond the many and hear the few." She held her hand up so that he could see more closely.

"Hear the few," he repeated, and reached into the sand and picked up a pinch of it, holding it between his fingers. As he held them up to his eye he saw small individual grains, and they looked to him like tiny boulders. More than what he saw, he heard a faint humming, a humming he realized he had been hearing without realizing it since they had reached the desert. It was a similar melody as that which he heard when singing stone, but it was softer, and somehow more choral. Instead of one voice, he heard millions.

"Take some time to block out the voices," Clodai said wisely, seeing his reaction, "To keep so many tiny stones aligned, so many millions all working towards the same goal is a great work of magic. It must have been a very powerful Stoneweaver to accomplish all this. I should very much like to meet him." Clodai sounded both awed and envious.

Chiave was pondering what he had learned from Clodai so much that when we was next aware of his surroundings, the group had stopped in front of a grand colonnade. The pillars in front of him, created in the likeness of desert creatures so alive that they looked as if they would jump and pounce on him from above. At the front of the group, Morge was speaking to Captain Warrek and the princess, who seemed to be hiding her vibrant hair by pulling up her hood. Captain Warrek came up to speak to the back half of the squad.

"All right, here's the deal. Inside, the Lothyn council will meet and decide what to do about us. I don't know what will come of it, but I've always thought that more talk is better than no talk at all. They're a suspicious bunch, these desert dwellers, and bringing in my regiment might not be the best way to say hello. Morge here has sent for guides, and they will take you to someplace where you can rest. Enjoy the beds; it will be the last time we truly rest before Haven City."

The council chamber was empty when Fionn stepped into the massive room. It was more like a grand amphitheater than anything else, with large wide steps rising toward the ceiling high above them. As they entered, men and women began to trickle in as if out of nowhere into the room. There were small doors along the walls he had not seen before, and, through these doors, came a steady stream of dusty, distrusting faces. It was amazing to him how many people of such varying ages and types could resemble their strange leader. It was as if the room were filling with Morges.

"I won't bandy about wit' you," Morge began, loud enough so the whole room could hear. "Lothyn was born of mistrust. We citizens of this fair city looked into the future and saw that this day would come. So we dug deep and built a civilization away from the prying eyes of the capital, away from the corruption that would eventually be its downfall. The council that sits around you are the wisest minds of Lothyn, and we make decisions as a clan. No one elf speaks for the city."

Fionn felt Mylena tense beside him, and looked down to see the fire of irritation burning in her golden eyes. "He mentioned nothing about having to dance before a council to prove our worth," she spat out the whisper as if it were something disgusting. He took her hand gently, and she squeezed his fingers with a surprising strength built from her frustration. Still she kept her head low and her identity covered. Fionn turned his attention back to the proceedings.

"Captain Warrek, you and your soldiers intend on striking at the capital of your nation, and request our aid. Why should we help the likes of you?" Morge swept his hand in a wide arc, indicating he was voicing the opinion of the council, and then nodded at Warrek to speak.

The captain stepped forward, his jaw set. He looked up at the people sitting above him, and addressed them directly. "It is true; we are going to war. We march on the very capital city I helped build with Thaniel of Eidalore all those years ago. But the city itself is not important. We of Shadowhaven can build elsewhere, as is the tradition of our people. But it is for the people that we fight. You say it is our capital, it is our nation, and that is true. But is Lothyn so deep underground that you have forgotten you too are elves?

"It is your elven brothers and sisters who are trapped within the walls of that city. It is they who are being tortured and starved for the sick pleasure of the tyrant. Make no mistake about it, whether or not you recognize the dominion of Shadowhaven, this pestilence called Sargon will not stop at the boundary of our lands. He will spread his pain and death until it seeps into everything you know, until it is your children who are hanging from the battlements. You don't recognize us, fine. But do not be fooled into thinking that you can hide in your caverns forever. He will kill you as surely as he has killed us.

"I do not ask your assistance. I am offering you a chance to stop this plague before it reaches you. The war is coming, and we aim to meet it head on before Sargon decides the city isn't big enough to hold his evil. Join us or no, that is your choice, but we march on Haven City with or without you." Captain Warrek bowed slightly and stepped back.

"Why should we follow you?" asked a voice from behind them. The group turned to see an elf dressed in rich blue robes sweeping into the room. He was accompanied by another elf as strange as himself, bound entirely in leather armor and carrying an intricately carved staff embedded with little gems. "Yes, I see that this evil must be purged, but I cannot see the benefit in following the Captain of the Queen's Guard when the royal family is dead."

"And you are?" asked Captain Warrek, affronted at this man's presumptuousness.

"I am Sojan of Kir'Midras. Our people are tired of the threat on our beloved realm, and are ready to fight. Yet under whose banner we follow remains another matter."

"The mountain elves of Kir'Kashel also recognize the evil that infests Haven City," said the second elf, punctuating his point by clanging his staff on the sandstone floor. "Warrek speaks the truth that we cannot expect such an evil to remain within the walls of the capital. But I refuse to follow a human upstart without any further connection to the throne. We need one of our people to lead us. I think it should be a clan leader, perhaps Rentyl there."

Rentyl stepped forward to join the other clan leaders, his scars glowing oddly bright in the shifting light from the torches. "You have heard of the attacks on Kir'Unwin. We have felt this pain greater than most, and have lost some of our best in the wake of this madness. I will not lead more soldiers to their deaths. Let that be for the captain, for the man trained for it." He waved his hand dismissively, sending the room into a roar of argument.

As the voices clamored and the men and women argued, Fionn felt Mylena's hand slip from his. He could feel the change in her, and suddenly felt as if the world had shifted on its axis. For so long this little slip of a woman had been running away from the fight, hiding who she was, pretending that royalty and her were completely unconnected. As she pushed through the crowd to stand in the center of the room, Fionn knew all the hiding was over. This wasn't Muirinn any longer. This was a princess. The thought bolstered him, but, at the same time, he felt a sadness creep into his heart. She was a princess. Where would there be room for Fionn in her life?

"You don't follow him," she said, her face still cast in the shadow of her cloak. She spoke quietly, yet all around her went silent as she stepped forward. "You don't follow him," she repeated, facing the council. "You follow me."

"You?" scoffed Sojan, tossing his chin in the air haughtily. "And who are you?"

"I," Mylena said, her voice almost a whisper, "am your queen." She threw back her hood, the mass of fiery red curl bursting around her as if waiting for that very moment. Mylena stood there, eyes sweeping the room, as if challenging everyone there to denounce her. There was nothing that could be said, her identity was unquestionable. No one else in Shadowhaven could have that hair. Fionn smiled at the sight of it.

A whisper swept through the room like a torrential wind, starting with those that could hear her, and spreading upward toward the highest benches toward the ceiling. She did not wait until they were quiet again.

"My name is Mylena Saebariela of Shadowhaven. I was born in Haven City, daughter of Saebariel the Warrior Queen and Thaniel of Eidalore. You may very well deny the captain of my guard your warriors, but you cannot deny me. I demand the support of your fighters as recompense for not coming to my aid. When we needed you most, every clan cut off communication with the capital. Why was it that the bravest of our realm were nowhere to be found when their queen was killed and their king lay wounded and in hiding? Did any of you think to send your warriors then? We hid among you," she turned to face Rentyl, "yet only one sought us. Only one came to bring support and aid when we needed it most. He is the bravest of you all, and you deny him your allegiance. Well, deny me if you dare. When I sit upon the throne in Illuminata Castle, I can guarantee I will remember the cowards in this room. I have an excellent memory. Are you willing to risk my wrath?"

Fionn took a step back and leaned against the wall. He had been wrong. Mylena wasn't a princess; she was a queen. She wasn't his; she belonged to Shadowhaven. As the room filled with applause and the clan leaders knelt before her, Fionn whispered a silent goodbye to the girl he had held tenderly in the Eye of the World.

The room they led Mylena into was dark, with only a few candles flickering weakly in the corners. From her days growing up in the castle she recognized this as a boudoir, although the furnishings were much starker than those that adorned the dressing rooms at Illuminata Castle. Everything in the room, from the furniture to the walls, seemed made of stone, and that included the women. They were brown and hard and barely looked at her as they undressed her and bathed her. They scrubbed her down unceremoniously, rubbing her with handfuls of sand until her skin was nearly raw. She was not even allowed to dry herself—that task they performed with their characteristic severity.

More than once, she tried to speak to the women, but they wouldn't give her so much as a glance. They had a job to perform, and had no time for the idle prattling of a girl who was not of the Sands. Even the pixie Gace seemed awed into silence; she hovered near the candles along the wall and wouldn't say a word. Without the distraction of conversation, Mylena just focused on the sensation of being waited on. Nearly four years it had been since she had stood and had a maid dress her.

Back in Kir'Unwin she would reminisce about those days and had always looked back with shame and abhorrence on how helpless she had been. Now, she realized that a small part of her missed the ceremony of it all, how luxurious it felt to simply let someone else dress her. She felt like a painter's canvas, standing there naked and unadorned, clad only in candlelight. The serving women rubbed her skin with oils that smelled of a sun-baked desert afternoon. Mylena closed her eyes and imagined she was standing not in a dark dressing room but out on the dunes, basking in the sunshine. The tugging of the bone comb they ran through her hair was, instead, the wind pulling at her curls, the stone beneath her bare feet was the sand of the dunes, wriggling between her toes.

Behind her, she heard a chest being opened, and turned to see one of the serving women reaching into a battered iron-bound chest. She pulled out a cloth bundle and set it on the stones at Mylena's feet and, with something akin to reverence, unfolded the outer protective layer as a flower unfolds in spring. Inside, lay the most beautiful garments Mylena had ever seen: A shift and overcoat woven from what looked like actual gold, a braided sash covered in tiny stitched flowers, slippers so delicate they looked as if they would melt when touched, and a diadem shaped into a vine of leaves and flowers. Against the walls, she heard Gace gasp, and the words "the Raiment of the Grove," escaped her tiny lips.

"What do you mean, Gace?" Mylena asked, her curiosity too strong to keep silent.

"I, uh," Gace stammered, and uncharacteristically appeared at a loss for words. "I'm not sure I should say."

"You should and you must." Mylena would not be denied an explanation.

Gace seemed to swallow hesitantly, although it was hard to see any expression on the tiny creature's face. Then, slowly, she began explaining. "The queens of the pixies have forever worn a special garment on the day of their coronation. I have never before seen it, except in paintings and tapestries. It is said that it was woven from the silk of a now-extinct species of golden spider, and that the cloth is so light you never feel it, but so strong it never wears out. They called it the Raiment of the Grove, since only those who ruled over the Pixie Grove were meant to wear it. However did it get here?"

Mylena puzzled over this as the serving women dressed her in each piece of the raiment. Gace was right; it felt as if she were wearing nothing at all.

One of the serving women stepped forward, and in a low, deep voice began to sing toward the water in the bathing basin. A thin sheet of water rose up out of the basin, forming into a solid, icy sheet, polished to a mirror's sheen. Mylena surveyed her reflection, as the eldest of the serving women placed the diadem on her head, nestling the golden leaves against her brow. The woman who stared back at her from her reflection looked nothing like her, despite having her features. She was regal, while Mylena was merely stubborn. She was beautiful, while Mylena was plain. She ran a hand down the golden gown, and then turned from the watery mirror. When she did so, she saw all the serving women kneeling, their heads bowed.

"My queen," they said in unison, and with a sad realization, Mylena knew it was true. She was their queen, in a way no other had been before. She was a child of the pixies and elves and a child of the humans; she knew them as if they were her own because she was part of them, and they part of her.

"Come," she said quietly, "the time has come to retake my kingdom." And she meant it.

# BOOK THREE

In the years gone by, I look back at the field of battle.
I float above the soldiers aligned in rows and feel their sadness,
See their spears and bows and swords as they stand facing the castle,
Hear their commander rally them, with vibrant words stir their blood.
In the quiet before the storm, the most oblivious of mockingbirds begins to sing
And I watch myself amongst them, so young and foolish smiling in anticipation of success.

It is no secret the tyrant must fall so that we may taste success.
His hubris and villainy have led us to this battle.
If I survive this day, of his evils I will no doubt sing.
But, for now, I shiver in the throes of a communal sadness,
Knowing the pain caused and how his hands drip innocent blood.
And so, I muster my courage and prepare to take back our castle.

The armies collide, writhing in pain within the shadow of the castle.
We clash with the unnatural army brought to ensure Sargon's success,

And leave their bodies behind, marching through pools of their blood.
As we push ever on toward our goal, we fiercely battle
Against our enemy, and slice them down in revenge for our people's sadness,
Knowing that should we fail it will be our laments they will sing.

Over the pulsing mass of bodies the elves raise their voices and sing,
Their Spell Songs call to the earth and echo off the castle.
Willing the elements to come to our aid and quell our sadness,
The magic coursing across the battlefield leads us toward success,
The power coursing in their veins is the greatest of our weapons, hidden in their blood.

Wounded, I stumble to the ground, my vision clouded by a stream of my own blood.
I search for a sense of sanity, while nearby the clashing swords sing,
Their terrible piercing dirge, gorged on the never ending battle.
I raise my eyes and realize we are within striking distance of the castle,
But my brothers in arms lay broken around me, our chance for success
Steadily seeps into the ground with our blood, and I choke on my sadness.

Though my battle-weary brethren hope to live on in tales of blood and glory,

Overwhelmed with sadness, I listen to a lone mockingbird sing,

While success floats away with the breeze that caresses Illuminata Castle.

- Battle Ballad of the Unknown Hero

## CHAPTER TWELVE

Within the span of a few days, the plans were set in motion. Chiave found himself in the midst of a massive battle plan, and it all made him excited and nervous. As a young man, he was thrilled at the prospect of seeing a grand battle play out before him, but he had seen so much death so far, he wasn't sure if he could handle any more.

The conflicting emotions disturbed his sleep, and he was driven to wander the streets of Lothyn'Kir in the early morning hours. The first night, he simply trudged around the neighborhood Warrek's band was stationed in, but the second night found him meandering down to the bridge over the singing sand river. Along the way, he scooped up a handful of sand to keep him company, and practiced singing the sand into shapes. He only managed a minor clump or two before the pile would collapse back into shapelessness on his palm. Again, he marveled at the power contained in the one who built Lothyn'Kir.

When he reached the bridge, Chiave was surprised to find he wasn't the only one drawn there in the middle of the night. The queen was standing there watching the sand slide off into the darkness. She looked up when he approached, and he quickly dropped his handful of sand and rubbed his palm on his trousers.

"Chiave," Mylena said in a soft, sad voice. Her eyes dropped back down to the sand river. "Sleep evades me in these dark days."

"I have a similar problem, it seems," he said, coming to stand next to her. He looked up into the dark expanse above them. "I cannot imagine living without the sun above you by day and stars above you at night. I have been here only a short time, and already I feel out of sorts with myself." He did not mention the vibration of every wall and column around him. He didn't think that was exactly germane to the topic at hand.

"Tomorrow, we will be marching on Haven City," Mylena said, almost to herself. He looked up to see her face clouded and darkened by something more than the shadows of the cavern around them. "All these soldiers will follow me to their death. So much has changed around me, I hardly recognize the world we live in. I miss our old life, Chiave, in Kir'Unwin. I miss living in a world where the biggest problem I had to worry about were the daily scrapes on Galenthail's clumsy nephew and the collection of sour grass by the creek."

"I miss the forest," Chiave continued the litany. "The Eye of the World is a beautiful place, but I miss running through the forest with my feet bare, feeling the grasses tickle my ankles. And I miss your father, teaching me all there is to know about the history of our peoples." He stopped there, fearing he had gone too far. So much emotion was tied to that man, to the man he had realized was his father. He needn't have worried, however, because Mylena turned to him, smiling despite the tears in her eyes.

"I miss him too," she said, and then looked surprised to hear herself say the words. "I never got the chance to tell him how much I cared for him. I spent so much time annoyed at his orders and his idiosyncrasies."

"He knew," Chiave said reaching for her hand. Suddenly it felt as if they were back in Kir'Unwin, standing in the doorway of her cottage instead of on a bridge over a sand river deep beneath the ground.

Mylena squeezed his hand and wiped away her tears, "I suppose so. He knew everything, didn't he? I feel better having you around, Chiave. Why is that, do you suppose? I'm always calmer with you nearby."

Chiave could hear the answer rising within him. Because I'm your brother. Because the same blood flows within our veins. Because being near family always helps when you are anxious. But he looked at her, and the hunch in her shoulders and the weight of an entire people in her eyes, and knew that one more revelation would just be too much to bear. Mylena already worried about the thousands of soldiers she led into battle. The concern over the welfare of a brother would be too much to deal with. No, better that he wait until everything was over, until they stood together on the balcony of Illuminata Castle. Then he would tell her. For now, he simply said, "I'm not sure, but I do know it means I should always stick by you."

Mylena smiled again, this time more openly. "You will be my charms then, you and your Joppa. I will have you both, one on each side of me, to keep me calm during the frightful days to come." She patted his hand fondly and looked out at the river one last time. "Oh, how I do miss the sea," she sighed, and turned her back on the river. "Come, little charm, take me home. I feel sleep actually creeping up on me."

Chiave took her arm, surprised to see how brash he had become since they had last been in Kir'Unwin together. So much had changed, he hardly knew what was the same. As they left the bridge and made their way to the apartments Mylena was using while in Lothyn'Kir, the pair did not notice that water now flowed underneath the bridge where sand used to race off into the darkness.

The next days were paced to move at lightning speed. Once the clan leaders agreed to fully support their new queen, warriors were chosen from the best of Lothyn'Kir. The leaders of Kir'Kashel and Kir'Midras left to assemble what they could lend to the effort, with the understanding that they were all to travel discretely across the lands and meet at the Laud'El monastery within two weeks' time. As Mylena had said, they were on the move the very next day, having only spent three days in total in Lothyn'Kir. That was fine by Chiave, as the residents were a skitterish, untrustworthy lot who rarely showed their face. He would miss the use of a warm bed and a steaming bath, but he was confident that he would sleep well once the war was over and done with. He would sleep well in Haven City, of that he was certain.

They had entered the city a small troop of battered elves and men, but they left the city an army triumphant. Mylena traveled at the forward edge of the column, visible to any who would see them march, her red hair the only banner they needed to follow across the pale desert sands. As she had said that night on the bridge, Chiave and Joppa were instructed to ride by her side, and, on occasion, she would converse with them about idle topics to pass the time. At one point, she and Chiave had a meaningful discussion on the strengths and weaknesses of a centralized government.

"While the city is certainly a jewel or, at least, was up until recent events, I wonder if my parents did something wrong in building Haven City."

"Why do you say that?" Chiave asked, intrigued. "The city itself is heavily fortified. Had the Betrayer not let down the defenses, I very much doubt she would have fallen at all."

"It's not a case of if the city was strong enough. I just wonder what it has done to the heart of the people. The elves were ever a migratory people, were they not? We pass by the ruins of their former settlements even now" Mylena pointed east, where a crumbling stand of stone buildings was slowly being swallowed up by the sand. "The need to move about this beautiful land is in their bones, Chiave. You know the lore of our people as well as I do. I just wonder if we somehow failed Kir'Tazul by asking them to live within unmovable walls. The city was young, yes, but it was still intended to be permanent. I think it may be this permanence that was our downfall."

"If this is the case, then you can change things, can't you?" Chiave bit his lip, thinking himself impertinent.

"Go on," Mylena said, prodding him to continue.

"What I mean to say is, you will soon be back in control of the country. You will have say over what is permanent and what is not. If you truly think the hearts of the people of Shadowhaven are hurt by the city, then tear down the walls and create something that will help the people."

She laughed suddenly, and then looked down at him with a wry smile, "I always imagined advisors to the throne would at least be old enough to grow a beard."

Chiave threw a false pout, crossing his arms over his chest in mock petulance. "I am working on that, m'Lady."

"Well go to, young man, go to! I command you in the name of my great self, Queen of Shadowhaven." At this, they both laughed, settling back into a comfortable silence.

Moving amongst a column of ten thousand soldiers felt akin to living in a mobile city. It was as if they had taken all of Lothyn'Kir with them, except the sand buildings. When they camped, great stretches of tents arose on the Plain of the Beyond, line after line of them until Chiave felt sure he would get lost in their multitude. He stuck therefore, to the campfire and his own tent, which he shared with Joppa simply because she refused to sleep elsewhere despite having a tent provided for her. The rhythm of the march and the camp repeating over the next week, without much in the way of happenings. At the end of the third night, Captain Warrek approached Chiave with a proposition.

"You've carried that sword to the ends of the world and back, boy. Would you care to learn how to use it?" His air was flippant, but Chiave saw past the smile. They were going into war, and Chiave would need more than a stone wall to defend himself with. So the nighttime lessons began, during which the captain began by teaching him to grip the pommel of the sword correctly, and then how to clean and sharpen it. The next night, Chiave was taught the weight of the blade, where it was weakest and strongest, but still not one lesson on how to wield it. The next night, Warrek worked with him on sheathing and unsheathing the greatsword, and Chiave finally snapped.

"What use is all of this?" he barked, after spending three hours sheathing and unsheathing his sword. His wrists were sore with the effort, but his ego was sore with feeling that he was being played with.

"You have to groom and tack the horse before you put a saddle on it," was all Warrek would say on the matter. Frustrated, Chiave turned back toward the tents.

"He got that sword from his father, you know," Warrek said quietly almost to himself, stopping Chiave in his tracks, "and his father from his." Chiave didn't turn around but, instead, stood still, letting Warrek's words wash over him.

"I always thought it strange for a scholar to carry a sword with him, so I asked him once about it. You know what he said? 'This sword has been passed through the men in my family for a thousand years. It is my connection to my people. It reminds me who I came from. Whenever I get wrapped up too much in my own troubles, I remember those men who fought on the battlefields of Eidalore. I remember that even an academic must be brave.'"

The silence stretched between them, and Chiave let it unravel as he returned to his tent. It was the last night he would show up for sword training. The sword remained, as always, strapped to his back, but he did not attempt to seek instruction from anyone on its use. On the eighth day, they arrived at

Laud'El, and Chiave put the sword training completely out of his mind but never the sword itself.

It had been two months since Warrek had set eyes on Laud'El, and the little battered monastery was beginning to feel like the only home he had left in this tumultuous world. He had left on a journey to protect a boy and his book, and, although that mission had failed, they still managed to bring a large army with them. It did his heart good to see the clans coming together. In addition to Morge's promised delivery of ten thousand soldiers, Warrek arrived at Laud'El to find Sojan along with three thousand soldiers, and Yar of Kir'Kashel with fifteen hundred. The massive city of tents surrounding the monastery was a welcome sight as they traveled over the rise.

Another surprise awaited him when Warrek entered Laud'El's main building. Captain Harridan was there to greet him, wearing a huge smile, a new scar or two, and a cloak made entirely of feathers.

"Corrupted by the latest fashions in Eidalore, I see," Warrek joked as they embraced.

"They're harpy feathers, my man," Harridan said, guffawing, and Warrek joined him in the laughter, knowing well the tribulations of traversing the pass.

"What news from the court of Eidalore?" Warrek asked as he settled down on a bench in the banquet hall turned hospital.

"The king is a pompous ass," Harridan said good-naturedly. "I wouldn't let him off without giving me less than twenty thousand men. It took some doing, but, in the end, he realized this bastard Sargon isn't going to stay in Shadowhaven. It seems you've had some luck on the recruiting end yourself. The clans are all here in some form or another. And was that the Princess Mylena I saw outside?"

"Outside?" Warrek, intrigued, made his way outside where indeed Mylena was walking amongst the women and men as then ambled about their tents. They whispered as they saw her, and knelt when she went by. "She's a queen now," he said to Harridan, distracted by the effect she was having on the warriors.

"Then shouldn't we compel our queen to come inside?" Harridan made to approach her, but Warrek stayed him. Mylena seemed compelled to greet each warrior, and Warrek could guess why. It was the same feeling he had had when he first had taken command. She was memorizing their faces. In a few short days, many of these warriors would be buried beneath the ground.

Suddenly, Warrek flashed to another moment where he watched a queen studying the faces of her soldiers. A sadness filled him suddenly as he recalled the last time he had seen Saebariel commanding her warriors. Nearly four years later, it was hard to believe that so much had changed, that he was standing on the grounds of a former monastery for a brotherhood of monks who no longer existed and planning to siege the very castle Saebariel had built. Scratching his chin, he turned his back on Mylena, very much needing a drink.

"Come, Harridan, there's work to be done," he said leading the way inside.

There was no evening or night or morning for Mylena that day. Something kept her down in the fields with the soldiers, talking with them, learning their stories. She felt compelled to know as many of them as possible. Sitting by the campfire with elves from Kir'Kashel enjoying their bitter cider and listening to their stories, she came to understand that she had wasted so much of her youth in petty self-interest. She should have traveled the land and learned about the clans. She should have spent the time as Chiave had, learning at the feet of her father. She should have followed her mother on campaigns and gleaned what knowledge she could.

There wasn't enough time to learn to be a queen, so she would work with what she had. She would soak up what she could in these final hours before these women and men would die for her. She would do her best.

When the sun filtered through the trees and the mist began to retreat from the ground, Captain Warrek appeared to collect her.

"It's time, your Majesty," he said in his low, harsh voice. It took her a moment to realize he was speaking to her. "I have given orders to the warriors to prepare."

Mylena looked around her, at those she had spent the earlier morning hours with, and saw they were strapping on their weapons and filing into formation. There would be no time for a meal, and many of these soldiers would have no such luxury again. She turned to Warrek, squaring her shoulders.

"I want to speak with them."

Warrek opened his mouth to say something, but something in her eyes and the set of her jaw made him reconsider. He only nodded, and with a sweep of his hand indicated that she should lead the way back to the buildings.

At the barn, Mylena's horse was waiting, as were Chiave and Joppa, and she smiled to see them. It would give her strength to have such companions on a day promising such bloodshed.

Bloodshed. Mylena sighed heavily and mounted her horse, barely noticing the direction she guided the animal, only that when she next took stock of her surroundings she stood facing the mass of women and men, elves and humans, magic singers and soldiers. Every single one of them had tasted the bitterness of life in an occupied land, and each of them was willing to give their life for the promise that the generations after them would not know such pain. Moved by this realization, she began to speak.

"We have come here today to this battlefield to fight for our brothers and sisters inside the city walls. Within Haven

City is a world of suffering we have only heard of from our spies. But we know it's there, and that is why we stand here on the threshold of war.

"Perhaps you are unsure of your purpose here. Perhaps you have wondered whether or not you truly belong amongst these ranks. Look around you. What you see is the product of a successful nation. You are the spirit of Shadowhaven, its heart and its sword. You do belong here, as much as I do.

"Twenty-four years ago two people met and fell in love. Out of that love sprung this amazing realm, a country built of choice, of tolerance, of union rather than disharmony. There is much Shadowhaven has that is unique, and it is exactly our advantages that have made us a target. Saebariel and Thaniel built Illuminata Castle over the font of elven power, but the Well of Zyn belongs to no one person, no one race. It is the physical representation of the spirit of our people. We need no Well to show us our true potential. We do not need to drink from the waters to perfect ourselves. That perfection lies within us already, in our veins and in our hearts. We do not fight for the Well.

"We fight for the people of Shadowhaven, for those in the city threatened daily with torture and disease, and for those outside the city, who must live in fear of demon attacks and worse. The Well is our birthright, but it is the people who are our treasure."

She paused then, looking over the faces of Captain Warrek, Captain Harridan, Vorynne, and Clodai, and finally, her eyes settled on Fionn. Fionn who had traveled across the world and back to protect her. Fionn who held her heart as closely as he held his bow.

"What I ask of you is not fair. It is not fair to be asked to lay down your lives for the sake of a future you will not see. But it is right. It is right that I ask you to do this, and it is my right as your queen. Today, we will fight the hired goons Sargon brought with him, and we will be victorious. We will fight everything he throws at us, and we will win. We will win because this is our home. Let's go home sisters and brothers. Let us return home to Illuminata!" As she ended with her arms raised and her voice calling to the throng, a deafening roar arose around her, a promise of assent and understanding of their goal, their purpose, their reason for taking up arms. These were her people, and her people were ready to fight.

Bolstered by Queen Mylena's words, Warrek led the forward advance down the valley toward the capital. He had no illusions about stealth; for anyone not completely mad, the sentries would have been alerted to the amassing of forces at Laud'El. Even Sargon must have at least a few attentive men in his strange, otherworldly army. No, there would be no element of surprise, but there would be the advantage that the mercenaries didn't have: the elves.

He was sure that once the fighting broke out, his remaining forces within the city would rise up in defense of their homeland. The warriors of Shadowhaven were wise women and men; they knew when to lay low and when to turn diplomacy into defiance. His only concern was the possibility that they were too weakened to fight, or had already been slaughtered, as his spies had mentioned Sargon was slaying the city's citizens.

He was proud to see Harridan joining him as he galloped ahead of the column. The young man certainly had grown up fast, but war will do that to you. His siren-feathered cape waved in the mid-morning breeze and made Warrek smile.

"Whatever is there to smile about?" Harridan asked amazed.

"I was just thinking about how best to defeat Sargon. I think I may have hit on the perfect strategy." Warrek waited for Harridan to take the bait.

"Oh? Do tell."

"We send you in with your ridiculous cape, and Sargon will laugh himself to death."

Sometime after that, they arrived at the final ridge before the valley Haven City nestled in. Dismounting, Warrek took his spyglass and his companion and ordered the rest of the column to stand firm. He approached the crest of the ridge on his belly, and writhed through the grass as would a snake newly born from the egg. When he reached the top, he parted the grasses and realized he didn't need the telescope after all.

"We brought 40,000 soldiers," Harridan whispered beside him. "That would make this, what, an eight to one fight do you imagine?"

"At least," Warrek looked down at a valley black with what looked like ants, but he knew they were men. It seemed that Sargon's army had grown in numbers, although he knew no new detachments had arrived from elsewhere. This would be quite a challenging day. "Well, it looks like we will have a good fight after all. And here I was worried this would go too easily." Back at their horses, he asked Harridan, "My man, how do you take down a charging bull?"

"Well, I've been told to take a bull by its horns," Harridan began, "but the horns are sharp and the head is the most powerful part of the animal. No, I would take a bull down by the flanks. Arrows work best in my experience. Hit where he is weakest and exposed."

"Arrows, eh? In the flanks? Well, we have one damned huge bull down there, and I expect it to charge on sight. Let us open our quiver, then, and see what arrows we have available."

From his position at the queen's side, Chiave had an excellent view of the battlefield. It had been about an hour since they had arrived on the ridge, and his first sight of the massive army opposing them made his stomach lurch. It seemed impossible that they should be expected to fight what looked to be about 350,000 men with their small number. He had thought the militia army massive up until that moment when he mounted the ridge and saw exactly what they were up against.

Joppa for her part took it all in stride. She spotted the armies, smiled up at Chiave, and said, "So many bodies to wade through. I certainly hope they won't stink up the castle. I would hate to sleep with the smell of rotting corpses in my bedroom."

"Do you mean we will succeed?" Mylena asked, suddenly keenly interested.

"Success is inevitable, mistress," Joppa said, her eyes bright. "Survival is the question." She then began to spin around in a circle until she got too dizzy to stand, and then fell to her knees, praying loudly, her arms raised.

Chiave listened to the rhythm of her chanting, the words of a language he didn't understand rolling off her tongue. He felt the voices of the rock beneath his feet, and Joppa's song mixed in his consciousness in an entwining melody of praise. It was as if the two strands of music were parts of the same song. Suddenly he wondered very much if there were ever differences between the elves and the humans. Perhaps Shadowhaven was simply the culmination of the inevitable. The worship of the elements and the praise of the El were separate halves of the same whole, manifest creation and unmanifest creator. Just as he himself was both elven and human, as was Shadowhaven itself. He knelt down to place his hand on the earth, and closed his eyes to listen to the music: Joppa's chanting and the Spell Song of the rocks below. It wasn't just similar; it was the same.

The epiphany shook him physically, and he turned to Mylena to explain what he had discovered but saw in her eyes a pain he didn't understand. He followed her gaze down to the valley below and realized that the battle had begun. The unit protecting the queen had stayed up on the ridge, his brother Fionn being the only elf among them. The rest of the group were swordsmen, their shields held close to their chests. He recognized Joppa's brothers among them, but their faces were closed off and tense.

Below, in the valley, the first units of the militia had begun to clash with the otherworldy forces Sargon had brought to protect his precious self. It was too distant for him to see the individuals, but he knew Captain Warrek to be down there, as well as his mother. He stood up and put his hand on the flank of Mylena's horse, using the steady breathing of the animal to steady his pounding heart. He knew many would fall today, and steeled himself for the possibility of never seeing his mother again.

His experience with battle had been limited and fairly unique. Involuntarily, his eyes grazed the sky as if the dragons would somehow appear here, now, to sweep down and pluck him from the ground. What he did know was the ceaselessness of it all. As he watched the masses of soldiers pushing against one another down in the valley below, Chiave could feel the tension on the bowstrings, the hoarseness in the voices of the magic users, the throbbing in the arms of the swordsman. Every foe defeated would reveal five more, and every time you thought you were safe, someone would come running in to attack from behind.

The initial skirmish looked like a total failure from what he could tell. The grey-skinned force was swallowing Warrek's soldiers whole, as if they were a small meal laid out for a massive black beast. Wherever they made progress, another group of mercenaries was there to surround them. From what

Chiave could see, it seemed as if the war would be before it had even begun. He found his hands clenching the mane of Mylena's horse so tightly his knuckles were white. Please, it can't be over this quickly, he begged the EL, the elements, anyone who would hear. We've come so far; please, help them.

As if his prayers were immediately answered, two huge divisions of the militia rushed down from seemingly out of nowhere to attack the mercenaries from their flanks. They flowed down the slopes, a river of elves, driving into Sargon's army and dividing it in two. In an instant, the tide had turned, and Chiave watched as the mercenaries were first divided and then pushed back toward the walls of Haven City.

From above, the battle seemed less like a group of people fighting another but more like a struggle of amorphous shapes. This militia blob was swallowing this triangular patch of mercenaries. Over on the other side of the valley the battlefield began to look a bit like a chess board, with patches of mercenaries interspersed with patches of militia. He couldn't tell how much progress was being made, but he could see the progress as the shapes he knew overtook the shapes he hated.

It killed Fionn to be standing still while others fought and lost their lives. His life was repeating itself all over again. While his mother and the other warriors of Kir'Unwin went off to protect the realm, he was forced to stay behind and guard their most precious possession. She was his most precious possession as well, to be sure, yet he felt conflicted. He knew that the most important place for him to be was there by her side, yet the action was down below in the valley. The Spell Songs echoed over the clash of sword on sword, walls of fire cutting paths through enemies only to have the next set of mercenaries encased in stone. Tornados sprung from a windless day to swirl through the ranks of the mercenaries. Every spell singer under Warrek's command was out there. Every one, save Fionn.

The darkness of his mood seemed to affect the weather, although he had no power over the element of air. Clouds rolled in with surprising speed, turning a clear day overcast and gray. The very air around Fionn seemed to be darkening, as if the sun were dropping below the horizon in the middle of the day. It was a strange feeling, and one he had not recalled having since that day in the forest oh so long ago.

"Prepare!" he yelled at his comrades. "The Ombrid approach!" Before he was able to explain what they were to do, a flood of demons surrounded their group on the hill, and poured into the valley in an unceasing torrent. There was no time to watch the effect on the battle below, the demons had swarmed their small group and were slashing viciously toward the queen. There were at least fifty of the creatures, and Mylena, who had shown such power defeating them before, appeared paralyzed with surprise.

In an instant, the war had come to him, and Fionn was knocking arrows as fast as he could to keep the shadowy beasts at bay. The swordsmen around him were providing a thin layer of protection, but it would not hold out for long.

Out of the corner of his eye, Fionn saw one of the monsters launch itself off the shield of a foot soldier, sailing through the air toward Mylena. Teeth bared, claws ripping the sky, its black eyes were focused only on her. Fionn jumped in hopes of blocking its attack, using his spine as a shield. Its shadowy form enveloped him. He collided with Mylena, throwing her to the ground, and everything went black.

When he was a little boy, Sargon used to collect butterflies. He was fascinated with the tiny, winged creatures, and had several jars in his room where he kept cocoons. It wasn't so much the flight that intrigued him, although flying was something he desperately wanted to learn about. No, it was the idea that a caterpillar, an ugly, disgusting little grub, could, through the sheer power of its will, transform into something completely and utterly different. Sargon wanted wings. Sargon wanted to be special.

Unfortunately, a tailor's son is rarely gifted with more than an extensive wardrobe. Having lost his wife to sickness some years back, Sargon's father tended to dote on him a little too much. He allowed the boy freedoms most parents in Eidalore would never even consider. When his child decided he wanted to study magical texts, Sargon's father sent away across the sea for tomes containing the illicit instruction. When his son wanted to start collecting magical creatures for research, the tailor spent a fortune hiring men to collect animals for his son. And when his tastes turned more macabre and Sargon requested bodies, both alive and dead, to experiment upon, the old tailor finally realized that he had indulged his child too long.

By then, it was too late, of course. Had Sargon restricted his curiosity to magical spells and creatures, he most likely would have become a great inventor. But, alas, his talent for figuring out the inner workings of things was allowed to roam free, and a darkness took hold of his heart that would slowly choke all the humanity out of him.

Even from a young age, there was an awful lot of Sargon to go around. His father had made sure that Sargon would want for nothing, and that included food. The rotund little boy grew out as well as up, and, by the time he was twenty, he had rejected the jerkin and trousers of the common folk for robes his father wove for him out of ornate silks. After his father died, worn out by Sargon's rapacious appetites, Sargon sold his business and bought a worn-down castle out in the mountains of northern Eidalore, and he made sure there was both a cook and a tailor on staff at all times.

For someone as indulgent as Sargon, tastes never change; they only intensify. His entire life had been spent in the pursuit of one thing: making himself transform from an ordinary tailor's son into a magical sorcerer of unspeakable power. The trouble was, Sargon soon found that magic was something innate. You were either born with it or you weren't. He was lumped into the second category, but he was too stubborn to accept his plight. He traveled the world, seeking the right answer to his question, and crashed on a remote seemingly deserted island one day to find the Zyn. The Zyn were a magical people, everyone born with abilities. The Zyn were the answer to his problems, but not in the way one might think.

The Zyn were originally from the old continent. These gray-skinned people spoke bitterly of how they had been forced out of their homeland, cut off from the wellspring that held their true power. One day, they vowed, they would return home and retake what was theirs. They would take the Well of Zyn by force if need be. But it would once again be theirs.

In researching these tales, Sargon learned that the Well of Zyn was not merely a legendary icon. It was an actual place, although the Zyn themselves had lost its location in the thousands of years of exile. Curiosity being his strong suit, Sargon dug into the Zyn's past, read every document explaining their voyage across the sea, and finally found one small notation at the end of an inventory list describing the amount of various textiles one of the ancient ships had carried. The notation read, "Silks from the Land of Shadow," and he knew exactly what it meant.

Standing now on the balcony overlooking the battlefield below Castle Illuminata, Sargon couldn't help but smile. He had come so very far, and was one step away from getting his hands on true magical power. Down below him, he could see the Zyn fighting valiantly against those who had invaded their homeland, had driven them out, had forced them into exile in a harsh land with hardly any resources to speak of. No wonder they were angry all the time. It was an emotion he could completely relate to.

His army was winning, and out there somewhere was the little princess. What was her name? Mylena. She was probably crying in frustration, poor little creature. She's lost so much, and now just as she's ready to take back her land, the Zyn have to go and ruin it for her. And not only the Zyn. There were also Sargon's pets, the Ombrid, an interesting result from some particularly dark experiments into the properties of magical blood. His little brood were out there now, sniffing her out. Find her, he thought to his pets, rend her to pieces, and bring me her still beating heart. His transformation was nearly upon him. His years of work and research were finally going to provide him with the gift he should have been born with. No longer would he be an ugly grub, digging in the dirt with the rest of the worms; At long last he would soar above them all like a glorious magical butterfly.

Turning his back on the battlefield, Sargon stepped away from the window and folded his fingers across his ample stomach. So much blood and decay down below. It was enough to make a man hungry.

It happened too fast for her to react. One minute she was watching in horror as her warriors battled bravely, pushing Sargon's forces back toward the city gates. And then they were surrounded by evil incarnate. Shadowy forms were everywhere, and then there was Fionn throwing himself at her, and it all went dark.

She was dreaming again, then, gliding through the halls of Illuminata Castle. She paused in the foyer, hearing the battle raging on outside the city walls, and then continued up to her old apartments. There at the window stood her mother, looking out at the sea. The sadness in her mother's eyes was deeper than the ocean she looked upon, and as she raised her eyes to look at Mylena, tears flowed from her eyes.

"The world is in so much pain, Mylena," her mother said, holding out her hands to her. Mylena approached, and as she took her mother's hands she felt them to be cold. "How could Thaniel and I have seen this coming? We wanted to create a realm of love, of understanding, and look," she gestured to the opposite wall, where a second bank of windows appeared instead of a doorway. Together they watched the soldiers fighting and dying far below and Mylena too cried. The shadow fiends were slicing the militia to ribbons, and Mylena cringed to see it.

"I'm so sorry, Mother. This is all my fault!" She threw her arms around her mother, sobbing.

"You're fault? No, what your doing here is the salvation of our people. You're succeeding, though you don't know it yet. You're what Shadowhaven needs now. You will make the difficult choice and save them all."

"The difficult choice? But I don't understand." Mylena pulled away a little so that she could see her mother's expression. Saebariel was smiling despite her tears, and ran a hand over Mylena's forehead as she used to do when she was a little girl.

"Yes, I've sent someone to guide you. Don't worry; everything will become clear to you at the right time. You've been brave enough so far, but you will have to be braver still. Remember Mylena, you must make the difficult choice. You have lost so much, my darling, and I am sorry to say you will still lose much more. But our time here is over now. It took me some time to break through, but at last my message has reached you."

"Mother, I love you," Mylena said as Saebariel stepped away from her, breaking contact at last.

"I love you," her mother said, but it wasn't in her voice. It was in Fionn's voice, and it startled Mylena enough to make her open her eyes.

She was lying on her back in a dark place she didn't recognize at first. It looked like she was in a cave, but she hadn't been near any mountains that she could think of. Something was pinning her to the ground. Mylena shook her head, trying her best to get her bearings. She remembered an attack, and Chiave throwing up a stone shield—When did he learn to do that?!—and Fionn...oh no, Fionn.

"I love you," Fionn said again, his voice weaker than before, and Mylena was brought back to herself instantly. It was Fionn who lay on top of her, badly scratched and bleeding profusely.

"Fionn," she said, "can you move? We need to get help; you're hurt."

He shushed her with a kiss, his lips weak and cool against her own. "I never truly sang until you came to Kir'Unwin.

Thank you." He lay his head against her shoulder, face-first, and she felt his slow breathing against her collarbone. The breath came in short gasps then stopped altogether.

"Fionn? Fi..." Mylena stopped, holding her breath. She hoped for any sign of life from him, but she could feel no more movement from him. "No, please! Please don't leave me," she sobbed, her tears turning into hysterical screams. "You promised you would never leave me!" she howled, beating on Fionn's unresponsive body on top of her. She pounded on his body until her fists were bruised, and she screamed until her throat was hoarse. Then she lay there, quiet in the semidarkness, breathing in her pain, and letting it take root within her.

When in battle, it was Vorynne's habit to clean her blade after every kill. This day, although it was nearly impossible to do so, she began wiping her sword on the backs of the fallen as soon as she saw the Ombrid sweeping into the valley. Soldiers by the dozens were slaughtered in seconds, and when the demons reached her, their shadowy blood began to gnaw through the steel of her short sword. From the moment she first came in contact with one of the dark, fanged monsters, she was fighting off five at a time. They seemed not to discriminate between their prey, and defenders and militia alike fell to their clawing and raking and vicious bites.

It is here, then, she thought to herself as she pinned another demon to the ground and spun to skewer another one with a fallen comrade's blade, here is where it ends for Shadowhaven. Somehow, the sad irony choked her. The land of light was to be ravaged by creatures created out of the darkness itself. How sad that everything they had built would crumble under the madness of one man.

Out of nowhere, a small fluttering creature appeared before Vorynne's face. Gace, the pixie messenger, had been useless since their leaving the Eye of the World. She had spent her entire time fawning over the queen as if somehow vying for a seat at court. As if there were seats at court and as if any existed small enough for one of her stature. Yet here she was, a little ball of light, shining in the gloom of the cloudy battlefield, bouncing on her toes in midair.

"They've come, just so you know," Gace said, doing somersaults above an Ombrid's head. She giggled as it snapped its jaws, attempted to eat her. Idly, Vorynne wondered what the monsters ate.

"Who has come, you annoying little insect?" Vorynne snapped as she fought off another group of demons. She didn't have the time for games, not now when all their lives were about to be snuffed out.

"Why, the pixie army of course." She pointed a tiny hand at the far side of the valley, where the air was swarming with points of light.

"There must be thousands," Vorynne said in amazement. She didn't think that grove could house so many pixies.

"Three thousand, to be exact. Silly elves and their biases. That's why Saebariel had to hide who she really was, you know. Because belief has died in the hearts of the elves. But they believe now, don't they?" As if to punctuate her point, Gace faced the nearest Ombrid, and, clapping her hands together, she sang a high-pitched song Vorynne had never heard before. Where the pixie's hands connected, a beam of light flashed forth, slicing the monster square in the face. It screamed in pain and then crumbled to the ground, dead before it stopped moving. "We're here to win the war for you. You could at least look a little grateful." Gace flew off, giggling into the chilly air.

Warrek had often thought about battle in terms of the sea. Perhaps it was the time he spent as a child on his uncle's fishing vessel back in Eidalore that taught him this analogy. Those lovely summer mornings out on the open ocean, where his uncle would explain the power of the tides, and how they brought the schools of fish close enough to the coastline of their little island home for the nets to gather them up. Only once had he been caught in a storm while fishing with his uncle. It was a strange and frightening experience. Great fists of water would rise up and pound at the boat, one after the other, until the sheets of rain and the crashing waves finally broke. Weather broke at sea. It didn't softly mellow out into a sunny day. The storm was there and then it wasn't. The instant the weather broke, the world was clean and clear and the most beautiful it had ever been. So beautiful, it made young Warrek cry.

When he went off to join the army, the memory of the power of the sea, that storm in particular, stayed with Warrek, and somehow got applied to his life as a soldier. The storm was pounding on him now; a great sea of shadowy creatures came flooding into the valley, cutting down anyone in their path. The waves of demons rose like ocean water over the women and men around him, and, just like the seafarers, most were drowned in the torrent. For hours, Warrek felt like that boy clinging to the mast of his uncle's fishing vessel, stretched in multiple directions at once, fingers raking any solid object so that he could keep his head above the tide. The solid object then had been the masthead, the great pillar of wood that formed the main support of the boat. Here, his solid object was his sword.

Almost as tall as he was, the greatsword cut through the creatures as the fishing net had cut through the sea, only he wasn't culling fish with each swing, it was death he gathered to him. Still they kept coming. With every swing, he cut down five or more monsters, and a dozen would flood the vacancy, until Warrek could see nothing but a writhing blackness all around him. He realized then that he was meant to drown in this sea. There was no escape, as the entire valley was teeming with these horrible creatures from the depths of man's darkest nightmares. Fine. If he were to die here, it was as good a place as any. He would die beside the castle he had seen rise from the rock face itself, fighting for a civilization he had sworn to protect. Here, he would stand until the sea claimed him.

But at that most dismal moment, when all seemed lost, the weather broke. Darkness had swallowed him, yet it spat him out again. He had been surrounded by an eternal sea of shadow, yet, in the blink of an eye, everything around him was lit by flashes of blinding white light. Warrek was sure he had passed on, and what he was seeing were the souls of the dead settling into their final sleep. However, pain still throbbed in him, and he looked down to see his sword smoking with of the black blood of his foes. His senses cleared, and he focused on the light searing through the sea of demons. There were thousands of little points of light, and great swords of light, slicing through the demons as if they were beams of morning sunlight dissolving the fog.

Warrek sifted through his memories for a correlation, something he knew that would connect with the fantastic scene before him. From the dark recesses of his mind, he pulled one word that explained it all, yet made him laugh uncontrollably at the realization. Pixies. The weather had changed, and there were pixies on the wind. The laughter took hold of him as he watched the tides recede, as every last demon was decimated by the tiny warriors and their swords of light. All his work, all his struggle had done nothing to stem the onslaught, yet here, these little flying imps were doing, in a matter of minutes, what his entire army could not do in hours. When the laughter faded, Warrek found himself standing in a smoking field dotted with triumphant balls of light. Only then did he finally let go of the masthead.

Forty thousand soldiers came to fight for their kingdom that day. They were a coalition of elves and men, born of the clans that had roamed Shadowhaven as free citizens for hundreds of years, proud people, who had raised a new civilization on top of their very ancient roots, who had seen the possibilities of the new woven upon the rich tapestry of the old. When the future generations look back on the siege on Haven City, they will speak of the strength of the warriors against an army ten times their size. They will write entire books on the determination of the clans to take back their homeland. They will sing songs about the triumph over Sargon's demon horde, of how the army of the pixie queen arrived to decimate the monsters just when all appeared to be lost.

Little will be told about the losses, as the lens of history often focuses on the most palatable of truths. When the queen's warriors finally breached the city gates, their number had dwindled to several thousand, and there was not one among them who was not gravely wounded. Had they been as triumphant of spirit as history claims them to be, what little shred of joy lay within them would have been stripped away by what awaited them once then entered Have City for the first time in three years.

History will tell of the salvation of the Kir'Tazul clan, who had formed the population of Haven City. History will mention the illness, that some had been claimed by the machinations of Sargon the Mad, but that the healing began virtually the instant Queen Mylena stepped onto the streets of the city. History will lie.

Within the city walls, arose a stench that gagged the siege force before they even passed through the city gates. Most, if not all, of the city's population were dead or dying; rotting corpses hung from walls and buildings, windows, and doorways in such numbers that it was hard to find a space that was not littered with the dead. Had the birds not succumbed to the plague infesting the city long ago, they would have been gorged fat on the bodies of the clansmen of Kir'Tazul. Instead, the insects were feasting in their place; swarms of flies clouded the sky so that the city looked to be in perpetual twilight. As the soldiers passed through the city on their way to Illuminata Castle, they wept tears of frustration and pain, mourning their sisters and brothers who could not fight back as they had. Kir'Tazul would be the last and most tormented victim of Sargon's demented campaign. There was only one pair of eyes dry that day as the remaining warriors reached the castle portcullis high above the city proper. Queen Mylena was alone in looking upon the devastation of her people with tearless eyes.

She had dreamt so long of this moment, this point in her life when she would return home. But Mylena had never expected it to happen like this. In her mind's eye, she saw herself entering Haven City, a carpet of rose petals leading up the mountain to the castle. Instead, the path was strewn with the bodies of her people, a carpet of an entirely different kind. She had thought she would be returning standing behind her father as he led the soldiers to a sweeping victory, one in which few would be injured, and the invading hordes would be pushed back with little effort. Owl-emblazoned banners would fly from the towers of the gatehouse as they entered the city, music would play, and the citizens of the city would cheer. This was her imagination, but nothing in her life had ever lived up to her imagination.

Instead, an eerie silence wrapped in the stench of death welcomed her, and she rode into the city at the head of the siege force instead of walking behind her father. His absence stabbed her in the heart almost as much as the carnage that awaited her around every bend in the roadway leading up to the castle. Somehow, she had not felt so very alone until this moment, until she traveled her own city as a stranger might without her mother's strength, without her father's guidance.

She was not actually alone, she knew. Captain Warrek was there, as were Chiave and Joppa, Morge, and Vorynne too. In fact, most of those who had traveled with her to Lothyn'Kir followed her up the death-ridden highway toward Illuminata Castle, except, of course, Fionn.

That was the knowledge that kept her eyes dry, despite the carnage that greeted her around every corner, despite the smell of decay that made her choke. There was one thing left to be done, one last task to perform before she could give in to the grief lying within her somewhere out of sight. And then she would be able to crumble in on herself, and let the darkness take her.

Expectation of resistance fled from her mind as she rounded the last bend and saw her beloved castle for the first time in four years. The portcullis lay open, and no mercenaries stood guard. It appeared as if Sargon had sent every last man down into the valley to thwart them, and, thus, was left unguarded in the end. Expectation of her opponent's sanity fled when she entered the castle foyer as she had so many times in her dreams, only to find Sargon standing at the top of the staircase, his dark eyes glinting, his rich purple robes stained with grime and waste. He grinned at the sight of them, and opened his arms wide as if to welcome his guests to an evening of merriment.

"I am so glad you have finally come, my dear!" he said, his tone jovial. "I have waited a very long time to meet you. I searched the entire kingdom for you, yet here you are. It is awfully rude of you, you know. If I had known you were going to simply arrive like this, I wouldn't have bothered looking. Oh well, I suppose you can't change the past, now can you?" He laughed lightly, as if they were exchanging pleasantries over a glass of wine.

Mylena glanced around the columned foyer, once so elegant and welcoming a room. The great domed ceiling used to radiate sunlight anytime of the day or night, feeding the flowers and shrubs living under its expanse with the illusion of warmth. The room was dark now, and the plants had long since withered away to dust. The blood of her people stained every surface, yet this was not as much an affront to her as the man infesting her home with his presence. She felt a disgust rising from within her cocoon of numbness, and she shivered with the power of it. Suddenly, she wished for the power to step back in time, to stand before the parents of this abomination and cut them down before they would have the chance to conceive such a monster. She wished she were capable of changing the past so that she would never have had to come to this moment, the moment when she truly wanted to kill someone. The power of such a desire frightened her, yet she still felt the weight of Fionn's cold body against her, the closest thing to a lover's embrace she had ever felt, yet the furthest thing from it.

Sargon saw the change in Mylena and instantly drew from his store of evil energies and lashed out at her, sending a wave of shadow magic at her that knocked her to the marble floor. He laughed then, a high-pitched cackle that echoed off the domed ceiling and bounced around the pillars. "You are so very young, little girl, and you know nothing about this world you live in. You're entire life you spent preening and primping, and I doubt you learned a single thing about the true power your people holds. Take heart, little girl. Once you are dead, that power will be in capable hands, and I will use it to bring every kingdom in this world under my control, and finally we will see the true potential of the races. So, in a way, you're not nearly the waste of space you once were. You're the instrument that will unite us all. Aren't you proud?"

"I am proud," Mylena said, standing and facing Sargon, "I am proud that my people have defeated you. You're dead, Sargon; you just don't know it yet."

"Your people? You've killed your people, little girl. Look at the city below. I doubt one person still breathes, and if they do, it won't be for long. If you had come sooner, none of this would have happened. But no, you were too scared, weren't you? Your people." He reached out, and a large hand summoned from the shadows coalesced around Joppa. It pulled her up the stairs and into Sargon's waiting hand. Holding her by the neck, he began to chant underneath his breath, unholy words that pulled the blood off the walls and up the stairs in a stream of gory intent. The blood pooled as if fresh around his feet, and began to smoke. The smoke rose around Joppa's limp body, crawling along her limbs toward her throat like a mass of creeping insects. "See what I will do with your people as I have done to thousands upon thousands before them. Witness true power, little girl." He was turning Joppa into one of his monsters. Right before them all, he was corrupting her into an Ombrid.

Mylena stopped thinking, her mind focusing instead on her repulsion, her disgust, her desire to see this man gone. "You will not harm her," she said, her voice harder than the stone underneath her feet. There was no chanting, no singing, only an inclination of her head, and a gust of wind pulled Joppa from his grip and deposited her unconscious form on the marble stones next to Mylena. Mylena walked forward, raising her hands, and, as she did so, the stones underneath Sargon flung him backward, pinning him against the wall with their petrified grip. The room filled with light, a brightness that seemed to radiate from within Mylena herself, and she could feel its warmth coursing through her veins.

"You will not harm anyone ever again. You have no power, little man, only the illusion of power." It became true the instant she said it. The blood that had pooled on the floor flaked away to dust and blew away, the shadows he commanded were banished from the room. There was only the light, and, as she stood before him, she saw true fear in his eyes.

Mylena considered mercy. Inside her, somewhere, she heard her mother's voice, telling her that the elves only fought as a last resort. She heard her father saying that, with the right knowledge, there was always an alternative to bloodshed. Wisdom and strength were her inheritance, the tools that had brought her to this moment. She considered the words of her parents, considered what they would do in her place. And then she crushed Sargon's head without touching him, the light reaching out and wrapping his head in a band of power, and slowly contracting. Sargon screamed until his throat was crushed, and then crumpled to the floor, limp and lifeless. The numbness returned and the light fled, and Mylena was left on the floor, weeping for what had been done to her people, and what she had done to herself.

## CHAPTER THIRTEEN

The war had ended, the struggle was over, yet it seemed as if their trials had just begun. The ruined city below Illuminata Castle begged for salvation, but, for the moment, its few remaining inhabitants were moved within the castle walls for protection. They would deal with the tragedy of Haven City, but not now. Things had happened too quickly for anyone to have a clear picture of what occurred, but it appeared that the siege had only been successful because Queen Ysle of the pixies had succumbed to Chiave's reasoning after all and overcame her fear of the outside world to join Mylena's army.

In the week that followed, most of the pixie army began the journey back to their grove. Only a small contingent stayed with their queen at Illuminata Castle; and their queen was a most demanding house guest. She took up residency in Saebariel's old apartments, somehow managing to make them livable again, and instructed that Mylena be brought there to rest and recuperate. At first, Warrek flinched at the idea, but realized that there were few people alive who could tend to their exhausted queen better than her grandmother.

While Mylena slept without waking, Warrek turned his remaining soldiers into stewards, and had them clean the castle from top to bottom. It was grueling and depressing work, but he wanted their queen to wake up in a castle completely devoid of Sargon's influence. In a small way, he was sorry he didn't have someone with Sargon's dark powers to summon the bloody stains from the walls. But, in the end, it was a combination of Stone Weavers and old-fashioned manpower that got the job done.

With the city virtually destroyed and the castle is such a state, Warrek ordered the soldiers to reform their tent city on the western slope on the city's outskirts. There, they were away from the carnage within the walls as well as the battlefield they had struggled so hard to claim. On the battlefield, they buried their dead by the thousands, and the mercenaries too. A forest of graves sprung up below Haven City in a matter of days.

Only one of the soldiers was not buried among them. Kanefionn of Unwin was buried atop a hill next to the castle, overlooking the city he had died protecting. Chiave himself wove his tomb from the stone of the mountain, just as he had woven the stone shield that had saved the queen from meeting Fionn's fate. The handful of warriors remaining from Kir'Unwin, Vorynne amongst them, raised their voices in lament, a song that was swiftly carried off by the ocean breeze into the hills and beyond.

For Warrek, the mourning could not be over until he himself traveled to the former settlement of Kir'Unwin to visit the final resting place of his friend, his king. Thaniel had begun this expedition 28 years ago, when they were both young and invincible. When they started out from Eidalore in search of their destiny so very long ago, they had promised each other that, on their dying day, they would drink to their old age, to their dozens of strapping sons, and die together, slopping drunk. While his soldiers swept the evil from Illuminata Castle, he ordered them to keep a lookout for wine, mead, liquor of any kind. It was five days before Captain Harridan knocked on his door in the castle barracks.

"I hear you're looking to get drunk," he began, his tone quite serious.

"I might be," Warrek grumbled, "if there were any blasted liquor left in the castle."

Harridan stepped into the room, brandishing a bottle and a small, mirthless smirk. "The castle might be devoid of spirits, but I'm not. This I lifted from the monastery at Laud'El on our way out. I thought it would be wasted on the infantry, and the monks are no longer around to enjoy it." He set the bottle on the table and turned to go.

"I'm sorry I didn't know him," Harridan said knowingly as he closed the door. "If he was anything like you, he must have been a blasted good king."

Warrek looked at the bottle, its liquid contents encased in glass too dark to reveal their true nature. He wondered at the nature of friendship, if it were always thus. Was one friend destined only to arrive after the other had left? Was friendship like the wine in this bottle, ever shifting, easily going to one's head, but never really sticking to one place? He put the bottle in his saddle bags slung over a chair in the corner, and left the room. He would keep his promise to Thaniel, but first, there were the living to attend to.

It was almost nine days before Mylena finally awoke. Chiave was informed of it by the pixie Gace, who fluttered into the battlefields to find him while he was digging graves for the fallen. He knew there were others who could complete the work just as well if not better than he, but he felt compelled to help the fallen find their final rest, to use what gifts he had been given to make their sleep more comfortable. The worshipers of the El believed that the body, once dead, returned to the earth from which it was born, that the cycle of life continued, and that, through our death, other things might live.

The elven beliefs seemed to center around the magic within a being. They believed that the element bound to a person called that person back to itself, wind called the Wind Callers back home, and the Stone Weaver was woven into the tapestry of the earth's stone. He wondered how the magicless humans would fit into their belief system and realized that, most likely, neither religion was correct. Perhaps there was a middle ground somewhere that would explain death to him in a way that settled right with his heart.

"Putting them in the ground seems a lot of effort," Gace twittered as she arrived. "What if they are Fire Callers? Then the fire will have to work through the stone to get to them. Silly, really."

"Is there something you want, little imp?" Chiave had grown a short temper in the last few weeks, something he was eager to sharpen on any unsuspecting subject. Gace would do nicely. "I have work to do, as you can see."

"Your queen has awakened," Gace said shortly, obviously offended, "And my queen has commanded that I remind you of why you called her here. You ought to be grateful." She flew off without another word, her bruised ego held firmly behind tiny crossed arms.

Chiave watched her go, anxiety blooming in his belly. Yes, he had been charged with a very important purpose all those months ago in Kir'Unwin. King Thaniel, his father, had thrust a book into his hands and sent him to speak to the queen of the pixies, to bid her come to Illuminata Castle to rebind the Well of Zyn. The ritual had been performed all those years ago with three of the royal bloodline, and Thaniel believed that it could be done again. So were his notes in the margins of the Testament.

Quickly making his way back to the castle, Chiave ran over in his mind the secret meaning of the makeup of the group Thaniel assembled for the Ritual of Rebinding. He had yet to explain to Queen Mylena his connection to her, and, in some ways, it still confused him why he was sent away at all. He was sent away to a place the king himself eventually arrived at. Was he meant to be protected? To be saved in case of an overthrow like the one that happened? Was it Chiave or the kingdom that Thaniel had meant to protect?

He entered the castle library, and looked about the ravaged shelves. The grey-skinned armies had plucked most of the shelves clean, using his father's precious books as latrine paper. What was left had been scattered about the room, and only recently rearranged by Warrek's company. The Testament had been taken here to the mostly vacant library, and placed on a pedestal formerly housing a history of Eidalore.

Retrieving the massive tome from its perch, Chiave hefted it down to the throne room, where he found Queen Ysle waiting, Queen Mylena slumped on her arm, as well as a small entourage of pixies and soldiers. The trees here had been stripped of their carnal ornamentation, but still had yet to grow any new foliage. He wondered if it were perhaps Saebariel's absence that kept them bare. Approaching the throne, Chiave placed a sweaty palm on the arm of the massive chair, and sung a supplication that the chair move aside for him. He felt resistance in the stone, a sense of distrust, since he was not its true master. He called again, his weaving song filled with his desperate need to make things right. The stone relented, and opened up a dark passageway into the heart of the mountain. Chiave stepped through, holding the Testament and a glimmer of hope to his chest.

"Captain Warrek," said Queen Ysle as she led her granddaughter into the cavern passageway, "I have an apology to make to you. I have seen my daughter's passing, and you had no control over such terrible events."

Warrek blinked in astonishment at so forward a revelation, and eyed Queen Mylena who Ysle held tightly. He had to make a conscious effort not to stumble as he made his way down the stairs toward the cavern floor.

"Your Majesty, I am honored that you think of me. I am but a humble servant—"

"None of that," she said curtly, cutting him off dismissively. "I didn't come to Haven City because of your feelings, young man." She brushed the limp curls out of Mylena's staring eyes. Although awake, it was as if the queen still slept somewhere within her ambulatory body. Warrek had serious reservations about moving the young queen, but Chiave had been very insistent that this ritual be performed the moment that she awoke. He relayed the sense of urgency evident in Thaniel's notes in the Testament, and Warrek was a wise enough man to recognize the voice of his king, and disciplined enough a man to honor the wishes of his liege even beyond death. Still, he was curious about several aspects of this procedure, and what brought them all down to the cavern beneath the castle.

"Why did you come then?" His question slipped away from him and echoed strangely off the walls of the enormous space they traveled into.

"My grandson is very persuasive," Ysle said, humor bubbling in her voice. She had been waiting for just such a question.

Warrek's shock lasted the entire length of the winding stairway and still had not faded for some time as he stood among the select group of witnesses to the ritual.

From the moment that she awoke, Mylena only wanted to fall back to sleep. In her sleep, Fionn was alive, she was not a queen, and they lay under the stars in the Eye of the World, far away from tragedy and loss. She was not allowed to return to sleep, however, and, instead, was bathed and dressed and brought down to a cavern she didn't even know existed beneath her childhood home. She watched the events unfold as if she were outside her body looking in on herself, barely conscious that it was her red head that lolled unresponsively down by the well.

Disconnected from the events around her, Mylena enjoyed a unique perspective. She watched as Chiave set down the huge book on the cavern floor, reading aloud the words in the margin she recognized as her father's strange shorthand notes. He took her hand, as did her grandmother the pixie queen, but another held her up so she would stand with them. Who was that? Oh, Captain Warrek, brave, strong, and loyal to the end. He looked odd from above, the gray hair at his temples glowing blue as it reflected the Well's light. In fact, everyone was tinted a little blue, and she laughed a little at the sight of it.

Chiave's chanting became a song, rising into the expanse of the cavern, past where Mylena's consciousness floated. It tickled her as it past, as a cat might tickle your face with its whiskers as it kisses you. She giggled at that too, at the feeling and the accuracy of the analogy, and then returned her attention to the group of people below.

Chiave concentrated every fiber of his being as he chanted. He knew what was at stake. If they didn't restore the strength of the shield around the Well, someone might very well come after Mylena, and then the power of the well would be theirs. Restoring the power of the shield was their last hope of peace, their last hope of success.

The song was hard to hold inside of him, it was wild and unruly and wanted to escape and rush out into the world. It wasn't a magic that he understood. It was a magic built by a magicless man, constructed out of Thaniel's methodical research of the land they lived in, of the customs of the elves. The Scholar King had sought to protect the people of Shadowhaven by creating the barrier around the Well, and that binding needed to be mended. Stone Weaving came naturally, came without thought or effort, but this song wasn't his, and, thus, didn't want to stay within him.

He held fast to Mylena's hand and to Ysle's, frightened by the weakness in the former, and awed by the strength in the grip of the latter. He felt as if he were the link connecting this uneven chain, and that if he faltered for one second, the chain would collapse. He continued the chant, blending the words with Spell Songs he had learned so that he might build from their strength. It seemed to be working; the shield around the Well vibrated with a strange white light, pulsing with power. He could feel the pulsing of the shield aligning with his own heartbeat, the two rhythms becoming one great pounding. It was working. They would do this, it really was working.

There was a final pulse of light from the shield, and then everything went black. There was neither light from the shield nor light from the Well itself.

In the blackness, he had time to hear Ysle quip, "Well that was certainly interesting," before being blasted off his feet by the force of a great wave of power. It exploded from the Well with such force, it knocked them all to the ground, leaving them struggling for air. It took Chiave several moments to come back to his senses, and when he stood and looked around him, everything appeared the same. There was the same strange blue light coming from the Well, as if nothing had changed.

The circle of people around him were looking to him for answers. "I don't understand," Chiave said, tears coming unbidden to his eyes. He reached out to the shield around the Well, felt only Mylena's energy, and pulled his hand away, disappointed. "I did everything he said, everything he wanted me to. Why didn't it work?"

He spent the rest of the evening sitting there in the cavern, pouring over Thaniel's notes. He paid no mind when Warrek came to collect him, saying everyone had returned to the castle above. There was no mistaking it. The ritual had failed. The reason for their failure escaped him, and would haunt him the rest of his days.

After the failed ritual, it appeared that Mylena's distractedness had passed instead to Chiave. She left the cavern under her own power, and in full possession of her faculties. She knew the ritual had failed, knew exactly what it meant. She was brought back to her senses by the blast, knocked back into reality, and that reality was a world without Fionn.

So she climbed the hill where he lay and stood in the afternoon sun on the cliff overlooking the ocean. The tomb was elegant in its simplicity, a fitting place for an elf such as Fionn. The day was so very beautiful, it mocked her with its brilliant sky and soft breezes scented with the sea. With her despair so great, she wished for thunder and rain, as she had invoked in the Eye of the World when Fionn had told her that her father had died, but she had no strength now to bring such weather to her. So she dropped to her knees and wept over the grave of the one she loved, mourning not only him but also the wasted moments they could have shared together. She had stupidly squandered their last weeks together, spending more time with strangers than with him. For the second time, she wished for the power to alter time, to fix what she had broken, to hold him one last time.

The hours of the afternoon bled into evening, and still she sat, awash in grief. So lost was she in her own thoughts that Mylena didn't notice that she wasn't alone on the cliff.

"How long do you expect to go on weeping like that?" A sardonic voice called from behind her. Mylena turned to see a girl, who appeared to be eleven or twelve, leaning nonchalantly against a rock. She was intensely beautiful, with flowing white-blond hair and large blue eyes set above chiseled cheekbones. Her sarcastic expression lent nothing to her beauty, but also, strangely, did not detract from it. She wore a long, black traveling cloak tied at the neck. Mylena was positive that she was alone when she arrived at Fionn's grave. How then did this child sneak up on her? Did she somehow climb the cliff face?

"I intend to weep for the rest of my days. Leave me be." Mylena turned away dismissively, making every effort to sink back into her black depression. She heard a cough behind her, though, and, irritated, turned again to see the girl had not moved, but was, instead, cleaning her fingernails with her teeth.

"I told you to go. As your queen, I command you!" She stood proudly, her regal stature perfectly silhouetted by the setting sun.

"You're not my queen," the girl said, spitting off the cliff edge.

"Who are you to dare speak to me this way?" Mylena demanded, rage rising within her.

"I'm your guardian. Do you not remember Fela?" The girl cocked her head to one side, and then another, as if changing profiles would make her more easy to recognize.

"Remember who? I've never met you before in my life."

"I'm hurt," and Fela oddly looked it. "Well, I suppose you were rather young. A baby rarely remembers much beyond its crib. Nevertheless, I've been charged with protecting you."

"Fine job you did. I was nearly killed three times in the last few months. Were you not charged to protect me then?"

"Yes, well, I was called sometime ago. I got a little, err, tied up, you might say. But I'm here now, and I've got a choice to present you with."

Mylena crossed her arms, incredulous. "A choice? Exactly why am I supposed to listen to you?"

"My word, you look so like her. Except for that horrid hair of yours of course, and the roundy ears. Suppose you can't help that with your father and all." The girl approached, looking up at Mylena, intensely studying her face.

"You make no sense. Look like who?" Mylena was quickly sinking into a feeling of helplessness, as if she were floating out to sea without a tether.

"Your mother, of course. It's she who sent me. She sent me a message," the girl said, unconsciously rubbing at her neck, "and told me to come and fetch you. I am to take you someplace safe."

"My mother sent you?" Mylena asked in disbelief. A vague remembrance of something familiar tugged at her mind, but she couldn't quite see clearly enough to understand what it meant.

"Aye," said the girl, pulling a chain from around her neck and handing it to Mylena, "and she asked me to give you this. Saebariel called it the Retulai. It's meant to dampen the power she said, and said you would know what that meant. Listen, I know it's all going to crap, this world of yours. The Well is in danger as long as you're here. That boy's chanti' didn't do a thing to restore the Well's shield, did it? Come with me and I will take you to a place where the maniacs like Sargon will never get ahold of you."

Mylena took a step back, looking at the object in her hand. It looked to be a crystal shard the size of her palm, inside of which swirled a constantly churning blue liquid. She had seen this liquid before. It was water from the Well of Zyn. Whoever the girl was, she was right. The Retulai pulsed with warmth in her palm, and she felt safer in contact with it. She felt more in control of herself. She dropped the chain around her neck, feeling the warmth pulse against her bosom.

"I need time to think," she said, looking distractedly out at the sea.

"Look," the girl said, "I meant to come sooner, but I got delayed. The time for thinking has been wasted, I'm afraid, and you yourself said your life had been threatened multiple times just in the past few months. There isn't time to think. You have to choose now. Leave, and this world will continue on safely without you. Stay, and you risk destroying everything you and your parents fought so hard to protect. You've lost so much already, haven't you, Mylena? Are you prepared to lose the rest if it means protecting them?"

Mylena clutched her head in her hands, trying to drown out the insistence of the girl's voice. It was a horrible choice. Of course, she wanted to see Shadowhaven prosper. That was just it. She wanted to see it for herself, to be there when the kingdom rose from the ashes. She wanted to see joy once again on the faces of those she loved. She wasn't alone as she had thought; she had her people, Warrek and Chiave and the others, her grandmother too. She had family here. Was she to leave all that? It was unfair. This was a difficult choice to make.

And then she remembered why this felt so familiar. She remembered her dream, in which she spoke to her mother at the top of the castle. Saebariel had urged her to make the difficult choice. It would be so easy to stay with those she cared about. But it would be selfish to remain here and put them all at risk. Shadowhaven had gone through so much in the last four years. She couldn't bear to think that it could happen again, and worse, that she would be the cause of it.

Dropping her hands to her sides, she turned to face Fela, saying, "I will go with you. But answer me this? Will they be able to continue on without me?"

Fela took her hand, nodding. "They will thrive without you. They will thrive because of you."

Fela led Mylena back into the castle, but through rarely used passageways and corridors that eventually led them back to the throne room. It was the last place she expected to end up, and she looked at Fela with questioning eyes.

"Ask it to open," said the girl, indicating the throne.

Mylena had never considered the possibility that she might be able to command the stone of the secret door to open, yet she stepped forward and said in a soft voice, "Please open," and the doorway instantly appeared.

"How is that possible?" she asked Fela as they descended the stairway she had only recently climbed.

"Did you not wonder why the shield charm failed? You are not like anyone else in Shadowhaven, Mylena. It is your very special blood that makes the shield invulnerable. Your father did a superb job protecting the Well, but he didn't really do the work. You did. Things happen around you, don't they? You have more power than any elf or human or pixie or dragon. It's you who protects the Well. Your father may have been the Owl of Shadowhaven, but it is his shadow that will keep this realm alive. You are that shadow, and your people will spend the rest of their existence protected by the shelter you provide them."

Together, they stood before the Well of Zyn. Fela continued to speak. "Your father once explained this as an artery of the world. This blue water is the blood of this world, and contains all the power that the world has at its disposal. A weakened strain of this runs through every elf and pixie and every magical creature, providing them a conduit to speak to the elements. I don't really understand it, but what I do know is that you are more connected to this Well than any other person."

Fela took Mylena's hand again. "You are the talisman that brought me here, Mylena, and you are the one who will open the door. Ask the door to open."

Blinking, Mylena faced the well, "Please open the door. Fela has somewhere to take me." The swirling liquid pulsed, and then solidified into a portal filled with shimmering light.

Fela reached out a hand to the invisible shield and, somehow, her fingers passed through. She smiled up at Mylena. "Here we go. I love this part!"

Together, Fela and the queen stepped through the portal and into the unknown.

## CHAPTER FOURTEEN

"Well, where the bloody hell could she be? A ruler doesn't simply disappear into thin air!" Warrek railed, and it wasn't the first time he had yelled at one of his lieutenants that week. It had been more than five days since the Ritual of Rebinding had failed, since Queen Mylena had stepped out of the cavern and vanished. His soldiers had searched the ruins of Haven City, the tents of the infantry, the entirety of Illuminata Castle itself with its many hidden passages, yet there was no sign of her. Just when he thought everything had settled down, it looked as if their queen had been kidnapped.

There was only one person in the castle who wasn't frantic about Mylena's disappearance. Queen Ysle was calm as you please, and it was beginning to irritate him. At the end of the fifth day of fruitless searching, when he was about to send search parties into the kingdom proper to find the girl, Ysle pulled him aside.

"You won't find her," she began without salutation. It was her bluntness that got under his skin more than anything.

"Is she dead then? Taken captive? If you know something, pray, your Majesty, out with it. To withhold information is to be an accomplice to the villainy your granddaughter had fallen prey to." He could be just as blunt as she was.

"There's no villainy here, and no, she isn't dead. She's left this world, but not in death. She's traveled elsewhere, as I once did at Chiave's bidding." She stopped and waited for this information to register with him.

Warrek thought back to that day in the Pixie Grove, when Ysle had stepped into the Reflection Pool, and then out of it again. "If she has gone someplace, will she return?" He felt the fury leave him, replaced by a sense of frustrated acceptance.

Ysle shook her head. "I doubt it very much. I expect Mylena has gone far away from her kingdom for its protection. She is currently the greatest threat to our survival. If she is safe elsewhere, then so are we."

"But how can we survive without a leader?" Warrek sagged into a nearby chair, all energy drained from him. He had struggled all this way only with the hope that the kingdom could be restored and harmony brought back to Shadowhaven. Without their queen, such a thing hardly seemed possible.

"Shadowhaven will have a leader. He is young, and he may not be Mylena, but he has the potential to provide the needed guidance this kingdom needs."

Warrek looked up at her, confused.

"My grandson will rule, Captain, and I expect he will do it well."

Six months passed, and spring flowed into summer at Illuminata Castle. It had been half a year since the war, and a new carpet of grass covered the battlefield turned graveyard. The cairns of the fallen looked little more than scales dotting the back of some massive creature lounging in the valley.

Haven City had been scoured of its dead, and they too had been laid to rest. The population of the city still resided inside the walls of the castle, but there were hopes that reconstruction would soon begin and they would be able to return to their homes.

Within Illuminata Castle itself, an audience was being held in the courtyard. The ranks of the King's Guard lined the battlements, and the citizens of Haven City filled the courtyard with their numbers. Many had traveled to the castle once word of the end of occupation had reached them. It seemed the citizens of Shadowhaven wanted to be near the heart of their government once again. They wanted to see for themselves that peace really had returned to the land.

Above those assembled, King Chiave appeared on a balcony. A cheer arose from the crowd, the triumphant voices reverberating off the castle walls. It took him several attempts to quiet them so that he could speak.

"Thank you for coming, my good people. It has been some time since I saw all of you gathered in one place, and it warms my heart to see so many of Shadowhaven's people together. You are the spirit of this great kingdom, and I am so blessed that I have been able to lead you in this time of peace and tranquility.

"Thaniel and Saebariel built this castle out of their love, and Haven City bloomed around it. It seemed that everyone wanted to be part of their union, and everyone who wished so was welcomed into their homes and their hearts. They wanted to build something permanent, something lasting, something new.

"But I am telling you today, they were wrong. As much as it pains me to realize, their good intentions were what inevitably courted disaster and brought villainy to our shores. The elves of Shadowhaven have long been a nomadic people, and it is that tradition that my parents strayed from. They did it out of love, but they built their kingdom on a shoddy foundation."

The king stopped and looked down at the throng, at the faces of those who looked so uncertainly back at him. These were the true treasure of the kingdom, as he had heard a very wise princess say long ago, and now was the time to protect them.

"We will learn from our past mistakes. This is the blessing of hindsight. I have thought long and hard about what is best for our people, and this is my decision: There will be no rebuilding of Haven City. Kir'Tazul and its sister clans will no longer be bound to one city, one location. The protection of the Well of Zyn is secure, so we no longer have to hover over it like a mother hen hovering over her clutch. Return to your homes, and to your traditions, people of Shadowhaven. Thrive in your ancestry, and learn from the mistakes of our past."

Laud'El monastery had fallen into disrepair in the months following the war. Weeds infested the once immaculate prayer gardens, and the barn was moments from collapsing. Mold had begun to work its way into the mortar supporting the building itself. It appeared that, very soon, nature would claim the little clearing before the mountain pass.

Only the chapel stood in a relatively intact state, sheltered from the elements as it was by the mountainside and by fortune. The altar and pews were stained with the blood of wounded warriors long since gone it was true, but the elegance of the structure remained eternal, despite the vines that crawled up its sides and threatened its windows.

It wasn't to the chapel that she came, however; it was to the graveyard. The solitary figure stood amongst the decaying gravestones, solemnly intoning the hymns of the monks who had once tended the graves. Then she began to speak, as if rebuking someone who was not really there.

"You ought to be ashamed, stealing like that. I'm a good girl, and Daddy never raised me to be no thief."

A deeper voice responded, yet still somehow her own. "I hardly call returning the writings of the El to their proper home stealing. I am the last remaining monk. I have a duty to protect the Testament."

The young woman crossed her arms petulantly, a challenge considering the massive weight in her pack pulled her shoulders backward. She reconsidered the gesture and, instead, dropped her shoulders so that the pack fell unceremoniously behind her. She then cried out in horror and spun around to retrieve the pack from the ground.

"You horrible girl! Do you know how vital this text is to our people? These are the words of the El! How could you treat them so?"

"I miss Chiave," she whined. "He never treated me as badly as you do. Makin' me your slave. Joppa take me here, Joppa steal this book. Joppa clean my grave."

"You can return to your precious king whenever you please. It's not like what I have been chosen to do is at all important. It's not like we're connected in any way, you and I. It's not like I'm your brother or anything."

"Aw, Abihu, don't be like that. Look, I'll clean off your grave real nice." And she did so, plucking weeds and dusting moss off the headstone that her other brothers had erected so that the name ABIHU JORAMSON was clearly distinguishable. Then she hefted the pack onto the headstone and pulled out the oilskin-wrapped book. Fingering the pages as one might the hair of a loved one, she spread open the book and turned to a page. There she began to do what no one in the kingdom had done in over a year, and what no one in existence had been trained to do. She began to read the words aloud.

"Although the darkness will shroud our land, the El has not forgotten you. Although all will appear lost, the El is with you. Although the land will shatter and the Chosen shall vanish, the El will send another. The El will send a mother for his people, and she will speak the Old Tongue and she will guide his people into peace."

It was then that Joppa knelt and kissed her brother's gravestone. When she rose, she was not Joppa, nor Abihu, but both. She was not a mad woman; she was a holy woman. Standing, Joppa closed the book, returning it to the pack and, slinging the pack across her shoulders, she turned her back on the monastery and began the journey back toward Illuminata Castle. She had come to Laud'El a mere girl. She left as the first Priestess of the El.

Mylena stepped into the Well of Zyn, feeling the warm, viscous water enfold her as she sank underneath the glowing blue surface. The water, if it could be called that, didn't suffocate her as she expected; in fact, it didn't even seem to be moistening her clothes. It merely held her in its liquid embrace, pulsing with its own strange heartbeat. She was filled with a warmth that seeped into her bones, and, as that warmth intensified, so did the glowing blue of the pool all around her. Now that she noticed, the Well seemed to be expanding, or, rather, the edges seemed to be disappearing. She could not see

Fela, though she felt the girl was nearby and safe. This place seemed to be a realm of pure sensation.

Slowly, the warmth coursing through Mylena's body focused into a ball right behind her breastbone, and something tugged on that ball, pulling her forward. She imagined this must be what a fish feels like being caught on a line, yanked through their placid, watery home toward points unknown. Whatever pulled her was strong, and getting stronger, until she was hurtling through the water at a breakneck pace. Were it not for the cushioning effect of the liquid around her, Mylena suspected this would hurt very much.

Then, suddenly, like a string breaking on a guitar, the invisible line connected to her snapped, and Mylena broke through the surface of the water, tumbled ignominiously onto a patch of prickly grass, and landed on her face. Pushing herself up on her palms and knees, she saw that she was in a forest clearing. It seemed to be daytime, but she couldn't tell the exact hour because the sky was filled with boiling black clouds. Looking at the violence of that sky unnerved her, so she stood, brushing wrinkles and leaves from her skirt, and saw Fela, leaning nonchalantly against a massive stone doorway. A familiar blue glow emanated from between the lintels, and she had the feeling that if she just took one step through the door, she would find herself back home.

"'Twas quite the tumble there, your Highness," Fela smirked, uncrossing her arms. "You sure you didn't break your royal nose?"

Unable to control the impulse, Mylena rubbed her nose just to make sure, and then noticed the glint of triumph in the little girl's eyes. Mylena quickly extended the movement, making as if she merely intended to smooth her curls. "Hush, you little weasel," she snapped, not bothering to keep the irritation from her voice.

Fela's smirk deepened into a wicked grin. "Weasel? I prefer cat." She laughed as if she had said something incredibly hilarious.

"I'm too tired for this," Mylena sighed, turning her back on Fela and rubbing at the beginning of a headache on her brow. "All I want is a bath and a meat pie and a soft bed. Think you can handle that, cat?" She put the full weight of her recently abdicated queenliness behind the question.

"Not sure I can, your Highness, considering where we are," Fela replied from behind her.

"Why? Where are we?" Mylena asked, turning around. Fela didn't answer, but then again, Fela wasn't there anymore. In her place was a black panther who, apparently, also had the capacity to lean nonchalantly.

This was the last straw. Mylena's rage flamed within her, an inferno she could not control nor wanted to. She had left everything she loved behind for their own good, traveled to who-knew-where to start a new life, and now she had to fight a panther?

"Enough! I have lost everything I care about, fiend! I will not be defeated now after all I have gone through. I will kill you where you stand. Do you hear me?!"

The panther growled low in its throat, and getting its feet firmly under it, turned and disappeared into the trees.

Shocked, Mylena was nevertheless too much in her temper to let it go. "You come back here! I'm not finished with you, you mangy fleabag!" She ran after the panther, hoping to take out her anger on her surprised foe. Pushing through the trees, Mylena had trouble seeing anything but bark and leaves. She was sure she saw the animal go this way, though, so she seethed her way deeper, until she saw daylight peeking through the arbors. Picking up speed, she ran straight into the clearing and nearly over the edge of a cliff. From out of the corner of her eye, the panther pounced, but, instead of attacking her, it jumped in front of her, stopping her from falling into the churning ocean below.

With her heart in her throat, Mylena backed away from the edge and realized that what she thought was a cliff wasn't actually attached to anything. They were floating above the ocean, the little forest island suspended in the air about two hundred feet above the waves. Below her spread a land she had never seen with jagged mountains piercing the sky and a dense forest pushing all the way to the seashore which wound eastward out of sight. Above it all, a massive floating castle dominated the skyline, its pale blue spires drawing lightning out of the ever-moving clouds.

Beside her, the panther changed shape, smoothly transitioning back into the form of the little girl Fela. She put a steadying hand on Mylena's elbow and her blue eyes, no longer crackling with mischief, were filled with a momentary sadness as she spoke. "Welcome to the Dark Plains."

## ABOUT THE AUTHOR

Amanda received her Creative Writing degree from the University of Southern California, learning her craft at the feet of David St. John, Aimee Bender and Carol Muske-Dukes. While at USC, she received the Middleton Creative Writing Fellowship for excellence in poetry.

For seven years she honed her writing craft as a video game journalist. In 2014 Amanda left the world of blogging behind to focus on her first love, fiction. Shadow of the Owl is her first novel, and she is currently writing a sequel.

If you enjoyed Shadow of the Owl, please join our email newsletter by visiting http://eepurl.com/bw4Cvz

Made in the USA
San Bernardino, CA
09 June 2016